The Flight of The Dragonfly

Dougie McHale

Azzie Bazzie
Books

To find yourself sometimes you have to have lost everything you hold dear

Contents

The Past

The Beginning

She slipped through my fingers. I lost my child and there was nothing I could do about it. But that's not how it began.

I loved the way he looked at me, his smile could melt the coldest heart. There was a definite feeling that we belonged together; our friends named us *the soul mates*. Sometimes, it uneased me that I could feel such a bond with another. I wasn't mesmerised by him, that's not the word, it implies we weren't equal. We were connected, physically and emotionally, that's what it was. I was the hand that fitted his glove.

We met at a party. I hadn't been invited to it, but my friend, Jasmine had, and she didn't want to go on her own, so she asked me to go with her. I wasn't exactly dragged along. I quite liked the idea of going out and the chances were I'd probably know someone there anyway. It was at a house in Corstorphine, a nice house, in a nice suburban area. I remember walking along a wide street with mature trees on each side. It must have been autumn because golden and copper leaves littered the pavement. It had been raining and they stuck to the soles of our shoes. The front door was painted black with a large silver knocker. It's funny how we remember certain details and others are obscured by time. I can't recall the host's name, but I've never forgotten him, after all, it was he who introduced me to Jamie that night.

My first impression of Jamie was he was shy, not painfully shy where he struggled to make conversation but reserved, I suppose that's a better word. Yes, that's a better description. He asked me my name, and when I said, Grace, his eyes lit up; it had been his grandmother's name. Then, he refilled my glass and enquired about what I did for a living. He seemed interested in my work, either that, or he was good at pretending to listen. I know now it was a bit of both.

I was a researcher at Edinburgh University, and we had just started a major project on the effects of plastics polluting the sea and its catastrophic effect on sea life. Looking back now, I probably did speak a lot about it. I was brimming with enthusiasm about the prospect of getting my academic teeth into it. Jamie asked all the right questions and smiled a lot. I remember he smiled.

I did eventually enquire about his job. He said it wasn't as interesting or globally effective as researching the environment, but he enjoyed it. He was a policy adviser for the Scottish National Party at Holyrood, the Scottish Parliament. He must have seen something in the look on my face as he almost apologised by saying it wasn't as grandiose as it sounded.

'So, you're one of them?' I asked.

'One of who?' he grinned.

'You know, a tartan warrior in a kilt who hates anything to do with the English, anything British.'

He looked at me with his piercing eyes and as he took a drink he said, 'Not really.'

'I'm sorry.' It was my turn to apologise.

'What for?'

'Judging you. I didn't mean to generalise.'

'Don't worry. I don't have the legs for a kilt.'

I laughed then. We both did. In a way, it broke the ice between us. I asked where he lived. He told me he had just bought a house in St John's Terrace. He asked me if I knew it and when I said I didn't, he told me it was a nice unassuming cul de sac not far from where we were.

I lived in a flat in Lonsdale Terrace, opposite The Meadows it was handy for walking to work and nowhere near Corstorphine, where Jamie lived.

'So, I can assume you're not a fan of Nicola?'

'Nicola?' Should I know this Nicola, I thought, and then it came to me. 'Oh. You mean Nicola Sturgeon. Your boss.'

'Who else?'

'Let's just say, I respect her because she's a woman in a man's world and doing well. In fact, she's doing much more than that, she's widening the parameters, but that doesn't mean I have to like her. I much prefer Ruth Davidson. She's a more likeable character, but I don't agree with her politics.'

'That's a relief. I never had you down as a Tory, anyway.'

'Why? Do they have a certain look?'

'No.' He smiled. 'Although they are irritating.'

'I'm glad you don't think I am, then.'

'Are you interested in politics?'

'I wouldn't call it an interest, but I've always had a soft spot for the Lib Dems.'

He pulled a face and rolled his eyes.

'I know. I know. But in their defence, their public image is improving.'

'It can't get any worse.'

I combed my hand through my hair.

'Are you hungry?' he asked.

That smile again.

'I saw when we came in, they've got a little buffet set up in the dining room.'

'There is, but I'd like to take you out, for dinner.'

'When?' I could feel my heart beating in the back of my throat.

He leaned forward. 'Now.'

The Present

Lesvos, Greece

Grace is looking at a mannequin in a shop window. It is wearing a dress she has admired for over a week now. Each morning, she stops and admires the cut of the dress and the way in which the fabric hugs the curves of the mannequin. It's a statement. Yes, that's what it is. Wearing such a dress, Grace thinks, is a measure of one's own confidence in who one is, it defines who you are.

She is not ready to be clothed in such refinery. It is too soon. There was a time, she would have bought the dress the minute she laid eyes on it, but not now. Back then, she was indomitable: fiercely independent, driven and resourceful. She had a propense determination to be optimistic, positive… she turns away from the shop window and sighs under her breath.

'Grace, I thought it was you.'

Grace spins around. 'Oh. Hello, Monica.'

Monica touches Grace's arm. 'Have you got time for a coffee?'

Grace checks her watch. 'I suppose so.'

'Good. I'm glad I bumped into you.'

Monica is in her late fifties and well presented. Her face is taut, and her skin has a polished sheen to it, a waxed complexion that reminds Grace Monica is not averse to the surgeon's knife. They sit outside under the shade of a parasol. The café is popular with the locals which means that the beverages and food are of a good quality.

'Have you settled in now?' Monica asks as she takes her smartphone from her bag and lays it on the table. She looks at it and frowns. 'I'm expecting a call… you don't mind I hope?'

'Grace shakes her head. 'No. Not at all.'

'So, the apartment is up to scratch?'

'Yes, I'm so lucky. There's a few bits and bobs that need my attention, but apart from that it's perfect.'

'I'm glad. There's nothing worse than moving to a place you haven't seen. I know it's just bricks and mortar, but it's more than that, don't you think? It's important to feel a sense of belonging, I feel.'

'Yes, you're absolutely right. I feel an attachment to it already, even though it's just been a few weeks.'

'Time flies, don't you think?'

'This past year has, that's for sure.'

'At least you're rid of him.' Monica smiles and then looks embarrassed. She glances at her phone.

Grace wonders if she is willing it to ring. 'Oh! thanks for the kettle.'

'You're welcome. I was glad to get rid of it. It was just taking up room. I had two sitting in the cupboard. God knows how I managed to acquire all those kettles. You don't want another one, do you?' Monica laughs.

A waiter approaches them, and they order two coffees.

'Would you like a cake or a pastry?' Monica asks as she scans the menu.

'I wouldn't know what to get. Why don't you order for both of us?'

Monica sets her mouth. 'Mm... I think we'll have a slice of *Melopita* and let me see... a Baklava.'

The waiter nods his head in approval before leaving them.

'You're not on a diet, I hope?'

Grace smiles. 'Not this week, anyway. What did you just order?'

'The *Melopita* is part custard, part cheesecake, it's a Honey Pie, you'll love it. Now, the Baklava is a classic. It's basically Greek pastry made with flaky dough and layered with a cinnamon-spiced nut filling and sweet syrup. It's very decadent, but it tastes like heaven. You'll love that too. We'll have half of each.'

Once the coffee and cakes arrive, Monica cuts the cakes into four pieces.

'Oh my God, that's delicious.' Grace dabs the side of her mouth with a napkin.

'Better than an orgasm?'

'What is that?'

'Has it been that long?'

Grace suddenly feels guarded, but she can tell she has caught Monica's curiosity. She hesitates before nodding.

Monica sighs. 'And is it important?'

'I'm enjoying my own company. I'm comfortable with how things are.'

Monica looks at her, as if weighing up the implications of Grace's words. Then, after a pause, Monica smiles and lifts her cup to her mouth. 'Then that's all that matters.' There is an awkward silence. 'So... you've settled in then, that's good.'

'I have. I've surprised myself.'

'It took me a while. I thought I'd never be happy here. The biggest mistake of my life, I kept telling myself. Eventually, I stopped missing London. I'd never go back now. This is home. It's been eight years now.'

'I didn't realise it was as long as that.'

'Yes. Arthur's been dead three years now, but as you know, I'm not on my own. Georgios and I are... very fond of each other.'

Grace thinks it is quite an old-fashioned word for someone like Monica to use, especially when referring to Georgios.

'I'll need to ask you over for dinner, Georgios as well, of course.'

'I'd like that.'

'Me too.' Monica's presence has been a comfort to Grace. In fact, she doesn't know how she would have coped if it hadn't been for Monica's continued support. 'I can't tell you how grateful I am.'

'We stick together. Especially in times of crisis. We muck in. I wouldn't have it any other way.'

'You've been a great support, Monica. I wouldn't have lasted five minutes here if it wasn't for you.'

'Nonsense, you don't give yourself credit enough. I've watched you change. You're not the woman you were when you first came here.'

'I suppose not,' Grace muses. She takes a sip of her coffee. 'But there's days when I just don't want to get out of bed. The thought of facing another day... it's like... well, it's hard, you know.'

Monica takes Grace's hand and locks her eyes on her.

'You're doing just fine, believe me. I could never have done what you have. I don't think I've got the courage.'

'I just don't feel the person you're describing.'

'And that's why you need to start having a higher opinion of yourself, Grace. Stop bringing yourself down all the time. You were like that as a child.'

'I can't help it. It's in my DNA, I think.' It is a statement that is instinctive, it is her default, but all the same, the familiarity sits uncomfortably on her tongue.

Monica rolls her eyes. 'Well, that needs to change.'

The Present

Something of Worth

The sun trickles through the shutters as Grace rises towards the surface of sleep, and just for a moment, she is in her bedroom in Edinburgh. Her heart pounds in her chest and she turns to see if he is really there, lying beside her. She can feel the cold dampness of sweat run in the dip between her breasts.

She remembers his eyes, piercing her resolve and staring down at her. He holds a knife in his hand. She tries to scream, but he has silenced her voice. He grabs a handful of her hair and hacks at it, viciously.

She closes her eyes. It was a dream, just a dream. The terror does not leave her. It fills the room. She does not want the memory of it to stain this new day, this new beginning, this new place.

After a shower, Grace makes a breakfast of toast and black coffee and sits outside on the balcony, just big enough for a chair and table. She watches as small groups of children, with sports bags strapped to their backs make their way to the local primary school. It is a building she came across the other day. At the time, she wondered how many classes it had, as, like most of the buildings, it was small and only two storeys. At the rear was a basketball court which surprised her, and she remembers thinking if basketball was popular in Greece.

The children smile and laugh, they are always talking amongst each other. It is uplifting to see children this happy, such innocence stirs fond images of her own childhood and a convivial warmth spreads through her.

A father, she assumes, passes below her, with a girl sitting on his shoulders. She has long dark hair that bobs with each step. Unlike the others, the girl's face is set, almost determined, Grace thinks. Her face has the look of natural beauty, like the young girls often portrayed in television adverts and magazines. The father looks up, more by chance than any interest in Grace and, to her surprise, smiles a reserved, *hello*. Grace returns the gesture. She resists an urge to raise her hand, her modesty restricts this, and she straightens up and pulls the soft collar of her dressing gown around her neck.

She presses her back against the chair and watches as they continue down the street. Grace releases her hold on the dressing gown and absently fiddles with the cord tied around her waist, as the man and child turn down a small lane that Grace knows will take them to the school gates.

It is already warm, and she can feel her shins tingle from the sun's glare. This morning, they look a bright red, burnt from yesterdays overexposure. She won't forget to cover them in sun cream today.

It has always been one of surprise and wonderment when, every morning, Grace gazes over the terracotta roofs towards a sensuous sea, cerulean blue, constantly amending and sprinkling diamonds like shattered glass. Her heart is embellished by the dazzling brightness and decorated surfaces of colour that adorn each archway, house and structure in luminous blue, alluring mauve, and brilliant white.

The baker's shop is only a few feet away and she smells the sweet aroma of freshly baked bread, pastries and cakes that transforms the air into a riotous bouquet that the ovens have fired. Each morning, her senses are illuminated with smells, tastes, sights and sounds that are becoming familiar, but always experienced new and unique to this space and time.

She decides that this morning, she will buy a loaf of freshly baked bread and then some jam from *Sofia's Delicatessen.*

She steps from the shade of the doorway and immediately feels the heat of the morning sun upon her shoulders. She crosses the street where it is sheltered, checks her bag for her purse and then ambles at a slow pace. She turns a corner that takes her down a steep hill where, in front of her, she can see tall masts and a myriad of boats, all shapes and sizes, hugging the harbour wall. She has forgotten the surreality of her dream and its residual impact, and now, amongst the sea air, she feels revitalised. Amongst the palm trees, traffic and pedestrians, the sun gleams off the pavements. She puts on her sunglasses and pulls her bag further up her shoulder. In places, weeds appear between the paving slabs, and skeletal cats lounge in the shade of doorways and under tables, where people sip coffee, and tea, and eat English breakfasts with chips, a peculiarity she can't get her head around.

She smooths her hair and readjusts the clasp that keeps it in place. She enters the delicatessen and slips her sunglasses onto her head. She takes a moment to adjust her eyes. Sofia is a slim woman, with dark wavy hair. She wears her make up discreetly and it compliments her features. Grace would place her in her forties. She knows she has a daughter, Grace has seen them together.

Sofia is reaching into her display and rearranging pastries and cakes when she looks up and smiles. 'Good morning.'

'Kalimera,' Grace replies.

Sofia's smile widens. 'You're learning Greek?'

'I'm trying. I can only say a few words.'

'It takes time and practice. I admire that, learning to speak the language.'

'Your English is excellent. Where did you learn?'

'I went to university in London in my twenties. I was able to improve my English every day, just like you will.'

'I don't think I'll ever be able to speak Greek like you speak English.'

'I thought that too. You'll be surprised how quickly you'll learn. You'll pick up new words every day.'

'I hope so.'

'What can I get you?'

'I was hoping you had jam.'

'I do. My friend makes it. She has her own business.' Sofia points to a shelf full of jars, each with the same logo emblazoned on the front. 'It's just over there. You'll find quite a variety.'

'Oh, I'm not that adventurous. I'm looking for raspberry.'

Grace picks up a jar. 'The jars are quaint all by themselves. It would be a shame to throw them out. I think I'll take two.'

'You haven't tried it, yet.'

'I don't need to, it's worth it just for the jars.'

Sofia takes the jars from Grace with a confident half smile. 'I'm sure you'll like the jam. I love it myself.'

'Well, that's all I need to know,' Grace says, unzipping her bag and taking out her purse.

'That's six euros. Do you want a bag?'

'Yes, please. I'm going to the bakers, I'll use it for that also.'

'Very environmentally friendly.'

'It was my job.'

'Really, what did you do?'

'I was a sustainability researcher at Edinburgh University.'

'Wow! How interesting.'

'Really? I don't normally get that kind of reaction.'

'It's a passion of mine. In fact, if you're interested, there's a group of us who clean the beach of plastics and rubbish every week. You're welcome to come along... if you want?'

Grace's eyes light up. 'I'd love too. When is it?'

'Tomorrow, in fact. We meet at the beach in the morning, around nine.'

'Perfect. I'll be there.'

Sofia hands Grace the plastic bag. 'This will be one of the last plastic bags I give out.'

'Oh! Why is that?'

'I'm changing to paper and encouraging customers to bring their own bag.'

Grace nods in approval. 'That's a great idea. The supermarkets back home have been doing it for some time now. If you want a bag, you must pay for one. It encourages people to use the same bag each time.'

'That's what I'm hoping to achieve.'

'Well, good luck. And I'll see you tomorrow.'

'Until tomorrow. Enjoy the jam.'

'Oh, I'm sure I will.'

When Grace leaves the shop, she feels uplifted. She thinks she will like living in Molyvos. She attributes this to having a purpose again. She is not just going to be engaged in the small things in life, she has found something of worth, something she believes in.

The Present

An Englishman in a Hat

The next morning, Grace strolls through the town on her way to the beach. She passes the bank, the church with its bell tower and the school. She smiles at an old woman in a headscarf, dressed in black.

The sun is a golden disk in the sky and already, the rising heat makes Grace feel flush, but she is happy.

As her shoes sink into sand, Grace can see a group of people up ahead. Someone is handing out what looks like large bags.

Sofia touches her lightly on the shoulder. 'Thanks for coming, Grace. I hope you're not allergic to latex?'

'No, not that I know off.'

'Good, take these then.' Sofia hands her a pair of blue latex gloves and smiles. 'Health and safety. You'll be surprised at what we find.'

Grace glances over the beach. Ahead, there are rows of umbrellas and sunbeds descending to the sea. Even at this early hour, sun worshippers pepper the beach, lacquering their skin with sun cream.

Grace estimates there are about twenty men and women of various ages readying themselves to begin. A keen enthusiasm spreads through the group and an older man in a straw panama hat raises his voice above the chatter.

'Right folks, we all know the drill. Our newcomer,' he nods towards Grace, 'can stay close to Sofia, she'll keep you right. What's your name, my dear?'

'Grace.'

'Well Grace, welcome to our motley crew. Okay, let's get started.'

'We walk in a row along the width of the beach and pick up the rubbish lying around. Sometimes we come across condoms, pardon the pun. So, keep the gloves on. If you find money, give it to Peter at the end of the clean-up. We use it to buy the gloves and bags. Anything sharp goes in the yellow tubs.' Several people are carrying yellow containers. 'We dispose of the glass we find and sometimes needles, I'm afraid, separately.'

Grace raises her eyebrows. 'I see.'

'Is there anyone here you know?'

'I don't think so.'

And then Grace sees a man bending forward, reaching with his hand into the sand. He is familiar, she is sure of it, yet she can't pinpoint how she knows him.

By the time they have finished, Grace's muscles are aching. She places her hands on her lower back and stretches.

'Well done, Grace, you did a grand job.'

'Thank you, Peter. I enjoyed it. I think I've used muscles I didn't know I had.'

'There's nothing like the sense of achievement. It gets easier. Will you be joining us again?'

'Try and stop me.'

'Good, we need all the help we can get. Please excuse me, I need to help with loading the bags onto the truck.' Peter tilts his hat and moves off.

'I forgot to ask,' Sofia says. 'Did you like the jam?'

'It was delicious.' Grace peels off her gloves. 'Do you open later in the morning, after this?'

'The shop's open now. I've got an older lady, Angeliki, she works a few hours in the morning.'

'Ah, I see.'

'What are you doing today?'

'I'm trying to keep out of the sun for a while.' She lifts a leg, slightly, to show Sofia her sunburnt shin.

'Oh, that looks sore. Best to stay out of it. The sun ages your skin, you know. Always wear a hat and keep out of the midday sun. In fact, when you come next time, remember, wear a hat.'

'I will. When is the next time?'

'Tomorrow morning. Not everyone comes each day. Most people have their regular days, except Peter, that is, he's here every morning.'

'He's English.'

'He is. You can't disguise that posh accent, but he's lived in Greece longer than he ever did in England. He used to be a tour guide on Zakynthos, you know. He's retired now.'

'I could imagine him being a tour guide and a good one at that. There's an authoritative, yet friendly presence about him.'

'Well, I've been told he was one of the best. Zakynthos must be a poorer place without him.'

'How did he end up here?'

'You'll have to ask him that,' Sofia replies, smiling.

'I love his hat.'

'Oh, the Panama. I've never seen him without it.'

The Past

Wishing Well

Edinburgh had always been home, I had never lived anywhere else. We bought a house on Colington Road. It badly needed renovating. The previous owners, an old couple, had lived in the house since the fifties and the décor hadn't changed much since then. It had a large garden, populated by mature trees and a fish pond. When we viewed the house, I was adamant the pond would be the first feature to go.

We acquired the house at a good price, a bargain, considering the inflated property market in Edinburgh, but we had to spend a small fortune on the renovation of every room.

I loved my house, we had made it our own, stamped our identity on it. It was always going to be a home for our children, our family.

The house was a short walk away from the Union Canal built to link the centre of Edinburgh with the Forth and Clyde canal at Falkirk. I loved to walk there, it also exercised my mind, amongst the dog walkers, joggers, cyclists and parents with toddlers on tricycles and youngsters on skateboards. Sometimes, canoes would spear through the dark murky waters, scattering ducks, as the solitary swan, I had never seen another, continued to gracefully glide amongst the reeds.

The canal flowed almost straight and narrow through the city and it had become a common walk of several miles I took most weeks into Tollcross, adjacent to Fountainbridge. I often bought wine gums at the Tesco Express for the walk back home, but before then, I'd visit Loudons, an all-day café and artisan bakery for a fruit scone with clotted cream and jam.

Occasionally, at the weekends, and if the weather was fair, both Jamie and I would walk the canal into town. We often went for lunch at a favourite bar or café, in the grass-market, or along Lothian Road, before doing some shopping, and then, depending if it had started to rain, we'd wander back, at a leisurely pace, talking about our plans: holidays, weekends away and starting a family.

We had a small group of friends that we shared. Really, they were my friends before I met Jamie. After several get-togethers, Jamie started to warm to the husbands and partners and we soon became part of the group, a couple, invited to parties, nights out and meals at the weekends.

It was a happy time for us both. When I think back, I could never say, *no*, to him, and that was my problem, it became our problem.

We went on long weekends to Skye and The Kyle of Lochalsh. We climbed Munros and ate lunch in little pubs, in villages, without a Post Office, whose names I couldn't pronounce. To be fair, I enjoyed most of it, not the weather, it always seemed to rain, and if it didn't, the sky seemed to be lost in a continual mist that seeped into my skin. All I really wanted to do was take long weekends in Rome, visit Venice or London.

We went to Majorca one year: Puerto Pollensa. A week in a four-star hotel, bed and breakfast. We didn't go full board, because Jamie wanted to eat out at the local restaurants and eat authentic Majorcan cuisine.

We hired a car and toured the island. I hadn't realised it was so big. I loved the weather. It was hot and sunny for the whole week, even though it was early October. Olivia was conceived on that holiday. We had been trying to start a family since January of that year and I was despondent at our lack of success. Jamie, on the other hand, was more relaxed about it, saying it can take some couples a year or two. I think he was enjoying the sex too much. By that stage, it was not lovemaking. It felt mechanical and purposeful. There was to be a product at the end of it, after all. I know you can't compare a baby to that kind of thing, but, well, that's how it felt at the time.

One day, we took a car trip to the historic village of Valldemossa. It was a charming little place with steep pedestrian streets and buildings with old stone facades. I remember it was mountainous and very green. On the way there, we passed gorgeous beaches and coves. Below the hilltop town, I remember a quaint little harbour at a little fishing village. We ate lunch there and the seafood, freshly caught, or so we were told, was delicious. I wasn't sure if it was a marketing ploy, or the truth, it didn't matter. I'd never tasted fish like it, or since.

After lunch, we visited the magnificent 14th-century Carthusian monastery. It housed a large well and it was the tradition for visitors to make a wish and throw money into its water. So, I did. Whether it was coincidence or not, my wish came true. It wasn't until, weeks later, when I knew I was pregnant, that I made the calculations, and then it dawned on me, our child was conceived that night after I made my wish.

The Past

Olivia

Incomprehensible speech, insistent. The midwife wiped her forehead with the back of her hand. I heard the word; *forceps* and it rang in my ears. Someone laughed, a loud explosion in another room. The midwife glanced at the machines, bleeping, numbers that were decreasing with each passing second. I had no real sense of their significance, but when the midwife's frown turned to alarm, I instinctively knew something was seriously wrong with my baby, my baby was in danger!

'What's going on? Why isn't the baby coming?' Jamie's eyes pleaded.

The midwife turned to her colleague. 'We need the consultant, now!'

In a second, the atmosphere had changed. It frightened me. My legs were being lifted, placed on something, I couldn't see what. There was an urgency that established itself in the tasks the midwife performed. I searched her face. I wanted her expression to relax, I wanted her to smile, again, as she had before.

How beautiful Olivia looked. Even in imperfection, perfection could be found. I lay with her, against my skin, for two hours. My gaze never left her. She had the finest of eyelashes, her skin unblemished, a button nose and the tiniest of hands. I'd never seen fingers and nails so small. I was reminded of the babies I had held, the curled warmth of their fingers wrapped around my own. Olivia was still. She was a miniature likeness of Jamie and me.

I didn't hear her cry, or watch with adulation, her chest rise and fall with each new breath. I was surprised at how much hair she had, black like the night and silky to touch. I stroked her forehead and told her how much she was loved, she was not alone, mummy was here, as my tears fell from my cheeks onto her delicate and milky skin.

I whispered her name, *Olivia,* and repeated it again and again, as if by doing so, she would open her eyes. Suddenly, for the first time, I realised, I didn't know the colour of her eyes and in that moment, I was engulfed in my loss for the child I would never have, the smile I would never see, the voice I would never hear and the reflection in her eyes I would never glimpse.

The midwife asked if we wanted to take photographs of Olivia. She said it often brought a comfort to the parents and if we wished, we could dress her in the clothes we had brought with us.

Olivia had a beautiful head of hair, dark and spikey. I brushed her hair, we washed and changed her. If all I could do was perform these simple tasks, then they would become an expression of my love for her.

I wanted to show her. I loved her more than anything in the world, this little person I had just met. In those precious moments, the world around me did not exist. It melted from me. Nothing mattered anymore, except this little person who my heart ached for.

We were asked by the midwife who was with us if we wanted to have some keepsakes, such as a memory box? I wanted to take my baby home, take her into her bedroom for the first time and place her in her cot. I didn't want to hear the midwife's words. I wanted to scream at her. I didn't, of course.

We kept Olivia's name band, a lock of her hair, footprints and handprints. I kept the blanket she was wrapped in. I smelt it constantly, trying to fill myself with her, to keep her close, to keep her with me.

We were asked to give our consent for a post mortem to be carried out. My mind swam in a whirlpool of confusion. I remember vaguely, the words, *chromosome analysis*.

We registered her birth and her death. This compounded our grief. It was an unnatural thing to do, but at the same time, it was real.

We both decided we wanted a funeral. We needed to say goodbye, celebrate Olivia's short life, show that she meant something, she had worth, she was loved.

I was Catholic but lapsed. Jamie was not religious, he didn't even know if he believed in God. He had never given it much thought. We decided on a Humanist funeral. Just close family and friends, an intimate experience we both wanted to share with those we loved and who were part of our lives.

I remember the white coffin, so small, so fragile. Both Jamie and I decided to choose a personal object and lay it beside Olivia in the coffin. For some reason, I'm not sure why I choose a small crucifix and chain I received for my First Holy Communion when I was seven. I had kept it all those years. Not for any specific reason, but in a way, it had been, I suppose. Jamie cut a lock of his hair and tied it together with a little band. We also put a photograph of both of us beside her, so we would always be close to her.

I tried to be strong. The medication helped a little. Inside, I was angry, I was hollow, I was distraught; mostly, I was numb.

I awoke every morning with the same thought, *my baby died.* I didn't think I could cry anymore, but I did, every day. I had never felt grief so raw. The image of her lying on my chest, so innocent, so pure, untouched, uncontaminated by the world would always be on my mind.

I constantly asked why? Why my baby? Why us? What did we do wrong? I saw mothers with their babies, couples walking with prams and it filled me with immense jealousy and even anger, at times. Grief can take many forms. I think I've experienced them all.

I built a small shrine to her: a photograph, a woollen hat I'd knitted, a soft toy... Most of the time I existed in a constant state of disbelief, overwhelming guilt that I could do nothing to save her. My shame suffocated me with every breath I took.

There was a continual stream of visitors, bringing gifts of homemade lasagne, chilli and curries. At one point, we had so many flowers and cards in the house, it was beginning to look like we lived in a florist or card shop. Friends were kind with their sympathetic words and selflessness, some even did the housework and our laundry.

Jamie and I spoke a lot about Olivia. She consumed our minds, our thoughts and conversation. I wanted my family and friends to talk about her too, to acknowledge that I had a baby girl and her name was... no, her name is Olivia. It was important to me because by doing so, it confirmed her existence. I wanted to show them the photographs we took of her. I wanted them to ask how I was coping. I wanted them to know it was normal to do so. And then, there were other times, I wanted to be left alone, with my thoughts, my memories. I wanted Olivia all to myself.

My body didn't know Olivia had died, so it went through the normal processes, losing lots of blood, feeling tired but worst of all, producing breast milk... that really was difficult for me to cope with. I was told I could take medication to dry it up, or just let nature take its natural course. I felt that to deny and stop the changes in my body, was in a way, denying that Olivia ever existed. I wept uncontrollably every time I had to express some milk. It got very painful.

I hadn't eaten properly for, well...a long time. I walked around with a great weight on my chest. I was exhausted every waking hour, yet, at night, I struggled to sleep. Every day my arms ached to hold her. I had never felt so alone in my life. I felt a failure, as a partner, but mostly, as a mother.

It felt as if Jamie and I had separated. We grieved in our own different ways. At first, Jamie spoke about her, but then, when he finally returned to work, he clammed up. He was always working, coming home late and drinking. It became a problem as did other things too...

He seemed to just... close down. At times, I felt the Jamie I knew was also dead. I had suffered two bereavements. I had lost him. We stopped talking, communicating. I had no idea what he was feeling. He was becoming a stranger. We should have been close, we should have been sharing our grief, supporting one another, listening, comforting. I realised we would never be the same people again. I tried to ignore it, hide from it, but as a couple, we weren't normal, not anymore. We had become like our friends; the ones we swore we would never turn into.

Being intimate was another change. We had stopped touching one another. When we did, he could not touch me without reacting like I had given him an electric shock. He said he just wanted to get back to normal, but our normal had changed and it frightened me. In my entire life, I had never felt so vulnerable.

The Present

An Undefinable Chemistry

She is holding her flip flops in one hand, dangling loosely, as her feet sink into the glassy, wet sand leaving perfect indentations, like clay models that the tiny waves breaking around her ankles cover and steal. Along the sand, smooth stones and pebbles pepper the shore, like miniature mountain ranges. Ahead, the headland looks like a dark shadow stretching and falling into the sea where a solitary white cloud melts into a pastel bleached sky. And, on the horizon, she catches sight of a white shape, a large boat, possibly a cruise ship, she thinks. She pulls her gaze from the sea to see a plane, streaking silver, catching the sun's light,

She loves these early morning walks, where she can stroll the fringes of the beach, quite alone, apart from the occasional bird that floats and bobs on the surf unperturbed by her presence.

Gradually, she is aware of the weight lifting, the darkness receding, the pain melting. Today is a good day; they are not all like this. She is not in control of it. She thinks it might have something to do with certain chemicals being released in the body and wiring up the mind again, like an internal electrician, the synapses and impulses, they all have an impact. Some days, her wires are disconnected, broken. Other days, like today, the pathways are connected. This is how she thinks of it. This is how she makes sense of it.

In the distance she can make out a figure, a man in shorts and t-shirt, laying out towels on two sunbeds, marking his territory for the forthcoming day. Once the towels are secured, he trudges up the beach. Grace wonders if he will now meet his wife, or a partner and have breakfast, secure in the knowledge that they have claimed their part of the beach. What a peculiar behaviour, Grace thinks to herself, marking one's territory, like an animal that leaves its scent to ward off others.

A covering of trees lines the fringes of the beach and, beyond them, rising towards a medieval castle, tightly packed lanes, sprinkled in a variety of illuminating colours, are lined with shops and doorways that lead to pot lined courtyards and decorative archways. Here there is an intimacy, unexpected to the visitor.

There have been times she has experienced the spasm of doubt. What was she thinking? she would berate herself, usually after something had broken in the house. She would question the logic of her decision to leave Edinburgh, the familiar surroundings, the job that defined her, friends, family and come to a country she only knew through listening to others who had holidayed on its islands, or the movies she had watched, *Captain Correlli's Mandolin* and the one with the Abba songs, its title always escaping her.

Of course, the reality is different. There have been many times she has thought of packing up and booking a ticket back to Edinburgh, back to the places that haunt her, even now. Yet, she is still here, she reminds herself, and on a morning like this, she is glad of it.

She registers an urge for coffee and decides to go to the taverna just off the beach. She has tasted all the coffee on offer in most of the cafes and tavernas in town and she has decided this is her favourite and the least pretentious establishment of them all.

Peter looks up from his paper. 'Grace, my dear. What a pleasant surprise, please join me.' He is wearing a crisp blue shirt, white chinos and tan loafers. His hat is on the table.

'Are you sure? I don't want to disturb you.'

'Nonsense. It's all doom and gloom in the paper this morning. I could do with some company.'

Grace takes a seat and flattens the front of her dress over her legs.

Peter gestures towards a waiter. 'What would you like?'

'Just a coffee.'

'Are you sure you wouldn't like a cake?'

'I'm fine, thanks.'

Peter orders the coffee in Greek. 'This is my little piece of heaven. I love coming here in the morning. It sets me up for the rest of the day.'

Grace smiles. 'I like it too.'

'We already have something in common. Will you be helping us again in our endeavours to clean the beach?'

She nods. 'I will. I was just down there, and it didn't seem too bad.'

'That's because we now have a new initiative to get people to become more self-aware and to help us keep the beach clean.'

'What's that?'

'You didn't see the sign, then?'

'No. What sign?'

Peter nods in the direction of a large placard perched against a small wall in front of the taverna.

Grace reads out loud. '*A free coffee if you collect a bucket of rubbish off the beach. Buckets available inside. Every little helps...* What a great idea. Was it yours?'

'Peter smiles. 'I can't take the credit for it. It was a collective decision, really. We have our weekly meetings here, you should come to them, Grace. Anyway, it originated from a discussion from one of the action plans we had. The owner, Vasilis, sometimes helps us on the beach. He's always enthusiastic when it comes to helping out.'

'I would have thought that was the council's responsibility.'

'It is. They clean it one evening a week. I'm glad they do, but as you've seen for yourself, it isn't enough. Budget restrictions, that's always the official line. It's like the roads and pavements, there are weeds popping up everywhere. They really need to get their priorities right. People are going to stop visiting if a certain standard isn't maintained.'

'That's why it's so important to do what you're doing.'

'I abhor the pollution of our world, Grace. I really do, and it's getting worse. It's constantly around us. Some of it we can see, like today, on the beach, but most of it we're blind to, or we choose not to see it. Take the sea, for instance, it's dying, as are the creatures who live in it. What we are doing here is on an individual level. I'm never going to stop climate change and eliminate microplastics, that needs governments to act, innovation, policies and funding. Individually, we're just small fry, but collectively, we can be an unstoppable force of change. Take our little beach for instance. By using initiatives like giving away free coffee, people are being proactive and actively contributing. Also, it gives us the opportunity to educate them, we are spreading our message. People can ignore it, that's their prerogative, but even if we just manage to prick their conscience, even if it's just one or two every day, in time, that message will spread and become an unstoppable force.'

'I agree with you, Peter, and there's no doubting your commitment.'

'Ah, here's your coffee.'

'Sofia tells me you use to be a tour guide,' Grace says, sipping her coffee.

'I still do a little. Just to keep the old grey matter working. Only once a week though, and just for senior citizens. We walk at a leisurely pace.' He frowns and smiles at the same time.

'It must take a lot of preparation. I don't know how you manage to do it all.'

'I love what I do, so there's no need to rest and take a day off. I live for the moment now. I don't care about the past or the future anymore. It's my coping mechanism, my safety valve.'

'I wish I had your outlook.'

'It might be an age thing. I think once you reach a certain age you start to see life with a certain clarity, you view it through a different lens. Well, I do anyway.'

'Have you always lived here, I mean since you came to Greece?'

'Oh no. When I was much younger, I spent a lot of time in Athens before I settled down in Zakynthos.'

'Did you live in Zakynthos long?'

'I did. Twenty years, in fact.'

'That's a long time. What made you move?'

He wrinkles his forehead remembering. 'A promise.'

'That sounds intriguing.'

Peter pats the newspaper with his fingers. 'I was a silly old bugger if the truth be told.' He breathes in deeply and looks away.

'I didn't mean to upset you.' Shit, I should learn to keep my big mouth shut, Grace chastises herself.

'Oh, don't worry. You haven't upset me. It's just... well, how can I put it, time isn't always a great healer.'

It's Grace's turn to be seized by the past. 'No. That's true.'

Peter gives a little smile, but he is too polite to enquire any further. 'So, to answer your question, Zakynthos was my home for many years, and I loved my job. I worked for one of the big tour companies who were based in Athens and well, to get to the point, they were cutting back, the recession and all that. I'm sure you've heard about it?'

Grace nods. 'It must have been terrible.'

'Being of a certain age I didn't fit the companies new branding, so I was offered a package as part of my severance. It didn't come as a surprise and I was grateful that I'd been offered such a decent amount of money, but it still wasn't compensation for losing my job. It was all I'd known, all I'd ever done in Greece. I wasn't qualified to do anything else, really. And, anyway, who was going to employ an old man like me?'

'You're not old, Peter.'

'Ah, thank you for your kindness, Grace, but it's the truth. Anyway, at my age, I wasn't looking to be swept off my feet, certainly not by someone fifteen years younger than me. Colin was… how shall I put it… he was gorgeous, he had a personality and he made me happy, for a while.' He lets out a small trill of laughter. 'I loved him.' Peter wipes his eye. 'Anyway, it's not a happy ever after I'm afraid. Colin persuaded me to go into business with him, not in Zakynthos, but here. It's funny how love can blinker you, steal your common sense, even the most rational of thinkers have succumbed to its lure. I certainly did. We… I should say, I offered various speciality tours, for those of a certain age. It was full on at one point. We were very busy. It surpassed all our expectations.'

'What went wrong?'

'Colin wasn't who I thought he was. He was seeing others. I knew, but somehow, I thought, let him have his fun. The trouble was, I could close my eyes to what I didn't want to see, but I couldn't close my heart to what I was feeling.'

'That's terrible, Peter. You weren't to blame. How can people be so nasty?'

'Because he was a con man, it's that simple, and a good one. Anyway, to cut to the chase, he ran off with most of my money and left me with debts I struggled to pay. And off he went, he just disappeared, no doubt to do the same all over again to some other blinded old fool. Unfortunately, I have thin skin.'

Grace can see tears in his eyes.

'It's not a secret around here. Everyone who knows me knows about it. They were here after all. If I didn't tell you, someone else would. That's how it works, isn't it?'

'I suppose so.'

'And that's why people are guessing about you.'

'Me!'

'Most are genuinely curious, that's all, although a few will make it their business to find out. You have a good friend in Monica.'

'You know her?'

'We have a little community here, ex-pats and all that. Monica is the salt of the earth, there's not many like her.'

Grace clears her throat. 'I don't know what I would have done without her to tell you the truth. I've known her since I was a child. She's been a saint really.'

'Saint Monica… she'd like that.' Peter laughs.

Grace knows Peter is too polite to ask about her past and normally, she would refrain from going there. But there is something alluring about him. He has safe eyes and his manner is old school. He is a gentleman, yes, that's it, he is of a bygone age, a typical English gentleman, and she has warmed to him.

'I had a baby daughter, Olivia.'

Peter can hear the sadness in her voice. He reaches and touches her hand. 'You don't have to tell me.'

'It's fine, honest. I want to. Sometimes, I just need to talk.'

Peter nods. 'I'm a good listener.'

Grace takes a deep breath. Should she be divulging her past to a man she doesn't really know. Why did it feel right? She believes when you meet certain people for the first time there can be an undefinable chemistry, a connection. She was aware of it the first time she saw Peter. She knew she would be able to tell this man her innermost secrets and he would guard them with his silence. Yes, this was the right thing to do.

She speaks for ten minutes, but she doesn't tell him everything. In that time, Peter never interrupts her flow; instead, he just nods, or occasionally, a half-smile crosses his face. As she speaks, Grace fiddles with her chain and the cross on it catches the light.

'The feelings still surface, even after all this time. I think they always will. The flashbacks have stopped, thank God. At times, I think I am going mad. The G.P. mentioned Post Traumatic Stress, but the flashbacks just lasted a few months.

'Separating is part of life. It's normal. Lots of couples do it. The important thing is, who have you become when you come out of the other side? How has it defined you? That's what counts, that's important, that's what matters… I think.'

Peter sighs. 'My heart goes out to you, my dear. You've been through so much in such a short space of time, yet here you are.'

'What do you mean?' Grace asks.

'It's okay to feel hurt, to feel ashamed. You're not weak if you cry. If you feel afraid. You can feel achingly vulnerable. It doesn't matter if you're having difficulty with the emotions your experience stirs. And so what if, at times, you can't find the right words to express them. Believe me, I know all about emotionalism and human connections. The important thing, my dear, is this… there will be a shift in all of this. One day, either next week, next month, it doesn't matter when, but what does matter is this, one day, you will recover. I promise you.'

Grace can feel a wet sting in her eyes. 'I hope you're right, Peter. I really do.'

'I've got experience. I've been there, several times. Believe me, Grace, one day what you're feeling now will pass.'

'How can you be so sure. I've lost everything I loved. The second I saw Olivia, she became the most important thing in my world, and I had to let her go.'

'I know...I'

'How can you know how that feels?' She looks away.

'I know because I've had to let go of someone who was everything to me, who was my world.'

She looks at him. 'What do you mean? A lover?'

Peter shakes his head. 'No. My son.'

'You have a son?'

'I know, hard to believe isn't it?'

'I didn't mean it like that. You surprised me, that's all.'

'Well... it's true. We're revealing quite a lot about ourselves. There must be something in the air or the coffee.'

Grace feels awkward and Peter has noticed. 'I don't mind telling you, Grace, after all you've shared with me. We have more in common than you know, my dear.'

Peter scratches his chin. 'I was eighteen and she was twenty. Her name was Sharon. She was my brother's girlfriend and well, one night when my parents were out, she and Freddy came home from the pub. They had both been drinking, obviously, but Freddy was worse for wear and fell asleep. Sharon came on to me. She said that she'd always fancied me, and it was me she should really be going out with. She tried to kiss me, and I politely pulled away, but she was very persistent, very determined.'

'So, what about... being gay?'

Grace's confusion brings a chuckle to Peter. 'This was my opportunity to find out if I really was. Oh, I'd known long before then I wasn't attracted to girls and I had several crushes on boys in the past, but sexually I was naïve. I was still a virgin. I hadn't even kissed a boy or a girl for that matter. So, you see, it was like a test, I suppose. Here was my chance to find out, to finally prove to myself that these feelings I'd carried around with me since as far back as I could remember were suddenly given this opportunity to finally prove themselves, one way or the other and as I said, she was a very determined young lady.'

Grace is looking at him, a keen expression crosses her face. 'You didn't do it with your brother in the same room?'

'She virtually dragged me to my bedroom.'

'And?'

'Well, obviously we had sex. She knew I was a virgin. To cut to the chase, it felt odd and obviously, there was the end result. She had to coax me a bit.'

'Too much information.'

'Anyway, after that night, I had no doubt in my mind about how I felt, about who I was. I knew deep in my core, the same as I knew I loved my parents and my brother.'

'When did you find out she was pregnant?'

'About two months later. Freddy was adamant it had nothing to do with him. They hadn't gone that far. That surprised me, given the enthusiasm she had shown that night.'

'What happened?'

'Well. My parents were devastated. My father, who was a prominent lawyer, arranged to set up a monthly allowance on the insistence that Sharon provided receipts that proved the money was being used to provide for the baby. Whenever Sharon married, this arrangement would stop. My parents and I were to be given access to the baby once a week. He was very thorough. Sharon had to sign a legal agreement, which she did, of course. It was a generous amount.'

'How did your brother take it?'

'He was relieved and glad it was me who had ruined my life, his words, as it could have easily been him.'

'Well, I suppose given the circumstances, he took it quite well.'

'Relieved more than anything, I would say.'

'What is his name?'

'James, after her father. Little Jimmie was the term of endearment she often used. Anyway, when James was two, she just disappeared. We were told she had met someone, an American. Seemingly, it had been going on for about a year. They moved to Chicago. It broke my mother's heart. In my young wisdom, I thought it was a good time to tell them I was gay. She never fully recovered. They were products of their time.' Peter takes a deep breath. 'My mother was worried I'd be carted off to prison. It was a different world back then to the one we live in now.'

'Thankfully.' Grace smiles at him.

Peter smiles back at her. 'It has its different challenges, today. I didn't come out to make myself happy or to confirm to myself I was ready for the people in my world to know. I did it to end the constant pain I felt. Afterwards, I felt peaceful, something I'd hadn't felt in a long time.'

'What about your son, James?'

Peter stares down at his hands. 'I never saw him again.'

'Oh, Peter. That's awful. I'm so sorry.'

'I was young, so young. I suppose I blotted it from my mind. But, as I got older, I thought about it differently, you know, at Christmas... his birthdays. I began to wonder if he looked like me? What was he like? Did he know his father lived in England? I ached for him. I still do. He'll be fifty-two, now. He might even have grandchildren.'

Grace reaches over and takes his hand. 'Did you ever think about finding him?'

'All the time. Something kept stopping me.'

'What?'

'He has his family. He doesn't know about me. I'm a total stranger to him, not his father.'

'You don't know that Sharon could have told him.'

'Even if she did, she's never tried to contact me; the ball has always been in her court. She knew where my parents lived. I didn't want to just turn up and expect to be part of his life. What if he didn't want anything to do with me? I couldn't live with that rejection.

'Life can be full of second chances, Grace. Take me for instance. I've met someone I care a great deal about, and I never thought I ever would feel those feelings again. We have lunch and dinner together, we have the same taste in wine, we both love listening to Frank Sinatra. It works because we compromise, we make the effort, we share experiences, we share our interests with each other, we make each other laugh. It has taken a long time, but I have found the perfect partner. I'm content in the here and now and I'm grateful for what I've got, and I try not to dwell on what I don't have. I don't *what if* the past anymore. I allow myself to be happy now and so should you.'

'I haven't felt the human chemistry of wanting and being wanted for a long time.'

'You will, you just haven't met the right person, yet. You're still young, my dear and you're attractive.'

Grace pulls her fingers through her hair.

'You're embarrassing me.'

'I didn't mean to be abrasive.'

'You're not, Peter. If anything, you're the opposite and captivating.'

'Now I'm the one who's embarrassed.'

'But that's the persona you create. So, how would you describe yourself?'

'Serious.' Peter leaves the word hanging in the air. He diminishes the finality of it with a lopsided smile and then says. 'But only sometimes.'

'Do you still see your brother?'

'He's dead now.'

'Oh. I'm sorry.'

'It's fine. He died when he was thirty-five, a car crash. It feels like a long time ago now. When we were growing up, we never really had much in common. For most of my childhood and teenage years, I felt like an only child. There was only a year between us. He played rugby and cricket and I liked to visit museums, read books and go to art galleries. We were polar opposites, really. Do you have any brothers or sisters, Grace?'

'I have a sister, she's three years younger than me. She's married, a boy and a girl, lovely kids.'

'Do you see her often?'

'Not as much as I'd like. She lives in London. Her husband, Tom, works in the city. It's going to be even trickier now I'm here.'

'And you're like being here?'

'I feel good about it, excited even.'

'That's good. I'm glad. When I left Zakynthos to come here, I thought it was the worst mistake of my life, initially, that is, and especially with what transpired. There won't be a next time for me, but if there was, I'd pause before leaping. It's turned out alright in the end. I'm an expert at adapting, I suppose.'

'That would make me a beginner, then. I'm just getting used to my new normal.'

'You're doing fine. I really admire what you've done, Grace. Not many people could do what you're doing.'

'I question the rationality of it, all the time. Sometimes, I'm close to going back home.'

'You're still here,' Peter remarks.

'I am. Meeting people like yourself has had a big impact on my decisions when I think about going back home. It's important that it's a daily choice. That way, I know I'm here for the right reasons.'

'That's a good way to look at it.'

'It's a new way of thinking, for me, anyway.'

He glances at his watch. 'Oh, I need to get going. I've got a group of twelve this morning for a tour. He picks up his hat and places it on his head. 'I think we're going to be good friends, Grace. Oh, and by the way, you must come to our next meeting. It's here if you're interested?'

'I'd like that.'

'Friday morning at ten.'

'I'll be there.'

'Good. I'll see you then, if I don't see you before.' He touches the brim of his hat and tips his head slightly. 'Have a good day my dear. I'll pay for the coffee, my treat.'

After Peter has gone inside and paid, Grace watches him as he heads off and she can't help feeling captivated by his endearing humility and it feels like something good will come out of their meeting, a semblance of hope for the future.

The Past

The past cannot be revisited, only reinvented

Descriptions become embellished, facts omitted, contorted or overlooked. Memory is a delicate mooring to our accounts of who we think we are. Within this serene ocean of our memory a trickle of oil drips, a continuous release, a continuous tap, polluting the ocean, until it is impossible to discern what is accurate and is invented.

Sometimes, I realised, with a surprise, my memories were but emotions I felt. They left me frantic, they could be soothing, they could be accompanied by regret, an irritation that lingered and I agonised over it for long periods.

In my eagerness to remember the intimate and precious time I had with Olivia in that hospital room, I played and rewound, played again, fast-forwarded, paused, over and over again, the images in my head. Sometimes, the details blurred, a cataract of the mind, drifting from me like a feather caught in the wind. Other times, the images were clear in my mind.

I remember Olivia's fingers were perfect. I counted them, even though I could see they were as they should be. I'd never seen fingers so small, and her nails, minute things. I stared at them, perfectly formed. That's what I could not understand, to me, she was perfect, how could it have happened? My voice quivered as I repeated her name, *Olivia.* The silence in the room exacerbated my heartache, pressing against me, a constant reminder.

I traced the tip of my finger along Olivia's hand and then strayed across her arm. My pain was unbearable. I had known nothing like it. I gulped for air and sobbed.

And even now, after all this time, fragmented images appear and fade, like the sun, suddenly obscured by a cloud.

To compensate, I often found myself sinking into a world of dreams. I heard her voice, saw the colour of her eyes, I combed her long dark hair and observed its shine, as it fell from the brush. I caught her smile, watched her play in a sandpit, and I was filled with wild joy as she laughed whilst sitting on a swing. Tentatively, I let her go, as she, for the first time, rode her bike without stabilisers and my heart ached with a warmth that radiated through me like no other feeling I had ever known. A protectiveness so strong it was impossible to describe.

I sank into my world of dreams and woke into an intolerable nightmare, an immeasurably sad and unthinkable reality.

At times, I felt suffused with an irrepressible rage, a heat and colour on the surface of my face my hands trembled, and my eyes glazed, possessed. Everything would be perceived as a wrongdoing, painful, chaotic, and I suffered. I'm certain I would have been capable of... well, who knows. Then came the bouts of melancholy, joy, abrupt assertiveness, I was a kaleidoscope of emotions. It's safe to say, that person is a stranger to me now. I've grown into my courage and confidence.

Jamie and I were insulated in a bubble of our own making but, within that existence, there was a hole that gradually appeared, and it grew bigger with each day, each week, each month. Eventually, as bubbles do, it burst, with all its repercussions and blame.

We were wrapped in our own individual grief. We stopped talking to one other. I mean, really talking, communicating as a couple. We had become two separate individuals by then, almost strangers, just existing alongside each other. Jamie was absent beyond understanding.

And then, the day came when I couldn't take any more.

I remember it had been a weekend, a Saturday. I hadn't returned to work by then, but Jamie had. He needed the normality that it brought. I was on medication, he went to work, that's how we both coped. It was the usual Saturday morning. Jamie slept late as was his routine. I, on the other hand, was always up by six; my cocktail of sleeping tablets and mood stabilisers hardly touched me. I was still able to see the funny side of it, and often joked I needed a prescription for an elephant.

I just came out with it. Thinking back, he was waiting for me to say something, He always did. Jamie hated confrontation. He was always the passive one. He made me feel guilty. I often ended up feeling sorry for him, as if it was my fault. This time however it was different.

'This has gone on long enough, Jamie, we need to talk.'

'What is there to say?'

'What kind of statement is that?'

'A truthful one.'

I looked at him in faint alarm. 'I don't understand, Jamie. Why have we let it get like this? You never open up. I don't know what you're really thinking most of the time.'

'That's not fair. I do.'

'You never tell me.'

He shrugged.

'You haven't come near me since...'

'You can say it, Grace. Since Olivia died.'

'Yes. Since then. You don't look at me like you used to. You're distant. We're so far apart. It's like you don't love me anymore.'

He looked away. I could see the guilt on his face as he rubbed his eyes.

'I've changed, Grace. I can't help feeling the way I do.'

'What do you mean? You're beginning to worry me. Is there something you're not telling me, Jamie? What do mean, Jamie, what do you feel?'

'Us! This! I can't do it anymore.'

I felt my abdomen contract. The beginning of a sickening response engulfed me.

He pushed his hand through his hair. 'I'm leaving.'

'Where are you going?'

He shook his head. 'No, no. You don't understand. I'm leaving you.' He looked away again and walked towards the window. He sighed and laid his head against the glass.

I leaned my hand on the table to steady myself. I felt like I'd been hit by a car. To say it came as a blow is an understatement. Three words. That's all it took to shatter my world. They continued to reverberate inside my head.

'It's not you. It's me.'

I could hear his voice, but my mind was still trying to come to terms with those three words.

He looked at me, concentrating on my face. 'Did you hear me? It's not your fault.'

'What does that mean?'

'Exactly what I said. I'm to blame for this.'

'I don't understand. What have you done? Are you seeing someone else?'

He opened his mouth, but no words came out.

I felt tired, suddenly exhausted.

'I should have told you before now. I'm sorry.'

'Who is she? Do I know her?'

'No.'

I glared at him. 'How could you? Your child has just died.'

'She's been dead for eight months, Grace. Christ!'

'Oh! and I'm just supposed to move on now. Am I? *Get over it, Grace. Life goes on.* Well, it certainly did for you, you bastard.'

It was a natural reaction. I grabbed a vase with lilies in it that I bought the day before and launched it at him. Jamie brought his forearm across his face and ducked, but I had a good aim and the vase smashed on collision. When I think about it now, I felt a warm satisfaction at the look of shock and alarm on his face.

He rubbed his forearm. 'I deserved that.'

I sank to my knees. The family I had eight months ago had just disintegrated before me. I began to sob and fold my arms around my head. He took a few steps towards me and leaned forward, his hand outstretched.

'Don't come near me,' I screamed.

He stopped instantly, almost frozen.

'I want you out of here.'

'I'll go to a hotel.'

'I don't give a fuck where you go.'

I pressed the palm of my hand onto my forehead. *Stand up, stand up,* I commanded myself. And when I did, I could see he was taken aback by my reaction.

'I'll pack a few things and come back later for the rest of my stuff,' he said as if asking for permission.

He came out of the bedroom with a small suitcase. It was the physical representation that proclaimed this was really happening. I was sitting at the kitchen table and glared at him, the man I loved, the man who had just obliterated my life.

The Present

Sofia

Grace thinks her life has been diverted. Where would she be? What thoughts would still fester inside her head if she had not come to Lesvos? It is hard to think of a more difficult time in her life.

She remembers standing in the kitchen, in Edinburgh, her eyes closed to the world, her world, and the small fragments and sharp edges, remnants of a present from a friend, scattered on the floor tiles, that had been imported from Italy. They reflected the inserted lights of her kitchen ceiling, each light worth a small fortune, each positioned with a precision that highlighted a certain ambience and tone.

Here in Lesvos, none of that matters now, it is trivial, self-obsessed, decoration to fit her compartmental life. In the aftermath of their demise, a new perspective is born.

She can hear a noise coming from the harbour, a low rumble, a murmur of voices and music from the restaurants and cafes. It is another still and warm night. The street lamps have just come on and illuminated the street in a soft glow. It is that time between dusk and the curtain of blackness that she knows will soon fall around her.

The early evening brings a crimson quality to the fading sunlight. Clouds trail the horizon, transfused in purple and pastel. She knows that soon, cones of light will twinkle on the water's surface and she will take a stroll down by the harbour.

She has heard about the power cuts that cover the small town in a blanket of darkness, yet, to her disappointment, she has not experienced one. She hopes she will. She has heard how vast the night sky can appear with no electric light to blot out the stars, veiled with hundreds of pinprick silver lights. She has been told they sparkle like diamonds. She hopes to see them in all their glory, one night.

She is thinking about this when from the street below her balcony, she can hear her name called. She cranes her head.

'Are you staying up there all night? It's a lovely evening, come down and walk with me.'

Grace smiles. 'Sofia! I'll be right there. Just let me lock up first.'

In the street, Sofia hugs Grace. 'How are you?'

'I'm fine and all the better for seeing you.'

Sofia links her arm with Grace's. 'I'm heading down to the harbour.'

'Perfect. Oh, I met Peter today and he was telling me about the meeting.'

'Are you going?'

'Of course.'

'Good. It will help to widen your social circle. It's good to get to know people. There's nothing worse than coming to live in a place and feeling isolated. It's bad for the soul, as well as the mind. You need an interest. A focus.'

'I do. You're right. I'm looking forward to it.'

Sofia looks at her seriously. 'I want you to know, if you ever need anything, just let me know. I'd only be too glad to help. I know how it feels. And, don't you dare feel indebted... I mean it.'

Grace smiles. 'I'll try not to. I promise.'

'Why do I not believe you?'

Grace shrugs. 'I want to be independent. I need to prove to myself I've made the right choices for the right reason.'

'I know.'

'That's twice you've agreed with me.' Grace looks at her with a suspicious eye.

'I haven't always lived here. There was a time I was just like you. I arrived not knowing anyone. I was much younger then. I didn't have much experience of life, really.

I used to live in a town called Argos, in the Peloponnese. My father died when we were babies, really.'

'Oh, Sofia, how awful.'

'It's fine, honestly. I never knew him. I've no memory of him. Eventually, when my sister, Magda and I were still young, my mother remarried.' A shiver steals over her. 'He was nice to us in front of my mother, but she never knew what he was really like.'

'What do you mean, did he hit you?'

'He would come to our bedroom at night. At first, he would just talk, give us sweets. Then, he'd ask us to touch him, do things to him. He told Magda and I that we could never tell anyone, no one would believe us. He said that if we didn't do what he asked, we would be sent away and never see our mother again.'

Grace looks shocked. 'Oh my God. He abused you and your sister.'

'With my mother in the other room.' Sofia's voice wavers and she looks away.

Grace can't imagine what this must have been like.

'It didn't happen every night. Sometimes, he wouldn't visit us for weeks. In a way, that made it worse. We never knew when he was going to come into our room.'

'Did you tell your mother?'

Sofia sighs. She breathes in deeply. 'I couldn't. She loved him. How could I destroy her world? It had been destroyed once before, I couldn't be responsible for that. What if I did and she didn't believe me? I protected my sister as much as I could. Sometimes, I was able to persuade him to leave her and not violate her.'

'By offering yourself?'

It takes Sofia a moment to respond. 'It was all I could do… I hated him, but I didn't hate my mother. I could not be the cause of that pain.'

Grace reaches out and takes Sofia's hand.

'After a few years, it stopped. We were older and stronger. Together we were stronger than him.' Sofia washes her hands over her face. 'When she was fourteen, Magda became ill, very ill. She was diagnosed with Leukaemia.'

'Oh, Sofia, how awful.'

'Magda died in hospital, just before her fifteenth birthday.'

Grace gulps for air. 'I'm so sorry, Sofia.'

'Several weeks after the funeral, he came into my bedroom. It had been a long time since he had done that and that night it would be his last.'

'What happened?'

She flicks a strand of hair from her face. 'He tried to force himself upon me. He had never penetrated us, but this time, I could tell it was different. He was forceful, insistent. I managed to grab a nail file and I stabbed him… in the leg. He screamed, and I pushed him from me. I don't know where it came from. I did it without thinking. He had fallen onto the floor and I stuck the nail file into his neck, just enough to draw blood. I wanted to push it into him. I wanted to do it for my sister. Blood started to trickle from him. He begged me not to hurt him. He promised he would leave me alone. Oh, how I wanted to do it. I wanted to kill another human being. I could see the fear in his eyes, real fear. I had control over him, after all those years I had the control. I was free from his threats. He was suddenly vulnerable and exposed. I saw how weak he really was. How small he had become. I knew then it would stop. I had taken his power from him. I told him that if he ever touched me again, it would be the last thing he ever did. I was eighteen. He was like a frightened animal in the headlights.'

'And he never touched you again?'

'No. Soon after that, I left to go to university. I couldn't stay. I felt for my mother. In a way, she lost her two girls.'

'It was a brave decision to make.'

'I didn't feel brave. I felt quite the opposite. I was scared and to start with, alone. I'd never felt so alone in my life.'

A family walk passed. The children, all under ten are eating ice creams, the father is on his smartphone and the mother is pushing a buggy.

'He'll fall in the water if he doesn't get his face out of his phone.' Grace smirks.

'Time is precious, especially when your children are so young. He doesn't know it yet, but that father is missing out on memories he'll never get back.'

'Did you regret your decision to leave?'

Sofia stares at her hands, clasped together. 'I did, sometimes I did. I always visited her whenever I could, but I missed her. There were times when I needed her, so I would phone, and she'd give me advice and ask if I still had friends and was I eating enough?' The memory of it brings a smile to Sofia. 'In a way, it turned out for the best, really. It made me who I am today. It gave me independence and choice.'

Sofia's words resonate with Grace. And she wonders if these are the things she is looking for? Is this why she is here?

'It also turned me into the mother I became.'

Grace can see that in contrast to Sofia's appearance there is an aura of toughness about her.

'After what I'd been through, I didn't want to be seen as a victim. I protected myself and my sister as much as I could and eventually, I found my own safety. As you must do, Grace… I'm sorry about your baby.'

This is unexpected, and Grace is not sure what to say.

'You remind me of myself. Grace.'

'I do?' she says, disbelievingly.

'We don't need social media around here to know the past of others. My shop's like Facebook. The old ones are the worst, always making it their business to know what's going on with this one and that one.' She shakes her head. 'Did you name your baby?'

'Yes. We called her Olivia.'

'What a lovely name.'

'I've got a photograph of her if you want to see?'

Grace taps the screen of her smartphone and, once she has located the photograph, she smiles and hands the smartphone to Sofia.

'Oh. She's beautiful, Grace. I can't believe how much hair she has.'

'That might have explained the heartburn I had just before she was born.'

Grace can see Sofia think about this. 'It's an old wives' tale. I don't know if there's any truth to it. It was probably just a coincidence.'

'I can see the resemblance. She has your eyes. She's beautiful, Grace.'

Grace looks away.

By now, they have reached the harbour.

'Do you know what I could do with right now?'

'What?'

'A drink. There's a nice bar just over here.'

Grace is glad she has met a good friend in Sofia.

'It will get better, Grace.'

The thought of this fills Grace with a surge of anguish because she does not believe her friend.

The Past

Becoming

The memory always returned to me like shrapnel. I had returned home from an appointment at the dentist. As I walked towards the house, a car I didn't recognise was parked outside the gate. I glanced at the driver, it was a female. She noticed me and looked away.

As I entered the house, Jamie was coming down the stairs with a suitcase in his hand.

The realisation struck me, the second I opened my mouth. 'It was her.'

Jamie fidgeted uneasily.

My heart stalled. 'How could you?' My voice was sharp. I looked at him in incredulous fury. 'How could you bring that woman here to our home?'

Jamie stared at me, torn between his need to explain and his desire for this to end.

'Answer me. I've got a right to know.'

He closed his eyes. When he opened them, he could see my face streaked in a red flush. I was furious with him and at the same time close to tears.

'Explaining my reasons won't make it any easier,' he said.

'For you or me?' I slammed my palm on the side table.

There was a pause and I waited for him to elaborate.

'Well then... for God's sake, Jamie.'

'Alright! Alright.' Nervously, he slid his hand through his hair. 'The thing is... oh God, Grace, I'm so sorry.'

'What!'

'I want to tell you before you find out from someone else.'

'Find out what?'

He paused. 'Look, come into the sitting room.'

For a long moment, we just stared at each other.

'She's pregnant,' he mumbled.

I must have looked like he had just told me my mother had died. Jamie lapsed into a silent pause again. I didn't reply and even though I was shocked I knew by the look on his face he felt he had torn my heart from my body, but it didn't help.

I stood, shaking my head.

'Grace,' he pleaded. 'Sit down, please...'

I interrupted him. 'I could have coped with almost anything, but not this, not this. Jamie, you have killed me.' I remember I covered my eyes and sobbed.

'I'm so, so sorry. Believe me, Grace, it's the last thing I wanted.'

I stiffened at his words. An image of Olivia, our baby, lying in my arms, swamped my mind.

'You've defiled Olivia's memory.' I spat at him.

It was his turn to shake his head. 'That's taking it too far.'

'Is it? She was your daughter.'

'Yes, and she's gone, Grace. We need to get on with our lives.'

'Oh, I see. So, it's my fault now.'

'No. I didn't mean it like that. This is not your fault.'

'So, getting on with our lives means fucking someone and having a baby with them. Well, does it?'

'You need time to absorb this, Grace. Look, I only came to get the rest of my things.'

'And you thought I wouldn't be here, so you brought her. Did she have a good look around?'

'I think I should go.' He stood up then. 'There's one more thing while I'm here.'

'It can't get any worse, can it?'

'I want to sell the house.'

I was shocked by his words, they were so final in their delivery. My eyes filled up again. I looked away.

Beyond the glass doors that led to the decking and then the garden, my eyes scanned the grass, the pots and stone path that weaved its way to an imposing acorn tree. I'd always imagined decorating that tree at Christmas with our children. I hoped that, in time, this would still happen, that another family would adorn its branches with lights and decorations.

I heard the front door close.

My legs and hands were trembling as I stepped out into the garden. His words played in my head like a loop, *'It's not your fault... it's not your fault.'*

I walked along the path and when I came to the tree, I slumped myself against its trunk. I felt abandoned, paralysed with self-doubt. I'd never felt so lonely in my life. Inside, I was aware of a rage building that suffocated any sense of rationality that may have remained in my thoughts. I wanted to cause him harm. I wanted him to hurt, just like me.

The following days and weeks passed in a fog of distress and incomprehension. Each morning, I awoke to an empty space beside me and I'd leaned over and buried my head in his pillow trying to breathe any semblance of him into me and then I'd become overcome with anger and betrayal.

The house would sometimes groan with the silence that inhibited it. How uncluttered it had become, now Jamie wasn't there.

The first thing I noticed was I would often speak to myself. If I was drying my hair, I would hear myself go through that day's tasks that needed to be done. I would instruct myself on a household task, such as, doing the washing up, retrieving the vacuum cleaner from its cupboard. When I think of that time now, I can see I wasn't going mad, but rather, I was filling a void, and the hum of the refrigerator, with my voice. The familiarity of it was a comfort, it reminded me of who I was, it was a map that stopped me from getting lost, it was the moat around my castle.

Even those closest to us don't get to know our innermost secrets, our innermost thoughts. These are uncensored, raw and unguarded. We let people get close, they may even touch our heart, they become precious to us, we identify with them on a level that is a unique investment in the emotional, cognitive, physiological and psychological acknowledgement of another human being. We may call it love, the colliding of two souls, or just human instinct, but we never truly give over ourselves to another. That is simply reason, I think.

Although I loved Jamie, certain thoughts were exclusively mine, remaining anonymous, invisible to him, only to be spoken in my inner world. They would remain wordless. They revealed the deepest qualities of my character that, at times, not even I recognised.

It has been a long time since I've thought of such things. Maybe I simply blocked it from my mind. I felt like a naked bulb shining in a long and dark corridor. Sometimes, I struggled to understand who I had become.

Where did we go wrong? Was it my fault? Did he just stop loving me? I asked myself these questions a lot. At times, I could remember certain things, and wondered about the triggers, the warning signs?

After Olivia's funeral, we argued more, both becoming defensive, protective of ourselves. I could see there was a conscious disconnection between us. We were both to blame.

I was anguished by self-criticism, it often plagued me in the moments of loneliness, where I felt powerless to change my life, to move forward and regain the worth of living without him.

Eventually, I thought, I would be able to tell others my story. It wasn't always like that. I was afraid, angry and lonely. He betrayed me. He broke me.

I couldn't change what had happened to me, but I could control my reaction to it. I could feel a courage growing inside me. I looked at my life without apology.

Separating is a part of life. It's normal. Lots of couples do it. The important thing was, who would I be when I came out of the other side? How would it have defined me? That's what counted, that's what mattered... I thought. I could see who I was becoming.

The Present

The Start of Something

'Once you smell the wild herbs… oregano, marjoram, thyme, and see the orange and lemon blossom, and the scent of the pine forests. Oh, the jasmine, the jasmine will just captivate you, Grace.'

Grace is not sure if it is the images that seduce her or Peter's words. Either way, she is held transfixed by his description and effervescent enthusiasm.

Large glass vases of fresh orange and lemon juice sit in the middle of the table. Freshly baked bread and olives accompany them under the sprawling vines overhead. Grace can feel the sun's radiant touch lace her neck and shoulders, as it finds gaps in the canopy above them.

She shifts and traces her fingers along her skin, rubbing an irritation.

Peter spears an olive and puts it in his mouth. Grace watches as delight spreads across his face.

'These are definitely the best olives I've tasted. I must remember to ask where Vasilis gets them.'

'I can help you there, Peter.' Sofia's eyes flash amusement.

'Well then, my dear, don't keep it to yourself.'

'They're mine.'

'From your shop! Of course.' Peter gestures with uplifted palms. 'Well, I need to become one of your regulars. These are exquisite.'

Grace smooths her dress along her thighs, enjoying the exchange between her two friends. She turns and sees a man appear from the kitchen with a bowl of bread and olive oil. She realises it is the man she sees most mornings taking his daughter to school.

He works here, she tells herself, and averts her eyes, as he nears their table.

'Ah, Vasilis, we're just about to start,' Peter says.

Vasilis places the bowl and oil beside the jugs and sits down opposite Grace.

'I was just saying; these olives are wonderful.'

'I can't stop eating them myself,' Vasilis agrees cheerfully.

'Now.' Peter surveys the table. 'I'd like to welcome Grace to our little gathering. Do you know everyone?'

'No. Not everyone,' Grace says.

'Well then, it would be rude if we didn't introduce ourselves. I'll start things off ...'

There are twelve people sitting at the table, most are British, who have either retired or are semi-retired, several are locals and Grace recognises them all from their morning clean-ups on the beach.

'Hello, Grace. My name is Vasilis.'

Grace nods and her eyes drop for a second.

'I hope you're happy in our little town?'

'I have been so far.' Their eyes meet, and Vasilis' mouth widens into a smile. 'Good. I'm glad to hear it.'

Grace allows herself to return his smile.

Once the introductions are over, Peter shuffles sheets of paper in front of him. 'I want to remind everyone, why we do what we do, in our attempts to improve the environment and protect the beauty and life in our seas in this little part of the world we live in.

'The other day, something awful came to my attention. A sperm whale that was found dead on the coast of Murcia in southern Spain had ingested twenty-nine kilograms of plastic waste. It died of gastric shock. In the stomach and intestines of this whale was found rubbish, such as plastic bags, raffia sacks, parts of fishing nets, ropes and even a jerry can. This poor creature was unable to digest or get rid of this man-made mass in its body and it died of peritonitis. This magnificent creature was thirty-three feet long and weighed more than six tons. Its death would have been gruesome and painful, and sadly, it was avoidable.'

'That's shocking,' a silver-haired man says.

'You're right, David, it is, but it reminded me that although our endeavours may seem, at times futile, in our small way, we are all contributing, doing our bit, as it were, in helping to keep the seas a cleaner and safer place. These plastics are the biggest threat to life in our seas.' He looks at Vasilis. 'First on the agenda. How is the incentive going, Vasilis? Have you given away a lot of free coffee?'

'At this rate, I might be out of business by next week.'

Peter's head is bent over his papers. He looks up. 'It's been that good?'

'Joking aside, it has gone well. Better than I expected.'

He is the owner, Grace smiles to herself, pleasantly surprised. With this unexpected knowledge, Grace is forced to adjust her perception of Vasilis.

'And... can you continue with the offer for another week or two? Be honest Vasilis. If you're losing money, then it needs to stop.'

'It's fine, honest. Normally, when they get their free coffee, they buy a cake, or pastry to go with it, so I'm gaining too.'

'Excellent.' Peter beams.

The meeting continues for another half hour. Once it is over and people start to leave, Grace's confidence is beginning to return.

It is good to be part of something again.

When she stands, Vasilis also stands from his chair. Their gazes meet.

'I might see you, tomorrow?'

Grace looks at Vasilis in surprise. 'You will?'

'On your balcony. I see you most mornings.'

'Ah. Of course. I suppose it's become a habit of mine.'

'It's a good way to start the day.'

'Yes. I think so.'

'I need to get back to work,' he says with a little smile.

'I need to get going as well.'

He turns and walks away. A waiter approaches him. Grace watches their exchange and then the waiter starts to clear the table.

As Grace says goodbye to Peter, she can't help noticing how he holds the attention of the small gathering around him. Peter is like a bonfire, people are attracted to him, drawn in by his glow. Grace smiles at this thought, as she leaves.

The Past

Lost

It was unlike me, and definitely out of character, but one night, I went out on my own. It was late, and I was about to leave, I can't even recall the name of the bar I was in. It was across from Haymarket station and I remember it was busy and noisy when he offered to buy me a drink. We spoke for a while and he bought some more drinks. He looked at me steadily and the expression in his eyes was all it took. It was a mistake, but my common sense was clouded. He bent towards me and kissed me. It felt good to be wanted again, to be desired, once more. I pulled away.

'We shouldn't be doing this,' I told him awkwardly, pushing him from me. 'I'm not ready for this.'

Undeterred, he placed his hand on the nape of my neck and pulled me towards him. If the truth be told, I enjoyed the attention.

We looked at each other for a moment. He lifted his hand to my cheek. My hair fell around my face. I imagined what this may be leading to and it alarmed me, it disturbed me and restored my sense of reality. He looked puzzled when I told him I was leaving, *alone*. I paid for my drink and left, relieved and ashamed. I didn't even know his name.

I let myself in and moved through the house still with the keys in my hand. I let my bag fall to the floor and slipped out of my jacket. My mind drifted, as it often did…

Moonlight broke through the shifting cloud, catching the foamed waves on a rocky South Queensferry beach. We marvelled at the spanning Forth Rail Bridge, illuminating the water in dazzling beams of yellow light. We were two diminutive figures. I braced myself from the breeze and

Jamie's arm encircled my shoulders pulling me into him, shielding me, protecting me.

The lights of a small boat twinkled in the distance, as we spoke above the rumble of a train crossing the River Forth, probably full of people returning to Fife from a night out in Edinburgh's pubs and restaurants.

I remember the overwhelming sense of togetherness. My happiness depended on this man. The word, fragile, comes to mind, when I consider now, as I often do, how unexpectedly shattering life can turn out...

Walking through the kitchen, I idly tossed the keys on the breakfast bar. I rubbed my forehead and stood staring out of the window into the blackness. I bit my lower lip and swallowed, rubbing my ringless finger. An ache slithered in my stomach. I feared losing my grip on life. In that moment, the only event that my life was leading towards, was the day I would eventually die. It seemed the only thing that was inevitable. I had no idea what was going to fill the space from now, until then, if anything.

The Present

The Meal

'That smells lovely, Grace.'

'Thank you, Monica.'

'What is it?'

'It's a Moussaka.'

'I didn't know you could cook Greek food.'

'I can't. I found an old recipe book in the kitchen. It must have been one of yours, so I thought I'd give it a go.'

'It smells delicious.'

'What would you like to drink? I've got wine and some gin.'

'Do you have red?'

'I think it's a Shiraz.'

'That would be perfect.'

'Where's Georgios?'

'He's not coming,' Monica sighs.

'Is everything all right?'

'I'll tell you later. Here, I brought this.'

Monica hands Grace a bottle of wine. 'And these.'

'Flowers, they're lovely. You didn't have to.'

'I know. I couldn't come empty handed. Have you got a vase for them?'

'Try that cupboard, I'll just check on the moussaka.'

Grace puts on oven gloves and opens the oven door. 'I think it's ready.' She bends and lifts it out, placing it on the kitchen top. The moussaka sizzles.

'Where's the bottle opener? I'll crack one open while you dish up.'

Grace nods towards a drawer, 'In there. You'd think you'd never lived in this place before.'

'I didn't do much cooking. I preferred eating out.'

Once the meal has been plated and the wine poured, they take it outside onto the small balcony where Grace has set the small table.

'It's one of the things I love about this country, eating outside.' Monica smiles as she sets her napkin on her lap.

'I have breakfast out here every morning.'

'You won't be able to do that in the winter, that's if you're still here.'

Grace clears her throat. 'Winter seems a long time away.'

'That's not exactly a confirmation of your intent to stay.'

Monica takes a mouthful of Moussaka and places her fork on her plate. She looks at Grace. 'That is sheer heaven, Grace. I didn't know you were such a good cook. That's a talent you've hidden from me.'

A smile dances over Grace's face. 'That's a relief. I wasn't sure how it was going to turn out.'

'Ah. We've digressed. You haven't answered me.'

'About what?'

'Do you intend to stay after the summer? Have you thought about that far off?'

She draws a breath. 'No. Not really. I'm just living from one day to the next, really. Do you think you'll ever return to the U.K. or are you here for good?'

'I'm happy here, more than I ever was in London and Edinburgh. I'm too old now to be starting a new life somewhere else.'

'Nonsense.'

'I'm fifty-five, Grace. I'm old enough to be your mother. The pace of life suits me now. I would never have said that when I was your age.'

'You're not old. The fifties are the new forties.'

'Anyway, you seem to be settling in. How long has it been now?'

'A month. It's strange. When I think of that length of time it feels long, but each day goes by really fast.'

'Wait till you get to my age. I've no idea where the time goes. I swear each year gets shorter. I hear you've been keeping yourself busy.'

'Oh, helping out on the beach.'

'Yes. Peter's very fond of you, you know.'

'He is?'

'Not in that way. Surely you noticed he's…'

'I didn't mean it like that. I didn't know you two knew each other.'

'The ex-pats seem to stick together. Strength in numbers I suppose. I've known him for years. When I first arrived, he took me under his wing. I don't know what I would have done without him.'

Grace smiles. 'Yes. He has that effect.'

'You've done wonders in here. I'd always been meaning to do it up, throw a few things out, but then, I thought I'd leave it to you, let you put your identity on the place, and you have.'

'I haven't really thanked you for letting me stay, that's why it was so important that tonight went well. I'm indebted to you, Monica.'

Monica shakes her head. 'Believe me, Grace. It was the least I could do. That's the problem when you have two places to stay, one of them lies empty.'

'I'm just so grateful.'

'We're doing each other a favour. You do know you can stay as long as you like, as long as you need to.'

'It's perfect. I have to pinch myself every morning.'

'I'm just relieved you're here. You really worried me. You know you'll always be the daughter I never had.'

'And you've always been like a mother to me.'

Monica takes Grace's hand. 'And you really are feeling better?'

'This place has been like medication, it's my daily dose.'

'I'm glad. I really am, Grace. You're free of him now.'

'It's behind me now. I used to think about him and... her. Not only is there a physical distance between us, he no longer occupies my thoughts as much.'

'So, you're not in love with him anymore?'

Grace thinks for a moment. 'Maybe with the memory of him, of our time together. I wouldn't have him back if that's what you mean.'

Monica smiles wickedly. 'I was just making sure, that's all. You've been through a lot, more than most of us...'

Monica thinks Grace is holding back. She feels she is about to tell her something, but shrinks from it, for whatever reason.

Eventually, Grace says, 'I miss some things.'

'You do?'

'Yes. If I'm honest, there are times I miss Edinburgh.'

She feels a cramping pain when she thinks of her house, her walks along the canal, the familiar street names, the myriad views of the castle, from the grass market, Lothian Road and along Princes Street. She misses the shops, the cafes and restaurants, the smell of rain, rising from the pavements, she even misses the trams.

'Not the weather, surely?' Monica tilts her head.

There's that wicked smile again, Grace thinks. 'No. It was home. All my memories are there.'

'You're making new ones, here.'

Grace's gaze moves towards the rooftops and the harbour beyond. 'I am.'

'You're making new friends, too.'

She takes a breath. 'I know. Oh, I almost forgot. Sofia has asked me if I'd like to start working in her Deli.'

'Oh!'

'The old lady that used to work for her is not able now. It's just for a few hours in the morning.'

'And have you accepted her offer?'

'I'm thinking about it.'

Monica searches Grace's face. 'Good. Good for you, Grace.' Suddenly, Monica's expression changes. 'Are you needing the money? Because if you are, all you need to do is ask. You know that, don't you? I wouldn't see you struggle.'

'No. It's not that at all. It would probably be good for me. I'd get to know the locals and I could practise my Greek, the little I know.'

'Well, I think you've made your mind up. Good for you, Grace.'

'You haven't told me what has happened between you and Georgios.'

'No. I haven't.'

'You don't have to.'

'It's fine. I'm sure most people will know soon enough. That's how it generally works around here.'

Grace can breathe salt and sea in the air. From the harbour, the sounds of evening meals and the muted tones of conversations float over to them on the still air.

Monica taps her fork on her plate. 'You know the saying, opposites attract? Maybe, there's some mileage in that. We were too similar. Together, we're both volatile, opinionated, argumentative. In full flow, we were like a tsunami. I'm too old for all of that. I haven't got the energy anymore. So, it's over. I finished it.' Monica leans back in her chair. 'He has a wife, he's married.' Her voice is sharp.

Grace's jaw drops.

'They're separated, fortunately for him.'

'But he never told you?'

'No. And if we were still together, he wouldn't have. I think it made him feel better. A bit of revenge, I suppose. He seemed pleased that he deceived me.'

'What a horrible man.'

'I think I was lucky, don't you?'

'Definitely better without him.' Grace smiles.

'That's precisely what I've been telling myself.'
Monica's lips curve. 'In fact, I'm finished with men. Better
without them. What about you, Grace? You're young, you
have your whole life in front of you. This could be a new
chapter for you. You can't always live in the past, after all,
you don't want to end up like me.' She looks at Grace
solemnly and then her smile returns. 'You need to be brave,
take your first steps into that big unknown world. There are
decent people out there, who are kind and gentle, they're
not all bad. The trick is, finding the right one. Don't close
yourself off to that possibility. You'll know when you're
ready.'

'Oh, I don't even know if I'm ready to even think about
things like that.'

Monica reaches over and takes Grace's hand. 'I know, I
know. What happened must have been awful, the worst
thing ever, but it doesn't define the person you are and who
you can be.'

'I know,' Grace whispers.

They sit for a while longer, listening to the sounds of the
night.

A tearful glaze covers Grace's eyes. She draws in a
breath. 'When Jamie left, I started to find out what had
really gone on. A month or two before he left me, he said
he was going to a conference in Rome, there wasn't one, of
course. Oh, he went to Rome, that part was true, but there
wasn't a conference and he wasn't on his own. He was with
her. It felt unthinkable at the time, but it happened.'

'How did you find out.'

'He often went to Europe. I thought nothing of it. It came
with his job. Anyway, after we split up, I bumped into one
of our mutual friends, he also worked with Jamie in the
Parliament. He told me he was going to Rome and I said

Jamie had been to a conference in Rome earlier in the year, and he said it was impossible because this was the first one. I could see by his expression we both realised what had happened. It must have been embarrassing for him.'

'Poor guy and what a way for you to find out.'

'I was beginning to find out he had been living two different lives. To tell you the truth, he surprised me. I didn't think he was capable, or as organised to do it. Now, when I think back, there were little signs, but I never thought anything of it. I suppose I thought it was just his way of coping with Olivia's death.'

'It's bad enough at any time, but after what you've both been through, how could he have done that?'

'It brings couples together or pushes them apart. I've learnt that much,' Grace says. Her voice is steady. 'He loved me only enough to let me think he did. And then he stopped. I don't think even he knows why.'

'Because he couldn't keep it in his pants, maybe. Sorry, that was crude. I shouldn't have said that.'

Grace shrugs. 'Don't be, it's true. Even now, when I think about what happened, I struggle with it, you know. Some days it feels like it was a dream.'

'Never feel like you can't talk about it. Remember, you're not alone.'

'I know. I've met some lovely people since I arrived.' She looks at Monica's plate and realises she is finished. 'Would you like a coffee?'

'I'd love one. I'll clear up here.'

'No, you won't, you're my guest. I'll do it later.'

Grace walks to the kitchen and Monica follows her.

'I think you'll be alright, Grace. You're doing exceptionally well.'

Grace starts to make some coffee. 'Life's too short to be angry and sad all of the time... well, most of the time.'

Monica smiles. 'I'd be worried if you hadn't added that.'

'I've had a long time to think. And sometimes it feels that's all I ever do. I'm going to tell you something and I've thought about this a lot, Monica. Imagine a circle and everything that is my life is in that circle. When Olivia died, everything in that circle was affected by her loss. As time passed, my grief just didn't simply get smaller and disappear, it stayed with me. What happened was my life started to grow around my grief, my pain. My life continued, and things happened. My grief didn't change, my life did. I didn't move away from my grief or pain, it didn't distance itself, it just became a part of my life.'

Monica can see the emotion in Grace's eyes and hear the intensity of her words.

Grace hands Monica a mug.

'Thank you.'

'The coffees' just instant I'm afraid.'

Monica takes a sip. 'It's fine, Grace. Don't worry yourself.'

Grace leans against the kitchen top. 'They had a boy. Jamie called him Zak, after his father. I found out through some friends. They were worried about telling me, thinking it would set me back.'

'And did it?'

'I'd be lying if I said it didn't. I cried a lot. I hated him then. How could he have a baby and with someone else? I felt like he had spat on Olivia's memory. I felt a failure, I felt worthless. That's when Lynn mentioned she knew a place I could spend time in and get away from it all. I thought she meant somewhere like Berwick. I never for one second thought she was talking about you and Greece.'

Monica smiled. 'Lynn phoned me to make sure the place was empty. She'd been over for a holiday last year and stayed for two weeks, so she knew it would be suitable for you. We had a great time. Anyway, that's when I phoned you. I should have thought of it before.'

'I'm just so grateful to you, Monica.'

'You look tired, Grace.'

'I am a bit.'

'Are you sleeping well?'

Grace shrugs. 'For some reason, I haven't slept too well for the past few days.'

'I'll help clear up and let you get off to bed.'

'I'm fine, honest. I'll see to all of this. It'll only take five minutes.'

'I insist.'

'It's not a problem. You finish your coffee.'

'Are you sure?'

Grace laughs. 'Look, if it makes you feel any better you can help with the washing up.'

'Good. I will. It's good to see you happy.'

Grace hesitates, she looks at the floor and then lifts her head. 'I want to be happy. It's about trusting myself and allowing myself to become the person I'm happy to be for the rest of my life. I just haven't found her, yet.'

Monica smiles at her. 'You will. Just don't be too impatient. Let it take its own time.'

Grace clasps her hands together and swallows. She can feel a burn in her throat. Time is what I have plenty of, she reminds herself.

The Past

Walking Away in Order to Arrive

I used to keep my favourite photograph of Jamie on the mantlepiece. It was the last remnant of him in the house. I couldn't bring myself to remove it. Until one morning, I took a deep breath, took it out into the garden and deposited it into the rubbish bin. It was a representation that I was eventually moving on, separating myself from my past. There was a change in me.

Time passed laboriously. I spent my weeks and months fretting. Ever since their baby had been born, I had been tormented, a knife twisted in my stomach.

Then one morning, standing in the garden, I looked back at the house. It was not the same house, everything had changed; what was once a home now looked sad, tired and dejected.

I think I awoke that morning knowing what I was going to do.

I knew the street and the house number. I was drawn to it.

I took the bus. It was the first time I had travelled on one for years and I enjoyed the novelty of it.

It was a tree-lined street. I passed only a few people, huddled into their coats, their hats and gloves. The road was eerily quiet as sleet fell onto my head, covering my shoulders and jacket. To my surprise the sun, that had been a yellow blot all morning behind the sombre sky, sliced through the clouds, illuminating the falling sleet in white morning light.

It was then, as I approached the house, the thought entered my head for the first time, what was I going to do? Was I just going to stand outside the house and stare at the windows like a stalker? I started to question being there in the first place. What was I thinking? Had I gone mad? Yet, something stirred in my stomach and my instinct was to get into the house.

I looked at the steps rising towards the door, the opened door. I stared, verifying what I had just seen, it was open, just slightly, but all the same, open. Jamie would be inside. Surely, they would feel the cold air and close the front door. I walked behind a tree and craned my head, scanning the door, the bay window and back to the door again. I waited for a few minutes. And then I saw a figure at the window, Jamie perhaps. He looked up and down the street and then he turned and looked in my direction. He had his hands in his pockets, casually observing the world outside. I was sure he hadn't seen me; his body language and posture remained passive. All the same, I waited a few seconds and pressed the side of my face against the bark of the tree before I looked again. He was gone. I shifted my gaze towards the door. It was still open. It was a heavy-looking door, blue and glossed. My heart jumped inside my chest, an electric impulse shot through me.

I edged up the pavement and registered the postage-stamp sized garden, bordered by a hedge expertly and neatly cut. I found myself wondering if they had someone to do the garden for them, as it was never Jamie's forte.

I reached the door and slid into the hallway. It was large and spacious, I remember the black and white tiled floor, the imposing side cabinet and the uncarpeted stairs with its black wrought iron bannister. The air was hot inside the house. My eyes glanced towards the rear of the hallway where I saw the kitchen and heard their voices.

My eyes shifted towards the stairs. I heard a low muffled sound travel down them and I felt myself climbing towards it.

I found him in a crib. It was their bedroom. Jamie's shirts were lying on the bed, freshly washed and ironed. There was a walk-in wardrobe, full of clothes, shoes and boxes. The dressing table had an assortment of jewellery, skin creams, bottles of perfume and brushes. There was a half-empty glass of water on the bedside table and a framed photograph. Jamie looked happy, they were both smiling. He had his arm around her, and she cradled their newborn. I closed my eyes. The hurt was unbearable. Had the love I had for Jamie not been enough? Had I not loved him enough? Or was it simply, he did not love me enough? I drew in a slow breath. Jamie had lived two separate lives. The times he worked late, went to conferences, he was with her. I never questioned it. I had no reason to. I trusted him completely.

I walked over to the bedside table and lifted the photograph. There was no denying it, she was attractive. I could feel a bubble of anger floating to the surface. They looked so happy together. He had lied to me, deceived me, but more than that, what hurt me to my core was he had deceived Olivia. I started to shake and placed the photograph back where I found it, face down.

I looked at their bed, the expensive duvet, the thick puffed up pillows. It brought memories of our bedroom, our bed, our lovemaking. Where was I to put these memories? They hung around me like a haunting.

I stepped closer to the baby and stood perched over the crib. I looked steadily at him and his delicate white skin. The baby was undeniably Jamie's. It had Olivia's mouth. My composure was about to fold. I brought my hand to my mouth and pressed my lips with my knuckles. I muffled a sob. The intense feeling of love that I had for Olivia announced itself in a sudden spasm. I caught my breath; a wave of nausea nudged my throat. My injury and my devastation were complete.

The baby was becoming fretful, impatient stirrings, mumbled cries. I thought about stretching my arms out and comforting him. It was then I saw the baby monitor.

I could hear the thud of footsteps on the stairs. A woman's voice. The next voice I heard startled me. It was Jamie's, travelling closer. I stood with my back against the bedroom wall. I craned my head. I could see the top of the landing. A tightening gripped my shoulders. I was trapped. I imagined Jamie's look of astonishment, the disbelief across his face. I had no idea what I'd say.

'I think he's gone off to sleep again. I can't hear him,' Jamie said, near the landing.

'Leave him then. He needs another half hour.' The voice downstairs suggested.

'I'll just pop my head in.'

Frantically, my eyes scanned the room. The walk-in wardrobe! I needed to hide in there. Tentatively, I moved towards it, moving passed the opened bedroom door. Once inside, I cautiously closed the door. In the confined space I felt claustrophobic. I had to concentrate on my breathing. It was dark. A slither of light came from the base of the door. I heard the toilet flush, the swish of water from a tap and footsteps reaching the bedroom. In the dark, I crouched, hugging my knees, burying my head in my arms. Amongst his clothes, I could smell him, as if he was crouched beside me. Small streams of sweat rippled under my arms. My mouth was dry, my nerves licked at me. I raised my head and listened. He was in the room. There was barely a disturbance or sound. I held my breath. I was hiding from the man I'd shared my life with. How had my life come to this point? I tried to process the rationale of it all, but my thoughts were congested. What was I thinking? What had possessed me to even contemplate this action? At that moment, it felt absurd, I felt fragile, brittle and not the person I thought I was. I realised then, I wasn't attaching my anger to Jamie, not anymore, my rage was turned inwards, this was who I had become.

I stayed there, crouched in the dark for a few minutes, unable to move. Eventually, I slipped out of the house, undetected. As I walked away from the house, I was aware I was walking away from Jamie too, but most importantly, I was abandoning the woman who had been in the bedroom, hiding, alone and scared. I no longer felt heavy and sodden in my grief, in my anger.

I remember grey clouds scudding across the sky. I drew my coat more tightly around me feeling enormous relief. In that moment of walking away, I had also arrived. Instinctively, I knew then what I had to do.

The Present

Devastation and Loss in a Beautiful Country

A breath of tepid air moves along her arm as she sips her coffee.

'You watch me every morning?'

'It's hard not to. You pass my house at the same time I have breakfast.'

'I have to take my little girl to school.'

'You do. And I like eating breakfast on the balcony, so, it is inevitable. And you sometimes wave.' Grace raises an eyebrow at him

'It would be rude not to.' Vasilis gives a little gesture with his hand.

'I suppose it would. What is your little girl's name?'

'Pelagia.'

'What a lovely name.'

'I think so, too.'

'I haven't seen her mother.' Grace has wondered why she has only seen Vasilis take his daughter to school in the morning.

Vasilis strokes the bristles on his chin. 'Me neither, not for a long time.'

'Oh!'

'She left us when Pelagia was two.'

'I'm so sorry.'

'Pelagia can't remember her mother. She rarely speaks of her. In a way, it's a blessing.'

'Yes, I can see that.' Grace rubs her forehead; this revelation is unexpected. She feels awkward and shifts in her chair. They are sitting in Vasilis' taverna. She had been on her usual walk when, passing the taverna, she met Vasilis who offered her an irresistible cold lemonade.

'It must have been difficult raising your daughter and running this place?'

'It runs itself, really. I've good staff, they've been with me since I started. They're like my family. I pick Pelagia up from school, make her something to eat. Sometimes, I have to work in the evening and my sister looks after Pelagia. I'm lucky, others are not so fortunate.'

Grace nods. 'All the same, it can't be easy. I admire you, Vasilis.'

'I have no choice. She is my daughter. Anyway, any father would do what I do. I'm not special.'

'I'm not so sure every father would.'

'Why not?'

'Oh, for some they would rely on their parents, grandparents even, to take care of their child.

'My parents are dead.'

'I'm sorry.'

'Don't be. They died before Pelagia was born. In a way, I'm glad they didn't have to experience what I went through.'

'I know it happens, but most women would never leave their child.'

'This is true. She had what I think you call a nervous breakdown. She was always highly strung. Hard work.'

'And she just left you and Pelagia?'

'She did.' Vasilis replies.

'She has never been in touch?'

'No.'

'Do you know where she went? I mean, I get the impression it was unexpected.'

'She went shopping in the morning. I took Pelagia out for a walk. When I returned, I expected her to be home, but she wasn't. I never thought much about it, but as the day went on, I started to worry. I imagined all sorts of things. I thought she might have been in an accident. She took the car, you see. I eventually phoned the police. She hadn't taken her smartphone which was unusual as she always did. I found it in the bedroom. The next day, the police found the car, I knew then she wasn't coming back.'

She looks down at her hands. Vasilis' account is a stark reminder that she is not the only one to suffer and, in this moment, she feels ashamed that she has been so selfish, probably at the expense of others, she now considers.

Their eyes meet and veer away. 'How long have you owned this place?'

'Five years now. When I first bought it, it was hard work, constantly trying to make it successful. It's easier now. I don't have to do everything myself.' He smiles self - satisfyingly. 'What about you, Grace, what do you do?'

'I work at Edinburgh University as a researcher,' she says, flustered. 'I'm taking a break.'

'Are you going home soon?'

'I'm not sure, really. I mean, I will go back to Edinburgh... I just don't know when.'

'Ah, I see.' But he doesn't really, and his expression confirms this.

'It's a long story.'

Vasilis smiles. Just then, one of the waiters calls over to him. 'Vasilis, the boat is going out.'

'I must go.'

'Where?'

'To the lifeboat,' Vasilis replies.

'To the lifeboat?'

'Yes. I have to go.'

With an urgency about him, he is rushing out of the taverna, leaving Grace wondering what has just happened.

She watches him disappear around the corner, and then she is aware of lipstick marks on her cup, and it is a reminder she is finally trying to be herself again.

Grace catches her breath. She has surprised herself. It is an emotion that has deserted her, lately. She had thought she had gained control over her emotions, her thoughts, the emptiness. This is different, uncharacteristic. But it is there, all the same, her inner voice is unrelenting.

In her mind, she has pored over his features and her stomach generates waves that are hot and liquified inside her.

She is not in control of this, it is as unexpected, as it is bewildering. She feels her sensibilities are being resuscitated, resurrected, it is inexpressibly unsettling, but at the same time pleasing. Such contradictions have not entered the black and white world she has constructed around herself. It has been her defence. It has become like walls around her and it has now been breached.

She spends the next hour idly wandering around the shops, and not with any real purpose. Her mind is preoccupied with Vasilis. Already, she feels she knows this man. They have both been victims. Both have lost, what in all respects were normal lives. They share a commonality in their past. We have both had to readjust and face the uncertainty of life's cruel twists and fragility, she tells herself.

As she stops at another shop window, she knows, of course, that another moment might not present itself where she will be alone with him. A thought steals her mind. She has been given the opportunity to reinvent herself.

As Grace contemplates what this might mean, she finds herself down by the harbour. A crowd has gathered, and Grace can feel a tension in the air. Something has happened or is about to happen.

Just then, a siren wails, growing closer with each second. Grace gazes out towards the water and she can see the lifeboat making its way back to shore. Voices are now raised and there seems to be a wave of excitement and apprehension that spreads amongst the crowd. Some people are standing in the restaurants that fringe the harbour, some pointing towards the lifeboat. It feels like the whole harbour is awaiting a great event that is about to occur.

As the lifeboat slowly glides alongside the harbour wall, Grace can see the pitiful sight of human beings crushed together. It is then she realises something has happened, something dreadful, and her heart jumps in her chest. Then, she can see Vasilis at the wheel of the lifeboat and for a second it is a reprieve from the horror.

People are running towards the lifeboat. An old man crosses himself. It doesn't matter if Grace believes in God or not, in that moment, she thanks him anyway.

She can do nothing but stare at the desolation that has spilt from the lifeboat. Two bodies are lifted from the boat. Within seconds, the quayside resembles a war zone. People and children are lying on the ground, wretched and sodden, villagers rushing towards them.

'Where is the ambulance?' Vasilis shouts as members of the crew perform C.P.R.

Grace can see a woman and a child. The child is lying on its back; it splutters and seawater jets, like a fountain from its mouth. The woman is motionless. Her arms flop like a doll with each forceful compression on her chest.

'Bring blankets. Where are the blankets?' Vasilis commands.

Grace has been so consumed by her surroundings that she hasn't noticed the stretcher being pulled from the ambulance, and it is only when she hears a command in Greek being barked at her that she instinctively moves aside to let two paramedics pass, as they rush towards the harbour wall.

Around her, even though it feels chaotic, with the crowd pushing forward to get a better advantage point, the policeman struggling to keep them at bay and the others, the men with serious expressions, pulling what looks like blankets of tin foil from bags, there is a sense of order and repetition.

She is aware roles are being played. Grace is not observing random actions, these activities have been performed before; there is a choreography about them.

To her distress, she sees a young child being held aloft by her ankles, hanging like a dead chicken. A man slaps the child's back, again and again, trying to release seawater from her lungs. There is a communal sigh of relief from those around Grace, as the man cries, 'Water is coming from her mouth. Get her a blanket. Cover her up. Hold her head.'

Grace recalls passing by this very spot earlier that morning. She remembers fishing nets fluttering in the soft breeze, rows of what she thought looked like octopus hanging from lines, like washing drying in the sun. Now, she thinks, this could be a different country.

A pleasant breeze wraps around them as Grace and Vasilis walk past solid stone houses crowned with red-tiled roofs. There is one small cloud in the sky. Grace has watched it for some time, it's like an island in a sea, she tells herself.

In places, the cobbled streets are steep and traffic-free, winding their way up the hill to the commanding Genoese fortress. At night, it is illuminated in the night sky by arresting light and Grace has thought many times it could almost be mythical.

They stroll around the market and Grace buys aubergines, courgettes and deep red beef tomatoes. They take their time along the narrow, cobblestone alleys, shaded by wisteria blooms and dazzling bougainvillea, crammed with craft shops and art galleries where tavernas offer striking panoramas of the sea.

When there is a gap in their conversation, Grace can sense Vasilis' thoughts are preoccupied with the events that unfolded earlier in the day.

As they walk, he has his hands in his pockets. 'They are leaving Syria because of the violence from the war and fear of persecution. Can you imagine what it must be like to see your cities, towns, and villages destroyed and turned into rubble.'

Grace is silent because she cannot imagine what these people have gone through.

'Some have even been raped, others tortured.' He shakes his head. 'They just want to feel safe and live in a place where they can live and work. Many of the refugees are young middle-class Syrians who want to contribute. They want to study and work just like they did back home. I've heard of dentists, teachers, and doctors coming off the boats. They just want to feel a sense of worth again.'

To her shame, Grace struggles to think of what to say. 'It must be horrific,' she manages, finally.

He gestures towards the sea. 'You have to be desperate to leave your home, your family, your job, everything that is familiar. They have crossed Turkey to end up in a dingy with fifty other people and they know they might drown; their children might drown. These people have witnessed things we could never imagine, Grace.'

There is a pause. All day, Grace hasn't been able to get the image of the little girl out of her head.

'Imagine being that desperate, you would risk your life and that of your child's, paying a lot of money to cross to Greece in a small dinghy. It can take up to three months to reach here. Many have walked from Syria. If they are lucky and have the money, I've heard some have taken trains as well. When they get here most of the refugees don't have any registration, so there's a real risk they could unwittingly fall victim to smugglers' networks, even human trafficking.

'You saw what they looked like. They suffer from dehydration, tiredness, lack of food and water, they've not had any kind of healthcare and a lot of them have sunstroke.'

Grace tries to imagine what this must be like, but she can't.

'The conditions at sea are better now it's summer, this is just the beginning. I've never seen so many people trying to cross the sea, it's unprecedented. This was the first time we've had to pick up a dead body,' he says quietly. He wants to tell her that he is glad she is with him, that he has not spent this day alone.

Grace can see the unmistakable look of despair on Vasilis' face. She turns and gazes at the sea, contemplates its dangers, and tries to imagine being cramped between bodies, feeling waves crash over the sides of the dinghy, being soaked through, terrified, not knowing if every passing second will be the last. 'It's going to get worse, isn't it?'

'We don't have the facilities or resources. We've been lucky. Other islands are struggling to cope. The numbers are increasing every day. We're doing all we can, but my fear is, very soon, it won't be enough. So far, most people have been sympathetic towards the refugees, but if the numbers increase, like in other places, I fear it could easily turn some people against them. There's the real prospect it could change people's sympathy towards them.' Vasilis pauses. 'Lots of families are being separated. Mothers separated from their children and husbands. I've seen unaccompanied children and young people now, and it's getting common. Most of them don't even know where they are when they get off the boats. They need to feel safe, have shelter, they need to feel human again.' He presses his lips together.

Grace reaches out and touches his arm. His voice is now coloured with emotion. 'This is not what we signed up for. We are used to rescuing tourists who have drifted out to sea and fishing boats that have broken down.' His forehead is furrowed, and his face is severe.

His eyes are seeing images Grace can only imagine, but really, she can't, how can she?

'When you look into their eyes, they reflect the war they have left. Families are torn apart, devastated and lost in our sea, our beautiful country.'

'Do you think it'll ever get better?'

'In 2002, twenty refugees from Afghanistan landed on our island. Back then, everyone one was talking about it, it was on everyone's lips, in the tavernas, the restaurants, the shops, the kafenion, everywhere. It's now completely different. How our lives have changed. We are now seeing hundreds of people coming in small boats. When we reach them, their eyes are wide, stricken with fear and exhaustion. They look like they've seen ghosts and maybe that is what we are to them, ghosts ploughing through the sea towards them.'

'If it wasn't for the lifeboat many more would have died. You are saving people's lives, Vasilis.'

'I know, but sometimes it doesn't feel like it. Today, there were two dinghies. One had taken in water and I could see five people in the sea. Three people managed to hang on to the side of a dinghy. The others were crammed into it, there was a lot of children, they were drenched in water, soaked to the skin. We threw our ropes to them so that we could bring the dinghies alongside the lifeboat.

'A child crying, a mother bewildered and desperate is the same in any language. There were babies as well, shivering, petrified. All around us all I could hear was crying, screaming, wailing, foreign languages. Some can speak English. When we pulled the woman from the sea, straight away, I could see she was in a bad way. She wasn't breathing, there was no pulse. We started C.P.R. We also pulled her child from the sea. She was unconscious but alive. As the crew worked on them, I radioed for an ambulance to meet us.

'As we headed back, an eerier silence fell over them. What can we do for them? They huddled together, trying to keep warm, bewildered. God knows what goes through their minds. At least, they are safe, and always, when I look at them, above them, the Greek flag flutters in the wind.

'This part of their journey is over, there'll be others to come. Once they are off the boat, life for them doesn't get any easier.'

'What will happen to them now?' Grace asks.

'There's a processing and accommodation centre, but really, we don't have the resources. We don't have the infrastructure for this. They aren't allowed to leave until their requests for asylum are processed. The camp is subsidized by the Greek authorities and international volunteers. They live in dreadful conditions, Grace. I've been told the air is heavy with the smell of urine and faeces. The few toilets there is overflow with human waste. Rubbish is left to rot. For those who receive asylum, they can go to the mainland and Europe; others, not so lucky, are sent back to Turkey.'

'How long do they have to live in the camp?'

'Usually, months and, even then, they might end up in a camp on mainland Greece.'

'It must feel like a prison to them.'

Vasilis shakes his head. 'Why is this being allowed to happen? We are not a third world country, this is Europe, for God's sake.'

Grace can tell that Vasilis' frustration has been marinating for a long time and she can't blame him. 'I can't stop thinking about that little girl. The one you rescued from the water.'

'She went to the hospital.'

'Have you heard any news? Is she going to be okay?'

'She's fine. They'll keep her for a few days.'

'What will happen to her?'

'They'll try and locate her relatives.'

'But her mother is dead.'

'She will probably still have family in Syria.'

'What will happen to her if there is no one else?'

Vasilis shrugs. 'These things could take years, Grace.'

'She can't live in one of those camps for years.' Grace is horrified at the thought.

'She won't. I'm sure they'll find a relative.'

'But if they don't, what will happen to her?'

'She might be lucky and get taken in by a family who will look after her until a decision is made about her future.'

'You mean, like a foster family.'

'Yes, that is what you call it, by a foster family.'

'I can't get her out of my head. I can't stop thinking about her. She must be terrified. She has lost everything she ever knew, her family, her home and her mother. It's heartbreaking.'

'She is being looked after. She won't be hungry anymore and she will be dry and warm.' Vasilis says, trying to reassure Grace.

'That doesn't make what happened any less shocking, does it?'

'No. It doesn't.'

'Are you sure there wasn't anyone on the boat who knew her?'

'There wasn't, I'm afraid.'

Vasilis looks at his watch. 'I need to collect Pelagia from school. Would you like to come?'

She smiles, trying to keep the image of the young girl from her and the shock and anger it evokes. 'Yes. I'd like that.'

'There she is,' Vasilis says as he rushes forward. Grace keeps a discrete and respectable distance between them as Vasilis scoops Pelagia in his arms. Grace smiles, feeling out of place and self-conscious amongst the parents and grandparents who are collecting the children. She scratches an irritation on her neck as Vasilis walks towards her, holding his daughter's hand. Grace can see the broad smile on Pelagia's face dissolve as they approach her.

'Pelagia, I'd like you to meet a friend of mine. This is Grace.'

Pelagia stands still and scuffs her foot along the playground dust avoiding eye contact with Grace.

'It's rude not to say hello, Pelagia.'

Although Grace cannot understand what Vasilis is saying, she doesn't have to, as the girl's aloof body language is no barrier, unlike Grace's understanding of Greek.

'Kalispera, Pelagia.' Grace places her palm on her chest. 'My name is Grace.'

Pelagia ignores her.

'I'm sorry, Grace. She's not normally like this.' And then to Pelagia, he says firmly, 'Say, hello to Grace.'

Pelagia bites her lip, still dragging her shoe in the dust. She shakes her head.

Vasilis gestures with an opened hand. 'I'm sorry, Grace. I don't know why she's being like this.'

'Think about it, Vasilis. I'm a strange woman she has never seen before and I'm with her father. What do you think is going through her mind? Maybe, this wasn't such a good idea after all.'

'Ah!' Vasilis exclaims, as if a great mystery has just been revealed to him.

He puts his hand on Pelagia's shoulder. 'I've made you your favourite dinner.' Suddenly, Pelagia's eyes light up and her smile returns.

Vasilis' face softens and, immediately he feels relief. He turns to Grace. 'Would you like some dinner too? I always make too much?'

Grace raises an eyebrow. 'Do you really think that would be a good idea?' She glances at Pelagia.

'Mm, I see what you mean.'

'Another time, maybe.'

Vasilis tries to hide his disappointment. 'Another time it is then.'

The Past

A New Feeling

The rain struck the pavement like missiles falling from the sky and lake-sized puddles appeared with every irritant step I took. I slipped into a café and shed my coat. Pulling my hand through my wet hair, I was annoyed that I'd forgotten to put an umbrella in my bag. I'd seen the forecast, for heaven's sake, and it had been raining steadily for two days. There had been a short lull that morning and I'd decided to go out and do some shopping, just a few necessities: bread, milk and coffee.

I sat at a window seat cradling my coffee and watched cars and buses spray the pavements. It had been several days since my incursion into Jamie's house, and now, having time to digest what I'd done, I didn't know that person, that me. I had some sort of breakdown? I'd become possessed, driven by a crazy desire that held no logic or reason.

Since then, I'd lived like a hermit in the house and when I finally ran out of coffee, I couldn't face the prospect of not having my habitual cup at breakfast. I was forced to venture out.

And here I was, soaked to the skin, my hair plastered to my head, trying to absorb the heat from the cup between my hands. I realised, at that moment, I hadn't spoken to another person in days. The only words I'd uttered were to the next-door neighbour's cat as it made its way through my garden on its early morning outings. The realisation was enough for me to catch my breath. I was taken aback. The truth hurt and, like the rain outside, it soaked into me. It was inconceivable, unthinkable, like snow falling in a desert. Who was this person I'd become? I caught my reflection in the glass of the window, and I was taken aback at the pale face that stared back at me. A shiver quickly passed through me. I was alone in the world.

I looked around the café and it didn't help that I was the only person on my own. A woman caught my stare and I slipped my eyes from her, embarrassed. It magnified my loneliness. The only voice I heard was the one in my head. The same one that spoke to me that day I made my hastily retreat from Jamie's house.

'I don't have to endure this. I've suffered, and I can walk away. I have a choice only I can make. I've been crazed and felt insane for months only I can change this.'

I took a sip of coffee and its bitterness slipped through my mouth. *Weren't we worth anything together, weren't we worth saving, he wasn't the only one in pain? He was fucking her right under my nose, and now… now… my fingers trembled around the cup. I breathed in a needed breath and thought, I don't have to do this anymore. I can't do this anymore. I don't have the stamina.'*

Everything changed in that little unassuming café. As I stepped outside and sniffed the wet air, just for a moment, my determination wobbled, but then I felt an intent resilience as I strolled along the street. I'm doing this for me, I told myself, and I felt an incredible strength of self-belief, the likes of I'd never experienced since before Olivia's death.

The voice I'd heard in my head for so long, didn't sound like my own. I was beginning to identify with the *me* I once knew. I told myself I would be alright. This new feeling quickened and intensified.

The Present

Reinventing Herself

That morning, the group combed the beach again, picking up plastics and rubbish. It was getting better, fewer people were discarding their rubbish and the group had revelled in a collective feeling of accomplishment. 'Finally,' Peter had told them, 'Our message is getting through. That's a vast improvement on yesterday's clean up.'

'How are you today? We're always that busy I never get a chance to speak to you properly,' Peter asks Grace as they sit in Vasilis' taverna.

Grace can see a satisfied smile grow on his face as he looks at her steadily.

'Oh, I'm good,' Grace answers him.

'That makes me glad. You look happy too.'

'I am, mostly.' She smiles at him gently. The components of her life are finally being assembled.

'It hasn't escaped me, nor others for that matter, that you and Vasilis are friendly. I'm just wondering if that has had anything to do with your new found... how shall I say, contentment, maybe, which I must say, is a most agreeable constitution.' It is a conscious prompting on his part and Peter is not in the least discomposed.

Grace feels a light flush on her face. She is still getting used to Peter's extravagant way with words.

'Well... I like him, and we seem to get on. He's a nice person.'

Peter looks at her with interest.

What she really wanted to say was: *I study his face, see every pore, every perfection and imperfection. I watch the way his mouth moves when he speaks, the shape of his lips, his teeth. I'm mesmerised by his eyes. I pour over every gesture. I don't think he sees me the way I see him. My feelings disturb me. Why would he even think of me as being different from the others?*

'Well, that's good. You need to make friends, Grace. Where would we be without them?'

'Lonely, probably,'

'Precisely.'

'I've never felt lonely since I've been here.'

'Everyone is so friendly. They look after each other, that's for sure,' Peter says brightly.

'It's surprised me.'

'Really?'

'Yes. I suppose I had this image that I'd be pretty much on my own, apart from knowing Monica, obviously.'

There is a slight silence. Peter clears his throat. 'Vasilis is a good man. I was just wondering if there was anything more than just a growing friendship between the two of you?'

She pauses, considering, then dismisses his compliment with a wave of her hand. 'What would he see in me? A paranoid woman with too much baggage, probably. No, he's not going to look twice at me, not in that way. Anyway, what's wrong with just being friends?'

'Nothing at all, my dear. Nothing at all. But why wouldn't he, Grace? Why wouldn't he see you in that way? You're also beautiful on the inside, you know, as well as the outside.'

Grace tenses immediately.

'You haven't answered me.' Peter smiles. 'Why wouldn't Vasilis think you're attractive?'

'Because, I just don't think he would, that's all,' Grace says dismissively. 'Not me, anyway.'

'You're always bringing yourself down. Why do you do that? You need to stop it,' Peter says, a trace of frustration evident in his delivery.

'I know, I know. I can't help it.'

'Why? Why do it?'

'Because I can't imagine not doing it.'

'I don't understand, Grace. I don't think it's because of your past. I think you've always been like this. Am I right?'

She nods. 'Even as a little girl. I never saw myself as being good at anything. I always saw myself as the ugly bug amongst my friends.'

'You're so frustrating. Do you know that? I might be getting on a bit, but believe me, my sexual orientation has never got in the way of being able to appreciate a good-looking woman, because that's what you are. You're a kind-hearted woman. Deep down, you're someone who needs to be loved, to be appreciated for who you are and what you are… you're a special human being,' Peter says in his genteel but opinionated way.

There are tears in her eyes.

'I think that's what I love about you, Grace, your modesty.'

'I'm scared, Peter.' She folds her hands on her lap.

'Of what, my dear?'

'Getting too close, again. Jamie ripped my heart out. It felt like I couldn't breathe for a long time. It felt like there was a corset laced around me.'

'Having the best intentions can at times be a recipe for disaster. We don't always choose who we fall in love with. Sometimes life chooses for us. You only have one life. Don't live it with regrets.' He reaches over and affectionately touches her hand.

'I don't want to, not anymore.'

'Well then. Happiness doesn't have to be temporary and conditional. It's about trusting yourself and allowing yourself to become the person you're happy to be for the rest of your life.'

Grace tilts her head and looks towards the sky, contemplating Peter's words. She sighs. 'My trouble is, I've been imprisoned for a long time by my self-doubt. But you're right, Peter, you're right,' she repeats, as if confirming the decision she has just made. 'I've been a passenger in my own life. I didn't feel in control of where I was going. I just wanted a quiet life. I suppose I wanted to be invisible, but I don't anymore, not now. I don't think I could have made that kind of decision back in Edinburgh.'

'Why ever not?'

'Because Vasilis wasn't there. He was here, serving food, and taking his daughter to school, and saving lives in his lifeboat.'

'So, now you must sail your own boat.'

She narrows her eyes, wrinkling her forehead. 'What do you mean?'

'A boat is not built to sit idle in the harbour, it's meant to sail on water.'

She laughs a peel of laughter. 'You have an amazing way with words, Peter.'

'I suppose all that private education hasn't been wasted on me, after all.'

From the corner of her eye, Grace can see Vasilis appear from the kitchen with a bunch of papers in his hand. He glances over and smiles. He sits at a table and bends his head to consult his paperwork. Grace studies his profile, his face, which she knows she is already in love with, but at the same time, she is scared by the thought of being abandoned again.

'I've watched you since you first came into our little group and I've marvelled at how your resilience has grown.'

'I was petrified, but at the same time, I felt an exhilaration about coming here, and now that I'm here, it feels like this place has slipped through the little gaps in my armour. It has reinvented me, I truly feel that. It was a leap of faith at the time, but it seems to have been a good one, so far.'

She remembers how things have changed. When she first arrived, she had an awful sense of dread. She felt she had made a huge mistake and coming to Lesvos was not going to help her desire to make sense of her life. Grace had never been to Greece before, therefore it was an open book.

'What do your parents think of you leaving Edinburgh and coming to Greece?'

'They're dead. Well, my mum is. I don't know about my dad, he could be for all I know. He left my mum when I was five. She was a nurse. She was amazing. She worked twelve-hour shifts, but I never missed out on anything. I don't know how she managed it. She was so young, and she managed to keep our lives stable, well-adjusted. I don't think I could have done what she did.'

'She sounds like a remarkable woman.'

'She was. I miss her. I wish I had more time with her, although I know she would have hated growing old.'

'Getting old isn't easy. It comes with its drawbacks. But being able to grow old is a remarkable honour. Too many of my friends and those I loved died too young. We spend our entire lives not seeing what is in front of us. Life is mystifying, changeable, invigorating and painful.

'Half the time we're so wrapped up in our own little worlds that we're blind to what's around us. Ageing is not easy, but dying of a disease, or losing a child is worse. I think I'm quite privileged to still be here. I never thought I'd live this long.'

She cocks her head to one side and smiles. 'I'm going to be rude now and ask you your age, Peter?'

'You're right, that's a rude question. But because it's you, I'll answer it.' He grins. 'The young end of my seventies.'

'That's not old, not nowadays. And you're still active, more than some people half your age.'

As they talk, the taverna is filling up with people having early lunches. Peter attempts to raise his voice over the disagreeable rattle of tableware. 'I saw you just then.'

'Saw what?' Even before she has spoken the words, Grace knows what Peter is referring to.

'You! It's cute. You're not even aware of it.'

'And neither is he.'

'Oh, I'm not so sure about that.'

'Is it that obvious?'

'You look like a teenager,' he teases her.

'No! Really?'

'Let's just say, when he came out of the kitchen, your face lit up.'

'That obvious?'

He nods.

'I wasn't aware of it.'

Peter looks at the menu. 'I'm hungry. I think I'll order some lunch. What about you?'

Grace takes in the menu at a glance. 'Mm, maybe another time. There's a few things I need to do.'

'Well, I'm going to have the grilled swordfish.'

Grace collects her bag and puts her sunglasses on. She rises from her chair. Peter stands and leaning into her, kisses Grace on the forehead.

'Take care, my dear.'

'I will. Thank you, Peter.'

'For what?'

'For showing me, I finally like who I've become.'

'I didn't do anything.'

'You listened. It's another one of your virtues I like. You always listen.'

The Present

Guilt and Doubt

'I've met some lovely people, Sofia. Present company included, of course.' Grace smiles. 'Take Peter, for example. When we're clearing the beach, he has a springiness about him, it's almost like a youthful energy, as well as his wit and mental agility, it defies his years. I feel like I've known him all my life.'

'He has that effect. He's intelligent and incisive, I'll give him that.' Sofia grins. 'But not when it comes to love. You do know his reasons for coming here in the first place?'

'Yes, he told me.'

'That boyfriend of his behaved appallingly. He broke Peter's heart. Underneath that intellectual mask, he can be emotional and touching, but it has left him scarred. It was harrowing to watch. But he never lost his faith in others. Not Peter.'

Sofia looks at Grace and can see excitement glitter in her eyes. 'I hear you've been getting friendly with Vasilis.'

As Grace is about to reply a customer comes into the Deli and Sofia serves her. Grace remembers her walk with Vasilis the day before. People smiled conspiratorially at them, as they walked along the path that led to the harbour. Grace reminds herself how things have altered. When she first arrived, Grace had an awful sense of dread, that somehow she had made a huge mistake and her coming to Lesvos was not going to help in her need to make sense of her life. She had never been to Greece before. She didn't know what to expect. All she had as a reference was an image in her mind made up of travel programmes and novels and online searches. She realises she feels protected. This small town has become a secure base. Already, she can feel an attachment to it. She has forged daily routines:

having breakfast on her small balcony, visiting the bakers each morning, meeting her group of friends, clearing the beach of plastic and rubbish, and her trips to the market. When performed, they leave her with a definite and distinct feeling of accomplishment. And then, there is Sofia, Monica, Peter, and of course, Vasilis. Inside, she is smiling, just thinking of him.

She remembers when she first saw Vasilis and looking to see if he wore a wedding band. It was a spontaneous reaction. How did she feel when she saw there was none? She thinks about this. She found it agreeable. How odd, she now considers.

Watching him from her balcony, something stirred in her. Even the first time she saw him. And now, thinking about this, Grace finds it remarkable. She marvels at him, this man walking his daughter to school, each morning.

She often finds herself wondering about Pelagia's mother, and always feels a harsh guilt descend upon her. A sensation, not unlike a tremor passes through her.

She speculates, if fate had engineered her life differently, these feelings would not be swirling inside her, and then, she thinks of the implications of these reactions, the responses, even she is trying to understand and make sense of. They can easily change everything.

'So,' Sofia says, now that her customer has left. 'You like him?'

Grace flushes. 'I enjoy his company... yes, I like him.'

'Maybe, more than, just like?'

When she spoke with Peter at the taverna, Grace's first instinct was to acknowledge her feelings, but now, she shrinks from it. Why this caution? It has touched a doubt she finds disconcerting. It takes her by surprise. It is complicated, and she is unwilling to examine it.

'Just friends.'

The Past

An Investment in my Happiness

I liked to get a tram at St Andrews Square and get off at the airport. Not only did I enjoy the ride, but it also had a purpose. I loved watching my fellow passengers. I'd make up stories about their lives, where they worked, who they loved, where they lived and whether they were happy or sad. I guessed at their personalities, often gauged by a facial feature, a gesture and the way they spoke. At the airport, I'd buy a coffee and watch the departure screens and choose which city or resort I'd like to visit: Paris, Rome, Prague.

All this is making me sound introverted. I'm not. I just liked the anonymity it offered. Since I'd been on my own, my close friends had rallied around me. To be truthful, I don't know what I would have done without them. They made sure, as far as possible, my weekends were busy. The times we weren't all together, they took it in shifts to be with me. But there comes a point where that is not real life, it's manufactured.

I wasn't ungrateful. God, I needed them. They were my safety net. My lifeline. As time passed, I realised I couldn't rely on them to fill my life with shopping and meals out and walks along Portobello beach and hiking up Salisbury Crags. I needed to regain a sense of who I was. I needed to design a life worth living, whatever that turned out to be.

So, my tram rides were my attempt at dipping my toe into the social world, the world of other people, of strangers. It was a tiny step to face, and hopefully, and gradually, would ease my anxiety, and untie the knots inside me.

In the beginning, when someone spoke to me or showed me the slightest bit of attention, it felt like a floodlight on me. I found it draining and exhausting. I often felt despondent, which I found difficult to shake off, but I persisted and unlike before, where I would dissociate myself from my surroundings, I was uncompromising in my will to go through with it. Gradually, I became more confident, as each new encounter and experience was conquered.

I began to experience a little thrill of excitement and a touch of triumph with each new outing. I was still extremely cautious, and I still am to this day, but being in control of my anxiety is an investment in my happiness. It is still there, like a pot put on a back burner for a while, simmering away. The difference is, I'm now in control of the heat applied.

The Present

Four Kilometres; All the Difference Between Life and Death

She sits on the balcony as she does most mornings, watching the early morning sun glance and shimmer of the tiled roofs, as she catches the deep sapphire of the sea. A pink light has dispersed the clouds over the horizon and Grace contemplates the promise of another hot day. She has arranged to meet Vasilis, once he has dropped Pelagia off at school.

For the last few days, Grace has been unable to get out of her mind the image of the little girl who almost drowned. She has found herself tormented over what has happened to her and the damage she will have certainly suffered after witnessing the horrors that were undoubtedly an everyday occurrence in her now, not so innocent, young life. How does a child's mind comprehend such a reality? She has lost her mother under the most horrific of circumstances.

Her mouth trembles a little as Grace thinks momentarily of Olivia and the loss, she will never resign herself to. She feels an overwhelming protectiveness towards this girl, whose name she doesn't even know. It is an intense but also gentle emotion, a dignified emotion, but at the same time, it has physically affected her like an itch whose effect is inescapable.

She catches the familiar figure of Vasilis coming around the corner, heading towards her. She allows her gaze to linger on him and she registers the inexplicable bubble in her stomach. She stands and waves, 'I'm coming down.'

When they meet on the pavement there is a contented expression lying effortlessly across his face. He has been listening to music on his smartphone, and as he removes his earphones, she is aware of his large hazel eyes contemplating her.

'I like your dress, the colour suits you.'

She is wearing a green dress, a new one that she bought only yesterday.

She smiles, enjoying his compliment. He leans towards her and kisses her on the check. Her surprise catches her tongue. Finally, she says, 'What were you listening to?'

'Vivaldi. I love listening to classical music, it always puts me in a good mood. That's why I try to listen to it in the morning.'

'Really? I never had you down as a classical music lover,' Grace remarks.

'I like other types of music too, but it's my favourite.'

'I'm not familiar with it. I know the usual names, you know the big hitters.' She laughs at her expression

'The big hitters?' Vasilis looks puzzled.

'Yes. Mozart, Beethoven, composers like that.'

Vasilis grins. 'I thought you were talking about boxing.'

'My knowledge of boxing is even worse than classical music.'

'When I'm out on the lifeboat I play it then. I find it relaxes me, keeps my mind focused.'

'What do the others on the boat think of it?'

'I think by now I've converted them to its pleasures.'

'Have you been out again, in the boat?'

He nods. 'Yesterday. Another dinghy overflowing with people.'

'And children?'

'Some. No one died this time, thank God and St. Nicholas.'

'St Nicholas?'

'He is the patron saint of the seas. I have his icon hanging in my boat.'

She meets his eyes, and she can see flecks of light reflected in them. She wonders why St. Nicholas lets a mother drown in the sea in front of her child. She thinks of confronting Vasilis with this contradiction but decides to let it slip from her.

He pulls a pack of cigarettes from his shirt pocket and lights one, taking in a great suck of smoke. 'In the nineteen twenties, over a million Greeks were forced to leave Turkey. Likewise, nearly half a million Turks were moved out of Greece. More than half of the people living on this island today are descendants from those refugees. This is why we are compassionate towards these people. Being a refugee is part of our history, it's also part of who we are.'

'I never knew.'

'Sometimes, I think the rest of the world is blind to what is going on here. It's not their problem, so they turn away from it. It will be Europe's shame.' A fit of sudden anger straightens his posture. 'These people do not want to stay here, they want to go to England, Germany, Northern Europe. A tsunami is coming Europe's way.'

'What would have happened to the little girl's mother?'

'I imagine by now the coroner will have done the autopsy and she will be buried.'

'Where?'

'In the cemetery.'

'Is it far?'

'No. Why?'

'I want to see where she is buried.' Grace can't believe it is her voice she is hearing.

He looks at her in utter bewilderment. 'Are you sure?'

'Yes,' Grace says simply. 'I'd like to see it very much.'

'But, why?'

'I don't know. I'm not really sure. All I know is, it's something I feel I have to do.' She chokes on the emotion she is feeling. 'Will you take me, Vasilis?'

'I'm not sure it's a good idea, but you seem very determined.'

'If you don't, I'll get Sofia to take me.'

'Okay, I'll take you if you're sure it's what you want?'

'It is,' she says, suddenly purposeful.

As they walk, they pass a group of children. One, a young girl of about ten years old, is teaching a younger boy to recite the alphabet. 'Alpha, Beta, Gamma, Delta, Epsilon, Zeta...' Her chant is like a hymn sung with conviction and passion. They pass a jeweller's shop, where an ornamentation of classical and Byzantine gold adorns the display window. Grace glances into a doorway and she can see an old man bent over with thick glasses painting an icon, the tabletop brims with small pots of paint and brushes. The streets are lined with poplars and palms, tiled courtyards are sprinkled with roses and jasmine. At the foot of a marble staircase, oranges litter the ground, fallen from trees that fringe the entrance to a house.

Soon, they are walking to the sound of birds and donkeys grazing in a nearby field, where rows of old olive trees are clamped by bulbous roots. As they near the cemetery, their pace slows, and Vasilis rubs the short bristles on his chin. He points to the cemetery. 'My father is buried here.'

Grace can see two men digging and clearing weeds. As they proceed further, they pass elaborate white marble graves, until, around her, there are only mounds of earth with white marble plaques. She notices there are no sentiments from loved ones carved into the marble only numbers written on them.

'These are the dates the person was found in the sea or washed up on the shore, the symbol determines if they are male or female and the next set of numbers is a three-digit DNA number,' Vasilis explains.

Grace is aware that most of the graves are marked, 'unknown.'

An old man, sombre in appearance, approaches them. He has been watching the two younger men as they dig the grave. His name is Theodoros Dimou. He walks with a stoop and Grace wonders if it is with age that his body bows or with the weight of the images of the bodies he has prepared for their final journey. He is the caretaker of the dead.

'Vasilis, how are you? Visiting your father?' Theodoros asks.

'No, not exactly. I was wondering where the young woman was buried. The one who recently drowned.'

'Ah, yes. You brought her body back, didn't you?'

Vasilis nods his head.

'She is over here. Come this way.'

They follow Theodoros, as he weaves in between the mounds of earth. 'They have survived a war only to drown in the sea. Four kilometres is all the difference between life and death.' He refers to the Mytilini Strait, that separates Lesvos from Turkey.

'What is he saying?' Grace asks.

As they walk, Vasilis translates Theodoros' words into English.

Theodoros sighs. 'We have nearly reached maximum capacity. We are running out of space.' He sounds like a man that is defeated. He points to a mound of earth. 'This is Zanaf. She was six. The boat she was in capsized and she was held above water by her uncle for eight hours. It wasn't until they were rescued that the uncle realised, she had died in his arms.'

They pass a grave with a round posy of white and red flowers. 'This is a mother, buried with her baby.'

Grace bites her lip. Her eyes are watering and she brings her hand to her mouth. 'How are they buried? They are Muslim. Who says their prayers?' Suddenly, Grace thinks how important it is that there is a proper and dignified burial.

'Even amongst all this needless death, there is a light. Moustafa is from Syria. He was targeted by ISIS at the beginning of the Syrian war. He had two choices, to reach Europe or die. This was his reality. He was one of the lucky ones. He got out a long time ago. He arrived with his wife to study in Lesvos, but now he works as a translator and body washer.'

'Body washer?'

'Yes. These people came here searching for a better life, the least we can do is to try and give them a dignified burial. Moustafa washes the bodies of the males and his wife washes the bodies of the females. It must be a woman that does this, and, in all cases, it is done in accordance with Sharia and they are all buried according to Islamic tradition. It has been a tremendous comfort to the surviving family members.' Theodoros points to a large white container at the edge of the cemetery. 'The bodies are washed in there. Ah, here we are. This is where the woman you asked about is buried.'

Grace looks at the small mound of earth and the white plaque with the date the woman died. She takes a deep breath and wonders at the courage this woman must have had to take her daughter on such an arduous journey through foreign countries and into the unknown.

Grace cannot comprehend the circumstances that would drive such an action, her fear for her daughter and the need for a future must have been bone-deep. Grace has seen the images on the news and in social media of the cities and towns whose buildings, houses and homes have been reduced to medieval skeletal structures. She tries to imagine, if those images had been Edinburgh, how would she have survived? No food, no running water, no electricity, no schools, no jobs, no transport, everything she took for granted, that made life comfortable and secure, had been disintegrated and wiped from the life she knew.

This woman awoke each morning knowing each day could be her last. She would have witnessed relatives and loved ones brutally killed, injured, maimed, disfigured and, most certainly, psychologically scarred. She would have seen children pulled from the rubble that once was a home, gasping for air, crying, dying.

How can a mother be blamed for taking her daughter out of that hell? Where morals, dignity and rights are only words. The endurance of such atrocities is beyond anything Grace has known.

This woman may have been a doctor, a dentist, a teacher. She was a mother, maybe a sister, an aunt, a colleague. She would have been a friend, she was a citizen and finally, a refugee, displaced. There is no choice, only necessity.

Mother and daughter endured terrifying months with little food or water, dwindling money, no medicine, the bitter cold, torrential rain, inadequate shelter, the threat of hyperthermia, hunger and sickness, beatings at border crossings, tear-gassed by police, the threat of human traffickers, criminal gangs, violence and rape, utter desperation, overcrowded rubber boats, dark menacing waves, the sting of the wind and its cacophonous roar, the sudden panic of being swallowed by the sea, submerged and struggling with the weight of water that presses against every inch of her body, burning lungs, screaming lungs… silence.

Where is the humanity? The understanding?

'Are you alright, Grace?' It is Vasilis' voice.

She has been crying, sobbing. She turns and sinks into Vasilis' chest. He puts his hand around her shoulder, bends forward and gently kisses the crown of her head. He touches her cheek with his finger. 'Let it all out.' His voice is gentle and soft.

'There's one more thing I need to do?'
'What is that?' Vasilis asks.
Grace lifts her eyes to him. 'I need to find the little girl.'

The Present

A Truce Before the Storm

Vasilis is up at six, an oblong of white light bathes the room as he sips his coffee. Sleep has become a stranger since the callouts have increased, as the boats continue to bring more refugees at an alarming rate. With each trip, the men on the lifeboat pray there is not another body to fish from the sea. He wonders how long the island's infrastructure can cope with the demands placed on it. It sits uneasily with him that the refugee camp cannot meet, because of the numbers, what are basic, but essential humanitarian needs. He can feel an anger stretch inside his chest. It is irrelevant because it will not change unless the rest of Europe comes to their aid. Some days, it feels like they have been abandoned, the capsized dinghies and the terrified faces of their occupants are invisible amongst the banquet of self-indulgence and celebrity the world is constantly fed. What will it take? What will be their moment of enlightenment and understanding? Dead children washed up on a tourist beach?

He frequently sees the images play out in his mind. He is often disturbed by the faces that haunt him, the paralyzed expressions attested only to a fear and terror he has never known.

He rakes his fingers through his hair and thinks of preparing Pelagia's breakfast, but a glance at his watch tells him it is still too early. Such domesticated chores would offer a momentary release, an adjustment to a normality his mind craves, instead of feeling he is always standing on the precipice of his own fear.

Pelagia is standing in the doorway of the kitchen, she is scratching her dishevelled hair; with her other hand, she is cradling a tattered teddy bear. Vasilis thinks she looks so vulnerable, with her long lashes blinking the sleep from her eyes. Occasionally, he sees her mother in his daughter's face.

'Pelagia, you are awake early.'

'I couldn't find you, Baba. I lost you and I was on my own.'

He stretches out his arms. 'Come here, it was only a dream.'

Pelagia shuffles towards him, sleep still hanging around her. She climbs onto his lap and as she snuggles into him, Vasilis strokes her long dark hair. 'I'll always be here, honey. Always.'

'Good.'

Vasilis lets a smile crease his lips. 'Are you hungry?'

Pelagia yawns and then nods. 'Can you hear my stomach grumbling?'

Vasilis smiles. 'Was that what that noise was! let's make some breakfast, shall we?'

'Can Teddy have some too?'

'Of course, he can.'

'Good, he's hungry as well.'

'I thought so. I can hear his tummy grumble too.'

'That was my tummy.'

'Oh. Well then, I'll need to make a really big breakfast. Does he like eggs?'

'Only if they are scrambled eggs.'

'Then scrambled eggs it is.'

As they eat their breakfast, Vasilis notices Pelagia's rosy cheeks and he says her name.

'What?' she replies.

'Nothing. Sometimes I just like saying your name.'

'But why?'

'I like the sound of it.'

'Grown-ups are weird.'

'I know.' He cherishes these moments, they cannot be relived.

'Baba, can I go and play at the beach today?'

'I don't see why not, but it will have to be after I finish at the taverna. And, before you ask, he can't go.' Vasilis points to the teddy bear.

'He doesn't want to. He's told me he's got more important things to do.'

'Oh. Like what?'

She crosses her arms and legs. 'He wants to help the people on the boats.'

Vasilis is momentarily caught off guard. 'Well, that would be a good thing to do.'

'Yes, that's what I thought. We've been told about them at school. I don't understand why people have to hurt each other? Why are people so cruel, Baba? I would be so sad if I couldn't live in my house.' Pelagia jumps from her chair and walks around the table. Vasilis scoops her up into his arms. She moves closer into him.

He tries to form the words that will explain to his seven-year-old daughter, but it is as if Vasilis' tongue is overcome by a great feeling of numbness. He dreads questions like this, not that they force him to admit the ugly truth, rather, it reminds him his little girl's innocence is being hacked away by the world around her. She is growing up, she is becoming more inquisitive.

He strokes her hair and tries to explain the best he can. Once they have cleared the table, Vasilis washes the dishes, Pelagia helps by drying them with a towel. Vasilis is aware that Pelagia is thinking about something, normally, she would be chatting away at him. He thinks she is probably pondering his explanation. As Vasilis reaches into a cupboard and puts the plates away, Pelagia is nursing her curiosity. 'Who was that woman you were with?'

'She is my friend. Do you like her?'

Pelagia shrugs.

'Do you want me to have friends?'

'Yes.'

'Well then, she is my friend.'

'But she is a woman.'

'Ah, I see. And does that make it different?'

'I don't know.'

'Do you have friends?'

'You know I do.'

'And are some of your friends' boys?'

She nods.

'And that's how it should be and it's the same for me, also. I can have Grace as a friend.'

'I suppose, but that doesn't mean I have to like her.'

'No, you don't have to like her, but it would be nice if you could. Do you think you could try?'

'I suppose.'

Vasilis has to hold back a smile.

A brief quiet ensues, a truce before the storm.

The Past

Am I Who I Think I Am? And Other Contemplations

I was sitting in La Barantine coffee shop on Bruntsfield Place when I saw her, Jamie's partner. She was wearing a floral slit skirt, with a white and turquoise print. Twenty-something years ago, if you were trying to make a statement with your clothes, floral attire said the opposite. I read somewhere that now it is called the rise of new wave femininity. And she did look empowered, as she strolled with her modern buggy, stopping occasionally to gaze into a shop window, before moving on.

It was an impulsive decision. I've made a few in my time, and now, with the benefit of hindsight, I should have stayed in that café nursing my coffee and scone.

I stayed on the opposite side of the street, sometimes, pretending to be distracted by a window display, but always, keeping her in my line of vision.

It was lunchtime, and the air rumbled with traffic and pedestrians. I reminded myself to breathe, as she disappeared into a shop. Should I go in? Would she recognise me? That would be an uncomfortable experience for both of us. It felt an eternity waiting for her to emerge. Finally, she did, a young man held the shop door open for her, as she appeared with the buggy and a newly acquired shopping bag. She smiled and thanked him. I can't remember what kind of shop it was, but I do recall she looked pleased with herself, she had a definite glow of self-satisfaction about her.

My throat was dry, and my tongue stuck to the roof of my mouth. I was aware of a tightening in my chest as she crossed at a pelican crossing. I had to stop walking and keep a distance to avoid an interaction between us. I stopped and stood at a corner, outside an Odd Bins on

Bruntsfield Avenue, for fear of being seen and I saw him then; he was no longer a baby. He had grown since I last saw him… in his bedroom, sleeping peacefully in his cot.

I noticed he now had thick dark hair, just like Jamie, hanging just above his eyebrows that enriched the radiant blue of his eyes. His eyes stood out, strikingly so, and his nose was like a button on his face. His cheeks were rosy, probably from the chill in the air and he clutched a toy teddy that was secured to the pushchair.

I allowed myself to glance at her. I didn't know her name. I never asked Jamie and he never offered it. I liked it that way. There was a distance between us.

I always wondered what Jamie saw in me What was it he was attracted to?

I have never seen myself as attractive, pretty in a normal way, plain maybe, but not someone who would turn heads.

I could see what he would have seen in her. Her chestnut hair was thick and wavy, falling around her shoulders in curls. Her figure had returned, and I wondered if she was a member of a gym. Both Jamie and I used to be, but the only exercise I partook in was walking, and my step count, some days, would be pitiful.

I could tell she liked to spend money on her appearance. Her make up accentuated her features effectively and I felt a tug of jealousy.

She leaned forward and said something to the infant and then carried along Bruntsfield Road. I followed at a distance. A hen party, all dressed in pink leotards, with the bride to be crowned in a tiara and L plate dangling around her chest, stumbled out of Papilio Italian restaurant, singing a drunken and tuneless rendition of 'Wake Me Up Before You Go Go,' by Wham. I weaved in and around them and when I looked ahead of me, she was gone.

I walked at a quicker pace, glancing from left to right. She couldn't have got far. I scanned along the street. You would have thought, it would be easy to pick out a woman with a buggy but, as my frown grew, I seemed to see everyone around me, everyone but her.

Suddenly, I saw her. She was trying to enter Cuckoo's Bakery, a little café that specialised in cupcakes, but the buggy was too wide to get through the door.

I waited and to my amazement, she left the buggy outside. I watched from a distance. A couple sat inside with their backs to the window. Then, one of them stood up, a woman, and went to the rear of the shop and out of my sight. I presumed she was going to the toilet. I moved closer.

There she was, not turning to check on her child, but on her smartphone, texting, engrossed. She grinned, and her fingers tapped the screen in succession. I couldn't believe she wasn't paying any attention to her child who was still sleeping.

She lifted her gaze and gestured to a cupcake and the young girl behind the counter leaned forward to scoop it out of the display cabinet with tongs.

It should be me. It should be my child, not yours. Why was I punished? She's not even looking at him. She's more interested in her phone.

The thought of Jamie touching her body, kissing her lips, being intimate with her, as we had been, made my heart tighten with torment.

I wanted her to suffer, just as I had. I wanted to hurt her. I glanced around. The man sitting at the window was engrossed with eating his lunch.

She was still grinning at her smartphone. I wondered then if she was texting Jamie?

I stared at her, she looked content, so happy. I felt anger tighten around my heart. The woman hadn't returned from the toilet. I shifted my eyes from inside the shop to the buggy. Even before I was conscious of deciding to do it, I had stepped forward, moving swiftly, my hands gripped the handles of the buggy, in one full motion, the buggy drew away and I was guiding it along the pavement away from her.

I was filled with a sudden wild joy, an elation I hadn't experienced in a long time. I imagined her screams, the sheer panic in her voice.

This is how it feels to have the one you love taken from you.

I knew it so well. It had been my constant companion. Now it was her turn to know how raw that pain felt.

I walked at a quick pace and crossed the road into Bruntsfield Terrace. I continued, quickening my pace and passed a traffic warden who was placing a parking ticket on the windscreen of a car. I veered off to my left into Bruntsfield Links, a large opened space of parkland. I pushed the buggy down an avenue of trees. On either side, people sat on the grass, eating lunch, reading books, children played noisily kicking a football and a group of students played cricket. I would have been viewed as just another mother taking her child for a stroll in the park.

I stopped and checked on the child. He was still sleeping peacefully unaware of what had transpired around him.

It was then I heard the siren and I walked away, leaving the buggy and sleeping child by a bench. I turned only once and, even though I was trembling, I smiled as I saw an elderly couple, one of them speaking into his smartphone, as they stood perplexed beside the buggy.

The police would be here soon. I felt a moment of relief, then of disbelief. I sucked in air, as I squinted into a ray of sunshine.

I kept walking until I came to The Meadows and then sat on a bench. Some distance away, an ice cream van was serving a growing queue of people.

I sat there for perhaps five minutes. I looked up towards the sky and the branches in the trees began to spin. I squinted my eyes away from the sun and I began to tremble. My breath caught in my chest. I breathed deeply the air around me, trying to quell the tide of nausea that threatened to spill from my stomach.

What was I becoming? That was not *me*, not the *me* I thought I knew. It was someone else. Being that other person was too terrible to contemplate.

It was not premeditated, the opportunity presented itself and I couldn't stop myself.

Somewhere, across the city, Jamie was being told his son was missing. He too would now feel my pain.

I often think about that day. I've tried to quantify it. Do I really know who I am? Do I know myself well enough to determine if I like who I've become?

What if, from the very beginning, I have been influenced by others, those I have known since I was a child, my teachers, my family, my friends, my work colleagues.

What if, I'm not who I think I am, but who I have been told I am. Are my memories and experiences legitimately mine? Or, are they painted with the brush strokes of others?

Am I the product of my imagination? Or am I who I'd like others to think I am?

You cannot be human without having faults, without making mistakes. It is a sequence we must tolerate. It is fundamental to our chemistry. It is inseparable from being whole. To being alive. These are the things that connect us. This is what I have come to understand.

The Present

Fragile

She has decided to enter the church on a whim. It was something that wouldn't have crossed her mind back in Edinburgh. The last time she had been inside a church was at a friend's daughter's baptism and she found herself uncomfortable with the theatrics of it all. Again, this time, hers is not an arresting experience.

An old man sits just inside the entrance, hunched over a wooden plate where visitors have obviously despatched a generous sum of euros. His face reminds her of the Easter Island Statues, glowering at her in his corner. He levers himself from the stool and standing, he gestures towards Grace's bare shoulders, and then towards a sign that asks visitors to be respectfully dressed. He is almost touching her nose and staring at her so much, Grace feels like she has entered his house without permission. At that moment, Grace's smartphone rings, and he frowns; it is enough for her to terminate this encounter and she turns and heads outside.

Sitting on the steps of the small church she squints her eyes from the sun's glare and rummages in her bag for her sunglasses.

She glares at the smartphone's screen, but it is too bright to see who has phoned. She removes her sunglasses. God, this phone is useless in the sun. She presses it to her ear.

'Hello, Grace speaking.'

'Hi, Grace. It's Greg.' Greg had been a colleague of Grace's at the university but had moved to Newcastle last year.

'Hello, Greg. What a lovely surprise. I've not heard from you in a long time. How are you and Melissa?'

'She's fine, I'm fine and you?'

His voice is tense, on edge. Grace can detect it and gets the distinct impression he hasn't called to engage in small talk.

'Look, I'll get to the chase,' he says, without waiting for her to reply. 'I need a favour.'

She can feel the sun beginning to sting her shoulders as if licking her with small flames. 'You do know I'm not staying in Edinburgh right now?'

'Yes, that's why I'm phoning you. You're staying in Lesvos, right?'

'Yes.'

'Do you remember my daughter, Natasha?'

'Of course. How is she?'

'That's the point really, I don't know,'

'Oh!'

'She went travelling during her gap year and ended up on Lesvos. She said she wanted to volunteer and help the Syrian refugees.'

'Yes. Quite a few people have done that. It's admirable really. You must be proud of her?'

'We are, we are, but also very worried.'

'Why, what's wrong Greg?'

'She'd always been phoning us, keeping Melissa and me up to date on what she was up to, you know that kind of thing. She was always regular with her calls. That's why we know she was staying in Lesvos. The thing is, Grace, she hasn't phoned us in three weeks. Melissa is frantic as you can imagine. I'm really worried.'

'Have you been in touch with the authorities on the island?'

'We have but they say that she is an adult. She's not necessarily missing, she has just not been in touch with us, which they feel is her prerogative. They were quite dismissive.'

'How can I be of help?'

'If she doesn't contact us within the next week or so, I'm coming over, but I was in touch with Robert and he told me you were in Greece for a while and when he told me you were staying on Lesvos then I just had to phone you.'

'Do you want me to see if I can get in touch with her?'

'I'd be so grateful if you could, Grace. It would be such a relief.'

'Do you know where she is volunteering?'

'I think it was that big camp that has been on the telly. At a registration clinic, helping the nurses and doctors with the refugee's health needs, that kind of thing. Do you know it?'

'I do. In fact, I'm going there tomorrow.'

'You are, my God, what a coincidence.'

'Is there anything you can tell me that might help?'

'She had met a young man, I think she called him, Neos, her boyfriend. She was staying with him in Mytilene.'

'I don't want to downplay what you've just said, Greg, but, maybe, she's just having a good time with her boyfriend.'

'And that would be fine, great even, but there's more to it I feel.'

'What do you mean?'

'She told Melissa and me, she was having these episodes where she would blank out for a minute or so. I told her to see one of the nurses or doctors she was working with, get them to take a look at her, but she dismissed that too easily. She said Neos was helping her. He was able to make her see things more clearly, to develop and heal her soul from the damage done. I've no idea what she was talking about.'

'Like what? What damage?'

'I don't know, she wouldn't say. When I asked if this Neos had a medical background, she got really annoyed. It was out of character, not like her at all. She said, he was helping her using Reiki.'

'What's that?'

'I looked it up on the internet. Seemingly, it's a healing technique that believes there's an unseen 'life-force energy' that we all have, and it flows through us.'

'Oh! I see.' But she didn't.

'Yeah. That was my reaction too. She's just broken all contact with us, Grace, and Melissa is at her wits' end. She's got an appointment to see the doctor this week. She's just not coping... she's very fragile. I haven't told Melissa yet. Natasha has shut down her Facebook account and changed her email address.'

Grace thinks about Natasha. She has an image of a happy and grounded young lady. She remembers liking her at the time.

'I just want to know what's going on. Do you have any idea, Grace?'

'I'm afraid not. Look, I can't promise anything, but I'll ask about her when I'm at the camp.'

'Thanks, Grace.' There is relief in his voice.

'Phone me in a few days. Hopefully, I'll have some good news for you.'

'I really appreciate this, Grace.'

'It's not a problem. You take care, Greg, and give my love to Melissa.'

'I will. Thank you again. Bye now.' She can hear his voice waver.

'Bye, Greg.'

The Present

Natasha

She feels angry, it feels good, it is a release.

Vasilis swallows his drink and peers at her. 'All I'm saying is, I don't think it's a good idea, that's all. What good can it do?'

She is frowning now her serious face set for a fight. 'I want to know she is alright, looked after. She still needs her mother.'

And that about sums it up, Vasilis shakes his head.

'You're not her mother, Grace and you never could be. They will try to find a relative, there are procedures they need to follow.'

'So, you're not going to take me?'

'I never said that.'

'You as much as implied it.'

He rolls his eyes.

'See.'

'See what?'

'It doesn't matter. I'm going anyway.'

'Yes. You've made yourself clear. How are you going to get there, you don't have a car?'

She sighs wearily and shrugs, all the time without looking at him. 'I could get a bus.'

'And the camp is on the bus route?'

'I don't know, I'll find out.',

There is a long silence between them. It makes her feel uneasy. God, why am I feeling like this? She searches for something to say but the words won't form in her head. Is it embarrassment or an anxious need to fill the defining empty space? She's not sure.

Her mouth is dry. 'I need a glass of water,' she says, finally and gets up, heading towards the kitchen.

She can feel his eyes on her, staring judgementally.

I don't need this, not now. She opens the fridge and takes out a bottle of water. When she turns, Vasilis is standing there. He smiles a slow, sympathetic smile.

'You didn't invite me here to have an argument with you. I've really enjoyed tonight. The food was delicious and the wine…' he lifts his empty glass, 'it seems to have disappeared.' He grins and says gently, 'If it means that much to you, I'll take you, of course, I will. Just be prepared, you'll see things you might not want to see.'

She doesn't exactly feel a warm glow of self-satisfaction.

'It's that bad?'

He nods.

'It's just that, I also promised a friend I'd look out for his daughter as well, she's volunteering at the camp. He's worried about her.'

'I know a few people. I could ask around for you?'

'Would you? That would help.'

When they arrive just outside the camp, Vasilis goes to a reception area whilst Grace waits in the car. This is different from anything she has ever seen. She can't just sit and wait. She steps out of the car and stretches her legs. She looks around and feels self-conscious. She is struck by the barbed wire perimeter fence. Vasilis was right. Nothing can prepare you for this. Grace has seen refugee camps on news bulletins before but seeing, and smelling, and feeling her surroundings sends her senses and emotions into another stratosphere.

Now that she is here, she is sure this is the right thing to do. Vasilis returns and tells her his friend knows Natasha and he will take them to her as she is working that morning.

'She is on her break and usually sits in the same place most days. My friend, Kyrios, said he would take us to see her.'

'That's good. What about the little girl? Can he take us to her as well?'

'That is not so easy. He will have to do some checking first. As we don't know her name, he will have to go through all the new arrivals within the last week or two.'

Grace's heart sinks. What was she thinking? There would be rules and regulations. Vasilis must have known this. She realised she could not just arrive unannounced and expect to see the little girl, just like that? This was going to be more difficult than she thought. 'Oh, I see.'

She can sense Vasilis thinking.

Vasilis smiles warmly. 'If she is here, Kyrios will find her.'

This promise seems to revive her.

They walk through a mass of United Nations High Commissioner for Refugees tents. The scale of the camp takes the breath from her. This is a town of tents. There are pallets everywhere, refuse bins overflowing with rotting rubbish. Mud is mixed with human waste and rotting food. Her eyes sting and water at the stench of garbage and smell of urine. Amongst this, washing lines add a sense of colour and normality. Everywhere she looks, children play beside piles of discarded rubbish bags. She is horrified at the thought of the vermin it undoubtedly attracts.

She glances at the opening of one tent where a mother is washing a child in a basin. She looks away, as not to make eye contact with the woman. At that moment, Grace wonders if she has been deceiving herself. She wants to escape this hell and realises she can, but those interned in this existence have no such choice. She feels crushed by this. A respect for the volunteers, who willingly come each day, grows with each step she takes.

'There she is, just over there.' Kyrios points over to a group sitting on a small wall.

'I recognise her. Thank you, Kyrios.'

Vasilis touches Grace's arm. 'I'll walk back with Kyrios. I'll see you back at the car.' Grace acknowledges Vasilis' awkwardness with a little compensatory smile.

As she walks towards Natasha, Grace is aware that the youthfulness once prominent in Natasha's face has been overshadowed by deep-set eyes and skeletal cheekbones where the skin is stretched and waxed. Although Natasha is still pretty, Grace feels a sudden alarm and she has to make an effort to smile a greeting. 'Natasha.'

Natasha looks at Grace. 'Hello.'

Grace is aware she doesn't recognise her. 'Hi, I'm a friend of your parents. It's been a while since I last saw you.'

And then it is as if a light has switched on inside her head. 'Grace! My God! What are you doing here?'

'I'm staying in Molyvos.'

'I've not seen you in years.'

'I know and look at you, you've grown into a woman.'

'Are you working here?'

'No. I've got a confession to make. This is not a chance meeting. Actually, your dad asked if I could look you up.'

'Really?'

Grace can tell by the tone of her voice, Natasha doesn't approve.

'He did, yes. Can we talk?'

Natasha glances at her watch. 'I've got five minutes.' Her look of disappointment leaves a bitter taste in Grace's mouth.

'The thing is, your mum and dad are worried that you haven't been in touch with them.'

She sighs and runs her hand through her hair. 'Jesus! Well, they don't have to. As you can see, I'm doing fine.'

'Look, the last thing I want to do is upset you. I just promised your dad... you know... he's a friend. I can see you're fine. After all, you're doing a really difficult job here.'

'What would you know about that?'

'Well… it must be hard.'

'I think it's worse for those living here.'

'Of course, it is. Look, Natasha, I don't want to get off to bad start and upset you.'

'I know. You're just being a good friend. I'm sorry. I shouldn't take it out on you.' She takes a packet of cigarettes from her pocket and offers one to Grace, who politely declines.

'Honestly, the last thing I want to do is upset you.'

Natasha lights her cigarette and inhales deeply. 'It's okay. It's not your fault.'

Good, she's starting to calm down. 'Why don't we just start over again. You know why I'm here and if you want me to leave then that's fine. I'll tell your dad you didn't want to speak to me.'

Natasha looks around and takes her by the arm. They wander away from the others.

'I've met someone. His name is Neos. I love him very much. We're staying in Mytilene. Neos has an apartment. He loves me too.'

'Your dad said you won't get in touch with him, that you've broken all contact. He's really worried. Couldn't you just phone and let him and your mum know you're alright?'

She shakes her head. 'Before I came here before I met Neos, I knew there was something inside me that was broken. I just didn't know what it was. I didn't understand my emotions. I didn't have any belief in myself. I couldn't let them out. Neos has let me see, he can make this happen. It's because I've been exposed to destructive forces. I've been emotionally abused.'

'By who?'

'By my parents. That's why I must disconnect them from my life. I don't need them, I don't need my friends. None of them. My relationship with them was damaging.'

'What do you mean, emotionally abused?

'I've seen the truth now and only Neos can help me. He can heal me. Only him.'

'I don't understand. How can he do that?'

'Don't you see? He has helped me recognise this. He puts his hands on my head to connect with my energy and sense the obstructions, the blockages. If my emotions are impeded, he can create a path, so that they can travel and emerge. It's about being aware of the energy points in our bodies. Neos is like a healer. He has helped me become aware that things happened in my past. I often get flashbacks. There was an auntie who used to hit me when I stayed with her. I was about five at the time. She died when I was about six. I've never told anyone about it. Neos helps me to open these memories instead of keeping them buried inside me. When this happens, everything starts to make sense. He takes me apart, emotionally and mentally and then puts all the pieces together in the right order.'

Takes me apart? Poor Natasha. Something is seriously wrong here. 'What about the absences? Have you been to see a doctor?'

'That's why I've not been well, physically. My body is reacting to my emotional damage. I used to get these absences before I met Neos, now I've not had one for months. It's all connected.'

After their meeting, Grace feels strangely depressed. This is way over her head. It is obvious the relationship Natasha has with this Neos is unhealthy, dangerous even. But the way she spoke about him frightened Grace. Natasha is blind to the reality of what is going on around her. Also, there is a clear dependency. Natasha needs him, that much is obvious, and Grace is frightened for her.

On their way back to Molyvos, Grace tells Vasilis of her concern for Natasha.

'What!' he sounds incredulous. 'This Neos sounds as if he is unstable himself.'

'She's besotted with him. She believes everything he tells her.'

'Getting someone to understand they are wrong can be difficult, especially if it is a belief about themselves. In my experience, they hold onto it even more.'

'She has been brainwashed. There's no other word for it.'

'What are you going to tell her father?'

'Good question. The truth is not going to ease his worries, and neither will a lie.' She has no ready, convincing answer. She tries to mull over a response. If it was her daughter, she would want to know the truth, no matter how difficult that would be to hear. She feels ashamed. 'I'll tell him his daughter is not coming home.'

Vasilis is intrigued. 'And that she blames her parents for whatever it is they have supposedly done?'

She thinks for a moment. 'Yes. I've no other option.'

The Past

A Moment of Weakness and Betrayal

I struggled with the key in the lock, clumsily holding my bag in my other hand. Once inside, I stood motionless and sighed. I walked through the house, flicking on lights, pressing the remote control for the television, dropping the keys and my bag on the kitchen table, before pouring a large wine.

I took a generous mouthful and walked over to the kitchen window. The sky was ablaze with a fiery red and orange glow.

Soon, it would be growing dark, I thought, as I looked at the garden, overgrown and tired looking, in the clutches of neglect. I had been meaning to source out an affordable gardener on the internet, but like many things, it never got past the thought stage.

From the living room, I could hear a Sky News journalist interview an MP about Brexit.

'I see you've let the garden go to rack and ruin. That's a shame.'

My heart thumped my rib cage, like the shock of an electrical current. I spun around in stunned disbelief, red wine splattering the floor. 'Jesus! Jamie. What are you doing here?'

He stood with his hands deep in his pockets. 'I used to live here, remember?'

'What do you want?'

He looked at me with an unnerving mixture of pleasure and suspicion. 'I thought that was obvious.'

I felt like I was in a dream. He was standing in the house. If I reached out, I could touch him.

'I don't understand.'

'Oh, but I think you do.' He pulled out a chair and sat down.

I leaned against the sink fearing my legs would buckle from under me.

'She saw you, Grace. By the way, her name's Jayne. She saw you in the coffee shop. You followed her, didn't you? I mean, it wasn't her best moment, leaving the little one outside on the pavement, but how was she to know what you were about to do?'

I drew in a breath, trying to suppress my nervousness. 'It wasn't planned. I wasn't thinking straight.' I felt tears rising to the surface. I attempted to formulate an explanation. 'I was… it was stupid, really stupid.' How could I tell him of the emotion that consumed me? I felt confused, unable to put into words any logical explanation. It was an impossible obstacle that clouded my mind. I felt a hopelessness struggling for a way to put it right. All I could say was, I was sorry.

'I know you are.'

'You do?'

'No harm came to him, and you made sure he was seen by that old couple. Jayne was in a state, obviously.'

'I would never have done anything that would put him in danger.'

'Of course, not, but the police don't know that, do they?'

'Have you told them?'

'Not yet. There's very little CCTV around that area, so in a way, you were lucky.' He stared out of the window and sighed. 'Jayne wants me to go to the police, she says, the police would be interested in speaking to you because you had a motive, but I've persuaded her to hold off, for now.'

'Why would you do that?'

'Because I wanted to speak to you first. I know you're not a bad person, Grace and, if I'm honest, I still feel guilty about what I did to you. In a perverse way, I deserved your revenge.'

I was astonished at this revelation, although it didn't diminish the gravity of what I did.

'Does she know you're here?'

'No. I don't think she'd be happy about it if she did. Cavorting with the enemy.'

'Is that how you see me?'

'No. I don't, but she does.'

'If you were in my position, what would you have done?'

He scratched his chin. 'But I wasn't.'

I placed my glass of wine on the bunker and noticed the pile of dirty dishes in the sink.

'How have you been?'

I wasn't expecting that. I straightened my back. 'I'm... I'm getting there, apart from my little blip.'

'I would say it was a big one.'

'Right.' I looked away from him, entwining and twisting my fingers.

'Have you met anyone?'

I shook my head. 'And I'm not looking.'

'Maybe you should.'

I stared at my feet.

'You deserve to be happy again.'

'Do you still think about Olivia?'

He sat back in the chair. His face tightened. 'I can go a whole day without thinking about her, and then, I remember her, that's when the guilt starts... and you?'

'Every day. I think I always will. Sometimes, I get into a panic. It's like her face slips from me and I struggle to remember what she looked like.'

'That's happened to me, too.'

'How's your son?'

'He's a lively one. He's trying to walk now. We need eyes in the back of our heads.'

It was surreal, asking about Jamie's son. I felt as if I had been dropped into another universe. Behind my civility, I was tormented.

He looked at me steadily and something in his eyes changed. 'You would have been the perfect mother.'

There was a sudden and strained silence between us. I held my breath, his words stopping me from breathing.

He was drumming his fingers on the kitchen table, thinking. He stood up and walked over to me. I looked at him in faint alarm as he lifted his hand to my face and slid his fingers through my hair.

'I'd forgotten how good you smell.' His voice was level, almost matter of fact. He leaned towards me and I could feel his breath on my skin and then his lips brushed my neck sending a shiver through me. To my shame, I was unable to resist. He caressed my neck with his touch, and it tingled with bewilderment and pleasure. He found my mouth and time collapsed on itself, beyond thought.

I drifted to the surface and opened my eyes. Morning light framed the closed blinds. Had I awakened from a dream? We were both naked in the bed. I listened to his breathing and felt the warmth of his body next to me. I realised I was holding my breath. Jamie stirred and turned onto his side, his face next to mine.

I was wrapped in contradictions: his presence disturbed me. The sensuousness of the night before stirred me. I regretted it, and I exalted in my mistake. My stomach plunged at the possible consequences, but my heart leapt.

I reached over to the bedside table and flicked my smartphone into life. I located the camera icon and holding my hand steady above us, I took a photograph, capturing us together.

Almost immediately, he stirred again.

He sat up, groggy, and rubbed the sleep from his eyes.

He looked at me, and I could see sleepy confusion cross his face. His eyes widened in panic. 'What time is it?'

'About seven.'

He sat up bolt and raked his hands through his hair. He wiped the edge of his mouth with the back of his hand. 'Shit! Shit! Shit! I need to go.' He clamoured out of bed and hastily began to change into his clothes. 'This was wrong. It was a mistake. I shouldn't be here. Forget this ever happened.'

'What if I can't?'

'You have to.'

'You used me.' I sank my hands into the duvet and brought it to my chest.

'I didn't hear you complain.' He fumbled with the buttons of his shirt.

'What if she goes to the police?'

He stopped buttoning his shirt and looking down at me said. 'Maybe, it would be better for you to leave Edinburgh, in fact, you should consider leaving the country. No. You will leave, Grace. I can't have you here.'

'What are you talking about? Where would I go?'

'I don't know, think of it as a new start. You either go or...'

'Or what? That sounds like a threat.' I stared at him in disbelief.

'I won't stop her going to the police.' He slipped his arms into his jacket. He turned and, in his expression, I could see a mixture of shock and sympathy. 'I'm sorry.'

I could hear his feet thud on the wooden floor and the rattle of the letterbox as the door slammed behind him.

The house was completely silent. Around me, the bedroom was spinning, my skin prickled and inside I wanted to die.

The Present

The Need to Be a Mother

Although something inside Grace tells her to forget her desire to find the little girl, she cannot let it go. It is an instinct. She thinks about this and it is conceptualised in her visit to *the lifejacket graveyard*. Vasilis took her there, after her visit to the camp.

It was a harrowing place and the symbolism was not lost on her. Thousands of life jackets, from every refugee that ever landed on Lesvos, were scattered over a great distance, and twelve feet high in some places. She saw many infant life jackets and she couldn't get the image of the little girl being resuscitated at the harbour out of her mind. It was then she thought, every life jacket can tell an individual story.

The memories of the camp will live with her for the rest of her life. It has made her want to see the little girl even more. She knows Vasilis is not in agreement with her. She, at times, has also asked herself, why this infatuation with her? For, if she is honest with herself, that is what it is. What good can come of it? Am I setting myself up to be unhappy? This has irritated her, and she is not sure why. Lately, her senses have not been her own. She has had restless nights and it is not only the heat that has forced her from her bed.

One such night, she sits at the kitchen table drinking water. It is the suggestion of innocence that has occupied her mind, tortured her thoughts. She knows this little girl is not unique in her suffering, but she is unique to Grace.

There is still a hole inside her and, right now, Grace is very aware of it. And there it lies; the need to be a mother is still pulling at her. She puts her hand to her mouth and sobs. She takes deep breathes, sucks in the air and wipes her tears. Her head throbs and it also hurts with the knowledge that she has tried, she has tried so hard to fill the void.

Her nose is running. She stands at the kitchen sink and blows her nose into a sheet of kitchen towel. She turns on the tap and, bending over, splashes her face with cold water. She allows herself to luxuriate in its effect on her skin. She stands erect, brushes her hair behind her ear and folds her arms.

The girl will be traumatised. The girl will be damaged. Will she know her mother is dead? Will she have been told? She needs her mother. She needs a *mother*.

The Present

Allowing the Future to Unfold

To celebrate the continued success of the cleaning of plastics and rubbish from the beach, Peter has organised a dinner at Vasilis' taverna. Everyone is there: Grace, Peter, Sofia, Vasilis and around another eight volunteers.

'So, Grace. What did you make of the camp?' Peter says, cutting into his Spinach and Feta pie. 'Vasilis told me he took you there.'

Her eyes meet Peter's. 'He did. And it was a revelation, to tell you the truth. I wasn't expecting to see conditions like that.'

'It's worse in the winter. Although it's just temporary accommodation, one gets the feeling it may be around longer than the authorities would want. It's not something they want the world's media to advertise. It's hurting the tourist trade, local businesses, hotels, you can imagine. The list is endless.'

'You can't blame the refugees for that.'

'I'm not, but others might.'

A waiter fills a glass with wine and hearing the conversation says. 'We are proud of our island's hospitality, we have a history of welcoming refugees, but there is only so much we can take.'

Vasilis sighs. 'I've heard demonstrations are being organised.'

'It's the last thing these poor people need,' Grace says. 'They've left their homes and families, not because they wanted to, they had no other choice. Surely people don't blame them, that would be disgusting, shameful.'

'People's livelihoods are at stake.'

'You of all people, Vasilis, should be more sympathetic.'

'I am,' he says as if he has been scolded.

Peter recognises this. It is an exchange between two people who have become closer, so certain opinions are expressed freely, more assertive in their delivery. He allows his eyes to linger on them. There is a certain spark that is ignited each time one of them addresses the other. Peter has the distinct impression Sofia has also noticed this.

'So, I was thinking, since our efforts have proven to be excitingly successful, I thought we should strike while the iron is hot, so to speak,' Peter says, looking at those around the table.

'What do you mean?' Sofia asks.

'Well, ours is not the only beach. We should expand our operation. I'm proposing that we need to tackle the whole island, clean all the beaches.'

'We can't do that on our own. That's a bit ambitious. I don't know if I'll be up for that,' an older woman at the end of the table says.

'No, but we can get others involved, likeminded people. I thought I might get some leaflets printed and distribute them, you know, get some organised groups involved in places like Eftalou, Petra and even Anaxos.'

Grace smiles. 'I think that's a great idea, Peter. I wouldn't mind helping you to distribute them.'

'Me too.' Sofia turns towards Peter. 'I don't mind helping with the writing and content of the leaflets.'

'Perfect,' Peter beams and lifts his glass. 'A toast, to our new adventure. Yamas!'

Peter pours more wine into the others' glasses. 'Would you like a glass of wine, Grace? I noticed you're just drinking water.'

'I'm fine. I'll just stick with water.'

'Do you drink alcohol?'

'I do like a glass of wine, but two is my limit. I only like the first glass really. After that, it doesn't taste the same.'

'I know what you mean. No more for me, Peter I'm working tomorrow,' Sofia says.

Peter grins. 'All the more for the rest of us.' He places the bottle on the table and sits back into his chair. Around the table, people chat amongst themselves. Vasilis is sitting opposite Grace and speaking to Sofia. He glances at Grace from time to time.

'Vasilis tells me you're looking for the little girl who lost her mother.'

'I am,' Grace says, without hesitation, as if she is prepared for Peter's interest.

'Do you think it's wise?'

'I just want to know she's all right.'

'Is that all?' he asks with a slight tilt to his head.

'What are you implying?'

'I just don't think it's a good idea to get emotionally involved.'

'How can I not be? Have you been there, to the camp? I hadn't expected to see conditions like that. I'd always thought of the camp differently. I suppose I was ignorant because of my distance from what these people are actually going through. The experience was… intimate.'

'Just be careful,' Peter says, putting his hand on hers just for a moment.

'I'm not going to run away with her.'

'I hope not.' Grace thinks she is being vaguely chastised but before she can say anything, Peter grins. 'Only kidding.'

After their main course, they order some sweets Grace and Sofia elect to have a coffee instead.

The sunsets, casting elongated shadows, the stars come out and the moon emerges from behind a cloud.

After a time, people start to say their farewells and drift away. The waiters clear the plates and cutlery. Vasilis is called over to the till to settle a dispute with a customer's bill.

'That was delicious, it always is, of course. I've told Vasilis he needs to pay his chef double what does, so he never leaves. Have you enjoyed yourselves?' Peter asks Grace and Sofia, the only two left at the table.

'It was lovely, and you're right, the food was amazing.' Sofia nods in agreement. 'I'd better get going.'

'Me too.' Peter rises from his chair. 'I'll walk you home, it's on my way.' He turns to Grace. 'Are you coming?'

'I think I'll go for a walk along the beach.'

'It's dark,' Peter says, concerned.

'I'll be fine. I'm a grown woman.'

Sofia leans into Peter. 'I don't think she'll be alone.'

As they leave, Grace gathers her bag and, as she stands, to her surprise Vasilis is standing next to her.

'You're going?'

'I thought I'd go for a walk.'

Vasilis tilts his head. 'Would you like some company?'

'Are you not needed?'

'I'm the boss.'

She smiles.

'I'll take that as a yes.'

As they walk, Grace can sometimes feel her arm rub against Vasilis' arm. His skin is warm, and she finds herself wondering what it would feel like to be in his embrace. She stops her mind from going there.

It is a hot night. They stay close to the sea, enjoying a light breeze.

'What is it like in Edinburgh? I've always wanted to go there, and London, I like London.'

'I'm biased, so I'm probably not the best person to ask. It's colourful, bustling, vibrant. It's not flat, it's a hilly city. It's steeped in history, it has a castle and a palace, a medieval Old Town and an elegant Georgian New Town, with gardens and Neoclassical buildings. It has museums, lots of shopping and places to eat.'

'Do you miss it?'

She thinks for a moment. 'I suppose I do.'

'Your description makes me want to go there even more.'

'What's stopping you?'

He shrugs. 'Life.'

'Well, lives too short, as they say.'

'I know. Maybe when Pelagia is a little older, I'll take her.'

'You should, especially at the festival, you should go then. She would love it then.'

'What's the festival?'

As Grace explains this to him, they find themselves in the harbour. The clanking of the boats, tied up and safely secured harmonizes with the clink of cutlery and wave of voices.

As they stroll further, music floats towards them. On a small wooden stage, a rebetiko band is playing and around them, people are dancing and clapping. Everyone is laughing and smiling. A young woman grabs Vasilis' arm and pulls him towards her. Her face is lit up, as she dances with him. Grace is impressed, Vasilis has rhythm and good timing. She suddenly feels a shaft of envy. She feels self-conscious and glances around looking for a place to sit. She finds an unoccupied seat and gladly sits down. On the table in front of her, she taps her fingers to the music.

She watches the dancers and her eyes train on Vasilis. She hasn't seen him like this. This is a new version of him. She looks at him with interest. Then, the woman dancing with Vasilis glances at her, and Grace thinks it is an interrogating look. It unease's her. When the music stops Vasilis and the woman embrace. She says something to him, and he laughs. She can see clearly, the exchanges between them are relaxed and familiar. Vasilis then looks around and, spotting Grace, he points in her direction. They both head towards her and Grace can't help noticing how the woman holds herself, she is tall, and slim, and has a certain stature about her that makes Grace feel awkward. She stands and runs her hand along her dress and watches them approach her.

'Grace.' Vasilis is slightly out of breath and he has droplets of sweat on his brow. 'I'd like you to meet Fotini, my favourite cousin.'

Grace can feel herself physically relax, this new information has eased her anxiety, but at the same time raised questions about her reaction. Why was I filled with a jealous admiration? What did it imply, that I love him? It was the truth. With a sense of surprise, she realises this as she thinks it.

'Pleased to meet you, Vasilis has told me much about you.'

'He has?'

Vasilis seems to shrink a little as if Fotini has given away a secret.

'Don't worry, it is all good.' Fotini smiles then, and Grace can see she has film star white teeth.

I'd have to pay a fortune for teeth like that and look at her skin, it's like a polished surface and there's not a wrinkle in sight. Grace offers her hand. Fotini's grip is surprisingly light.

Vasilis brings over another chair from a nearby table and they all sit.

'Fotini works at the camp with Kyrios, she has some news for you.'

Grace's heart accelerates. 'Have you found her?'

'Kyrios told me to tell you, he has.'

'And is she well?'

Fotini nods. 'As well as could be expected. Physically she is fine... she has lost her mother, as you know. She hasn't spoken yet, but we do know her name. One of the others on the boat spoke with the mother, he told us her name is Rasha al-Ahmed. She is from Deir Ezor. It's a city in Eastern Syria.'

Grace exhaled a long breath. I know her name.

'I'll get some drinks. What would you like, Grace?' Vasilis asks.

'Just a lemonade, thanks.'

'I suppose you'll have your usual.'

Fotini tilts her head. 'Of course.'

'Have you ever tried Ouzo, Grace?' Fotini asks.

'I'm afraid not.'

'Then you must try some.'

'Oh, I'm fine. Just a lemonade.'

Vasilis raises his hands. 'That's like me visiting Edinburgh and refusing the offer of a whisky. Come on, Grace, just have a taste.'

She doesn't want to offend him. 'Alright, but just a little drop.'

Vasilis heads towards the bar.

'Vasilis told me, you were there the day the girl came ashore,' Fotini says.

'Yes. I was.'

'You know, she is not the first child to have lost a parent. There are many like her and she won't be the last, unfortunately.'

Grace rubs her forehead. 'I'm well aware of that.'

'So, what is your interest in this girl?'

She sighs. 'I can't get the image of her out of my mind. She seemed so helpless, lost and alone, so dreadfully alone.'

'You are not responsible for her.'

Grace can see a small frown on Fotini's face.

'I know that. It doesn't stop me from wanting to see her.'

Fotini gives a small sigh of exasperation. 'I know about your baby.'

'Vasilis told you?'

'He is worried about you.'

This fact seems to distress Grace. He has no right to do that.

At that moment, Vasilis arrives with three glasses and a bottle of ouzo. 'I thought I'd just get a bottle, it will save me going back to the bar. I'll take whatever is left home.'

He turns to look at Grace and her eyes meet his. 'Are you alright?'

She is angry with him, she can't deny that he broke her trust and it sinks into her as a stone dropped into a pond. She tries to push her anger back to where it came.

'I'm fine,' she lies.

As Vasilis pours the ouzo into the glasses, he mixes Grace's with water to dilute the strength. 'We make over half of all the ouzo made in Greece here in Lesvos and it's the best in the country. It's our most popular drink.'

He hands the glasses out. 'Here, try it. See what you think, Grace.'

Grace puts the glass to her nose and sniffs. Tentatively, she takes a sip.

'Well, what do you think?'

'It tastes like liquorice.'

'Do you like it?' Fotini asks.

'Yes. I do. It's… very pleasant, but strong, even with the water in it.'

Vasilis grins. 'Good. I'm glad you like it.'

Grace smiles. She doesn't want Fotini to see that she is annoyed with Vasilis. In fact, what he has done, stings her.

'What will happen now, to the girl… Rasha?'

'We think the mother was coming over to meet a relative, her brother.'

'So, she has an uncle here on Lesvos?'

'Yes. We have located him, but unfortunately, he is in hospital.'

'Oh. What happened to him?'

'He had a heart attack. He was in the camp at the time.'

Grace's heart aches for Rasha. 'And does she know?'

'No. Rasha has not been told. This wouldn't be the right time.'

Relief fills Grace, but only briefly. 'Of course.'

'Your request is unusual. Normally, it would not be allowed, but since you are with Vasilis, and he can vouch for you, if you want you can see her, just to put your mind at rest.'

'When would I be able to see her?'

'In a few days. She's still being assessed.'

Grace turns to Vasilis, she has him to thank for this. I can't be angry with him now. 'Thank you, Vasilis.'

He is smiling faintly. Just then, the music starts up again. Vasilis offers Grace his hand, a gesture that is an invitation. 'Dance with me.'

Her answering nod has embarrassment about it. 'I can't.'

'Everyone's dancing.' He stands up and moves around the table. 'I'll be gentle with you,' he whispers in her ear.

As the music plays, it is as if the musician's song is infectious and she can't help herself from being immersed in the tempo and melody.

Soon, she gets over her nerves. Vasilis is smiling at her, she is elated. She can feel the length of his arm around her waist. A level of excitement rises within her that she has not felt in a long time. Vasilis is joyous, there is delight in his eyes and charm about his smile.

Vasilis says something, but she can't make it out over the music. He bends his head to her ear, 'If you were ever to leave Lesvos, I think my heart would break.'

He walks her home, it is late, and their route takes them past sleeping cats sprawled around the foot of a lemon tree. Around them, the air is still and sultry. Grace feels lightheaded and she can't decide whether it is the effect of the three glasses of ouzo she drank or the curled warmth of Vasilis' fingers. As they approach her door, Vasilis gazes at her searchingly. There is an expectation to his look. He is standing so close to her that Grace can feel his breath on her skin. He lowers his head and gently presses his lips to hers. His mouth is soft and warm, as Grace brushes her lips against it. He places his hand behind her head and pulls her towards him. It is a kiss but beyond the sensual and physical act. She is allowing herself a future to unfold.

The Present

A Disagreement

Whenever Vasilis isn't needed at the taverna and Pelagia is
at school, Grace spends time with him, eating lunch at the
harbour and watching the fishing boats unload their catch
of sardines, mackerel and tuna, destined for the markets
and restaurants. They amble around the warren of stone
houses and shops, where washing hangs from balconies,
limp clothes drying in the sun. Every so often, Vasilis is
greeted by a shop owner or a waiter, and he stands and
talks, always introducing Grace with a broad smile. The
days are getting hotter and Grace is grateful for the shade
provided by vines of wisteria that hang overhead, sheltering
the cobbled lanes and dining tables.

They are sitting outside a small café and, even though the
street is really but a lane, a scooter passes them, its
occupant helmetless. Vasilis lights a cigarette and looks at
the menu. 'They have some nice pastries here; would you
like one?'

'No. I'm fine. Just water for me.'

'No coffee? I'd recommend it, they do a strong one, it
gives you a kick.'

'It's too hot, just water.'

A waiter comes and takes their order.

'Pelagia asked me this morning if I was seeing you
today.'

'Oh?'

'I think she's getting used to the idea now, you know,
that I can have female friends too.'

'Bless her. It must be difficult. She's a credit to you.'

'She's had a lot to deal with. She has a big personality
and that helps. She's quite settled at the moment. There was

a time when her school work suffered, and she didn't go to school. That's all behind us now, thankfully.'

'You must be proud of her?'

'I am, I'm her father. I know it's difficult for her not having a mother. The saving grace about all of this is she doesn't really remember her mother, she was too young.'

'In a way, that will help, I'd imagine.'

'Sometimes, at night, when I'm putting her to bed, she'll ask about her. She'll want me to tell her stories about her, what was she like? What did she like? What was her favourite colour? Silly things, really.'

'But not to Pelagia. Even the smallest detail will be precious to her.'

Vasilis nods. 'I suppose.'

'What's her name?'

'Drosoula.'

There is a pause as the waiter brings their drinks. Then Grace tips her head forward. 'Has Pelagia seen photographs of her?'

'I've shown her a few. I don't have many, really. When I think about it now, Palagis has never really said that she loves her.' He smiles sadly. 'She would often ask why did she leave us? What could I say, I don't know the answer to that myself? She once said it must have been because she didn't love her. As a father, you want to have all the answers. She needs me to protect her, keep her safe and part of that is to be able to make her happy. I can't always make her happy. I wish I could.'

Grace reaches out and takes his hand. 'You're doing the best you can, and I've seen you with her. She couldn't have a more caring and loving father.'

Vasilis smiles at her and then says, 'I hope she doesn't hate her. A child should never hate their mother.'

'If you have loved someone and stop loving them, I think it is then easier to hate them.'

Vasilis inclines his head. 'Personal experience?'

Hate is such a strong word... resentment? Not strong enough. 'I did hate Jamie, I don't anymore.' She looks at him seriously. 'What about you? Do you hate your wife?'

Vasilis stubs his cigarette out in an ashtray. He doesn't want to be reminded of her. 'I don't hate her for what she did to me. Not anymore. I do, every time Pelagia is sad, every time she cries, when she is happy, when she has achieved. I feel it for Pelagia because she is the victim and her innocence pains me even more.'

Grace bites her lip. 'That's exactly how I feel about the little girl, Rasha. That's why I need to see her.'

'And then what? She will still be living in the camp. If her uncle recovers, she will at least have someone she loves with her. If he dies... if she is lucky, they will find a family that will look after her.'

'A foster family?'

'Yes.'

'I would do that.'

'You can't.'

'Why not?'

'You're serious?'

Why on earth had she not thought of this? 'It makes perfect sense to me.'

Vasilis shakes his head.

'You don't think so?'

Vasilis tries to keep his voice steady. 'There are strict rules, Grace. You need to have lived in Greece for a long time, you will need documents, family records, financial records, doctor's certificates, residence permit, even then, social workers and psychologists will assess you. It's not as easy as filling out a few forms.'

Grace shrinks from the coldness in his voice.

'You're obsessed with this girl. It's eating at you.'

'No, it's not.'

'It's all in your head. You have to stop this.'

Grace meets his eyes.

'What's the purpose of all of this? When you meet her, what then? She can't even speak. She's in shock.'

The leaves of a nearby orange tree flutter as a breeze picks up.

'I know... it's something I just have to do. Do you understand?'

'No. I don't. The girl is well. They have found her uncle. She won't be alone anymore. That's what I understand.'

There is a silence between them.

'This is all about you, Grace.'

'Well, I'm sorry if I disappoint you.'

'Why would you say that? Have I ever said that?'

She can feel tears in her eyes.

'I don't expect you to understand.'

'How can I understand, you need to speak to me first.'

'It's difficult. Even I don't know why I really feel this way. I don't know what to say.'

'You can't replace, Olivia.'

Grace looks away. 'I know. Don't you think I know that, but it doesn't make it any easier? This whole business with the girl has just brought it back. The feelings I thought I'd dealt with are still inside me, they're resurfacing, that's how it feels.'

'So, don't you think it would be better if you didn't go? You need to work out what's best for you, Grace. I can't do that for you. If it was me and I was in your position, I would want to heal my wounds and not open the scars.'

'Is that how you see this?'

'Yes. It is.'

Grace can feel pressure on her chest.

'When my wife left me, it felt... it felt as if she'd died. On the day before she left, she was with us doing normal everyday things. There was nothing to suggest something was wrong. She gave me no reason to suspect anything. I had no idea what was about to happen. Then, she simply walked out of our lives… she was gone and Pelagia never saw her again.'

Jamie strangely surfaces in Grace's mind.

'We can't replace her. She is Pelagia's mother, she is still my wife. Olivia is still your daughter, but whatever you do, however you try to fill the void, she has left in your life, you can't change what has happened. Somehow, we all need to crawl out of our swamps of unhappiness.'

She feels an ache by the simplicity and certainty with which he speaks.

'My mother died when I was eight years old,' he says. 'I was brought up by my grandmother. Whenever I was going through a tough time, she always reminded me that life is not what happens to you, but what you do with what happens to you. I've always tried to live my life that way.'

She feels a moment of panic. 'What am I going to do? I cannot go on like this. Vasilis is making sense. He can see this through a clear lens, where my mind is clouded with fog and I am sluggish with an immense drag of guilt.'

The Past

I'm No Longer the Victim but the Enemy

We had shared so many intimacies and experiences that, sometimes, it was a struggle to imagine the unbreachable expanse we had built between us. When did he know he was going to leave me? When did our life together become unbearable? I wanted to ask him so many questions. He must have lied to me on many occasions to cover up his deceit, his betrayal. Did he think about her when he was with me? When we spoke? When we made love? When we planned for a future that was never going to be fulfilled? Did he ever wonder who would put me together again when he shattered me into pieces? Do these things matter anymore?

At first, the text messages arrived every other day. Then every day, twice a day, four times a day. The language he used was threatening and sinister in its tone.

This was the man I had shared my secrets with, my multiple thoughts, my complexities, my ambition. He witnessed my vulnerabilities, my strengths, what drove me to succeed, my likes, my dislikes, my politics, my love for reading romantic novels, even though my favourite book was James Joyce's *Ulysses,* my guilty pleasure watching chic flick movies on a Friday night, and the crush I had on Ross from *Friends.* I'd told him my earliest memories, he knew what made me happy, unhappy, scared, my most unappealing habit... telling the truth, mostly. He knew I was bullied at primary school and developed an eating disorder, that my best friend died in a car crash at the age of sixteen and I recited a poem I had written at her funeral. We shared the joy of my pregnancy and grieved over the death of our child. At that time, he knew me as well as I knew myself. He knew the deep interiority of who it was to be me. It would have been a dream to have woken each morning permeated in existential joy, but that never happened.

The first text would always be sent at eight in the morning, while I was having my first coffee of the day. After a while, I wouldn't look at it straight away. I'd wait, that way, I still had some control.

At first, he sent the same message, *'Are you still here?'* Then, after a week, he expanded his vocabulary. *'Are you still here? A woman on her own is an easy target! Watch your back!'*

He gambled that I wouldn't go to the police, after all, that had always been *his* threat. I had hoped he would stop, but as the volume of text messages increased, I realised, one day soon, he might just carry out his threats. He was trying to scare me into leaving, he was trying to wear me down.

Then, one afternoon, when I came home, the front door was open. I knew I had locked it, as I left the house that morning. I could feel the blood leave my head. My first thought had been I'd just been burgled, but then, I noticed, there had been no forced entry. Whoever had been in my house, or who might still be inside it, had a key. A mixture of adrenaline and fear seeped through me. My hand trembled as I set it against the door and gently eased it open, just enough to let myself in.

In the hallway, I stood very still. All I could hear was the rasp of my breathing. Everything was how it should be and in its place. The pictures on the wall, the framed photographs and lamp on the oak unit, the umbrella stand in the corner next to the stairs. I glanced into the living room. The house was silent and still. I was suddenly aware I was pressing my nails into my palm. It was then I smelt it. It struck me in the face like a heavy mist, a pungent, and stomach-turning stench. It was coming from the kitchen.

As I moved through the house, it filled my nostrils. I covered my mouth and nose with my hand. I felt a wave of nausea ebb inside me. I stared at the kitchen table in utter shock and disbelief. Someone or something had defecated on its surface. My stomach wretched. Then, my smartphone bleeped, a text, '*Have you found the present my friend has left you? Your time is running out. LEAVE!*' I felt defiled, my home had been violated, it had become polluted.

I phoned a locksmith and, as luck would have it, he was finishing a job a few streets away. I got my locks changed that very day. I still didn't feel safe.

Where would I go? The house was now full of memories of a life passed and my daily existence only accentuated what I had lost.

Maybe it was time to move on, begin again, find me again. The *me* I had become was not the person I had been. Was that just a natural progression, after all, I had been through?

The protection I sought would come from my own initiative and intuition. I remember quite clearly, the moment it was decided when I was seized by the thought.

I was sitting alone on a tram, it had just passed Haymarket station when I pressed the photo icon on my smartphone and scrolled through images until I found it. I stared at the image.

This is madness, I thought. My mind went into a momentary paralysis. Could I do this? And then I thought, of course, I could. I had no other choice. It had been forced upon me.

When I closed my eyes, I could still see the photograph I took. Jamie lying on the pillow, a small trail of saliva glistening at the side of his mouth. His hair sticking up at odd angles, flat in places. A shadow of stubble imprinted across his face. He looked content, so peaceful. I, on the other hand, just stared at my smartphone, as I took the photograph.

It was unthinkable, yet it had to happen.

I got off the tram and went into Boots. A few minutes later, I deposited into my handbag two printed photographs of the image of both of us lying together in my bed. I bought two A4 sized envelopes and first-class stamps. Originally, I'd decided to post one to Jamie and the other to Jayne. The more I thought of this, it troubled me.

I sat in a café in Hanover Street, an idea formulating in my mind. I phoned Alistair, Jamie's best friend. He was surprised to hear from me. I explained that I needed to get in touch with Jamie. He wasn't answering his phone and I was wondering if Alistair had Jayne's number, as unfortunately, I had some bad news for Jamie regarding a close mutual friend. It was a long shot, but it worked.

Alistair was very accommodating. I felt bad that I used him, but when he relayed Jayne's number to me, and I wrote it down, I was suffused in a self-gratifying feeling of accomplishment.

My finger hovered over the send button. In that moment, I felt my mind transform itself with the most incredible sense of power and, at the same time, a sickening discomfort of dread. I remembered being struck by how relentless and hateful Jamie had been and I wondered how it was possible that, at one time, he had loved me. But now, everything was different.

I thought about leaving a message for Jayne, with the photograph of Jamie and me. It would say, *I didn't mean for this to happen. It's not what I wanted. I'm sorry.*

But that wouldn't have been true.

I stared at the attachment and thought of the image it contained. I felt a prick of sympathy for her. Around me, there was a stillness and quietude. I clicked the button.

I knew, of course, what would happen. I could see it as if I was there.

I pushed down on the handle of the door to the toilets. I had my eye on a cubicle, but my stomach curdled, and I knew I wouldn't make it. I moved towards a sink and just in time I bent over double. The retching came in relentless waves, my stomach strained and burned, my throat was scrapped and raw. I tried to hold my hair back from my face.

Once it had finished, I washed my face, and the water felt like a new covering of skin. I rinsed my mouth, dried my face on a paper towel, and then stood, regarding myself in the mirror. I scrutinized myself. My skin had acquired a taut and stretched look. My eyes were heavy and shadowed. I'm no longer the victim. I'm the enemy.

Everything had changed.

The Present

A Life Worth Living

She wakes to the early morning light slipping under the shades. After her shower, she cradles her first coffee of the morning sitting on the balcony. The air is soft and moist, and she wonders if it has rained through the night. The sun is already warm. Above her, the sky is a deep blue and cloudless. Her eyes skim the rooftops and take in the sea. She can see the shiny white mast of a sailing boat.

On the narrow street below, an old man passes astride a donkey, twigs and branches strapped to the animal's side. He is wearing an old tattered and worn cap that others would have replaced by now and Grace finds herself speculating about its history and its attachment to memories. As the old man passes, he is unaware he is an object of scrutiny.

She thinks of the phone call to Natasha's father, Greg, and a familiar knot forms in her stomach. She spoke to him a few days ago on the phone. Greg queried her continually. She tried to tell him the facts with a steady voice, and she recollects his incomprehension that he is to blame for his daughter's refusal to contact him. When Grace informed Greg that Natasha accused an auntie of abusing her, when she was six years old, Greg was beside himself. He said this was impossible, as this auntie died when Natasha was only three years old.

Greg is convinced the man Neos has an unhealthy hold on Natasha. He is making her believe things that never happened, he is controlling her, Greg had cried out. Grace had no words to counteract his assertions, she too fears for Natasha. Grace felt obliged to promise Greg she would stay in touch with Natasha, but really, there was little she could do.

She presses her lips together.

Will Greg travel to Lesvos? She ponders this with unease. If she was my daughter, I would have to see her. I would be determined to confront Neos. Yet, all the indications are that Natasha's mind is set.

These thoughts are not the only ones that make her stomach drag. Monica has informed her that she is to return to Edinburgh. In fact, her flight is this morning. Monica's mother has lived in a private home for the elderly for several years and now her health is ailing at an advanced rate and she has been given weeks to live.

Grace brings her knees to her chest and wraps her arms around her legs. With Monica gone, she has lost the only connection she had to her old life. Tears brim at her eyes. She tries to fight them off, but it is hopeless. The thought of not having Monica's presence in her life, at this moment, constricts her chest. She wipes the tears, takes a deep breath and releases it slowly. This is an impediment she must bear and rise above.

She turns the corner and enters Sofia's shop. Sofia is sitting behind the counter. She looks up from reading her magazine.

'Hello, Grace… are you alright?'

'She's gone,' she blurts out.

'Who is gone?'

'Monica. She's gone back to Edinburgh. Her mother is very ill. She just found out, only yesterday.'

'And this has upset you?'

'Well… yes.'

'She'll be back, won't she?'

'I don't know. I was just getting used to her being back in my life. It was a surprise that she had to go so quickly, that's all. I know I'm being silly, and she needs to be with her mother…'

'But you need her too?'

'I didn't realise how much until this morning.'

Sofia studies her. 'Is that all that's troubling you?'

Grace sits on a wooden chair in the corner of the shop, her hands rest loosely in her lap. She bites her lip and hesitates. 'Vasilis.'

'What happened?'

'Nothing yet. He just doesn't understand.'

Sofia looks at her carefully. 'You're going to have to tell me what he doesn't understand.'

She starts to tell Sofia of the day she saw the lifeboat return with the refugees, the commotion that ensued, the little girl whose name she now knows is Rasha, learning of the death of Rasha's mother, the undignified existence in the camp. She tells Sofia she feels haunted by the Rasha's fate, she can think of nothing else, she is possessed with a sense of urgency to help the girl. She has dismissed Vasilis' doubts. Something is happening to her that, at this moment, she does not understand, but she has no control over it. Vasilis has told her that this is all to do with the turmoil of her past. The way in which Sofia is looking at her tells Grace she may agree with him. This worries her, it alarms her slightly.

She shakes her head, sadly. 'Do you think he has a point?'

Her question disconcerts Sofia.

Grace looks at her steadily. 'You do, don't you?'

Sofia takes a breath. 'Grace, I think you need to take your time over this before coming to a rash decision. Seeing the girl like that, almost drowned, must have been a traumatic experience for you, especially after what you've been through.'

Grace folds her hands on her lap again. 'I see.'

'I know how difficult this must be.'

'I'm surprised. Of all people I thought you would understand.'

'I think I do, Grace.' Sofia makes her way around the counter. Before she reaches her, Grace stands abruptly.

'I need to go.'

'Grace, please stay.'

Just then, two women enter the Deli and Grace brushes past them.

Outside, her head is spinning. She steps from the pavement and some oncoming moped swerves around her, its horn blaring, as she feels a rush of warm air. Her temple aches and she is struggling to breathe. The trembling in her body is such that she is forced to clasp her hands together.

Grace moves aimlessly through the narrow lanes, past the trinket shops, tavernas and bars. She is oblivious to the glance of an old man who is watching her speculatively, sitting outside a shop, where around him, a colourful array of rugs and linen sprinkle the walls. Beside him, an old woman embraces a young girl in a white dress and a cat dozes in the shade.

Grace is climbing a gradient, steps that curve around houses and balconies. She suddenly stops and leans against a wall. The heat from the stones radiates against her palms. Around her, there is an abundance of flowers, spilling from ceramic pots, on ledges and steps. Grace walks briskly and almost falls over a chair. She crooks her arm over her forehead to shade her eyes from the glare of the sun. She can feel the tickle from a line of sweat on her spine and she decides to sit on some steps that lead to an imposing blue wooden door. She wraps her arms around her legs and rests her forehead on her knees. She thinks of the girl, the camp, and Vasilis, and doubt creeps into her thoughts. She shakes her head.

Everything she has been through she has sealed behind a veneer of normality. Her nightmares, her confusion, her self-doubt and self-blame have not left her, they have followed her to Molyvos. Her fear is like the size of a continent, she has tried to bury it, she has tried so hard.

At her worst, back in Edinburgh, she felt the world had closed its door on her. She remembers the shame, the agony. The bitterness she expelled became a poison. There were times when she couldn't move from her bed.

Grace thinks about the loneliness, she thinks about the silence, the silence of others, of friends and family. She was lost to the pain, the fear, the shame. She was adrift on an overwhelming ocean of grief.

But, here in Molyvos, the door has begun to open, each day, slowly and slightly, a light gradually peers through. The door can't close, the door mustn't close. I have a life that is worth living.

The Present

Becoming Closer and Other Possibilities

Grace is lying on top of her bed, surrounded by a palpable heat. She feels clammy, as her t-shirt sticks to her, like a second skin. Her head is swimming. She shouldn't have run this morning. Three miles covered. It's too hot. Next time, she'll wait until early evening.

She puts her hand to her forehead and feels it pulse, it is almost in time with the cicadas beat that floats through the opened window. It is an effort to stand. She feels her calf muscle twitch and bends to rub it. She undresses, tosses her top and shorts into the washing basket and heads for the shower.

As she dries her hair, she thinks of them. Her world is full of ghosts; Jamie and Olivia. Sometimes, their absence is beyond understanding, and now Monica has left too.

Her hair dried and styled, she slips on a sky-blue dress that draws her eye to her waist. She considers her image in the mirror. Is it possible, she wonders, to ever feel again the love she had for Jamie? A sensation, an ache in her chest presses against her, it consumes her. Will she ever share again the intimacies and exhalation of pleasure that felt so natural with Jamie?

There was a time she would have found such a thought incomprehensible, it would have been met with disbelief. Yet, here she stands, observing herself in a mirror with the luxury of time to fully understand her situation. She has lost her trust in the word love. There are many forms of love, she is sure of this, and each is displayed in different ways.

Since she has met Vasilis, she has been aware of a seed lingering inside her.

He is changing me. Grace understands now. *I feel different when I'm with him, less guarded.*

She runs her hand through her hair and watches it fall back into place. *Whatever happens, I'll let it happen.*

There is an air of finality about this.

She hovers at the door before knocking and is seized by an urge to check herself, but she doesn't have a pocket mirror in her bag, so she makes do by smoothing the front of her dress. The anticipation of the door opening causes her heart to race. When it finally does, Vasilis smiles at her. He invites her in and comments on how nice she looks. Grace has never been in Vasilis' house and she is pleasantly surprised that it is tidy and neat. In her mind, she has had an image of domesticated neglect, fine dust covering surfaces, unwashed dishes languishing in the sink and dirty laundry neglected and strewn around rooms. In truth, the house has a bright and airy feel, an almost feminine touch to it. She wonders if the furnishings have his wife's influence.

He takes her to the kitchen which is illuminated in a wash of light. In the middle of the kitchen table, there is a vase of red and white roses. The work surfaces are shiny and clean and everything has its place. She realises, to her shame, she has subconsciously constructed a stereotypical impression that is far from the reality she is presented with.

Vasilis gestures for her to sit.

'Your home is lovely.'

'Thank you. I can't take all the credit, I've not done much to it since... well, since Drosoula left.'

The mention of her name lies like a wall between them before it dissipates as Vasilis offers her a drink.

'Orange juice would be lovely.'

While he pours their drinks, he asks her if she'd like to sit in the garden instead.

They sit in the shade of overhead vines and a skinny cat rubs itself on Grace's leg, purring contentedly.

'What's this little one called?'

'That's Pomona, she's the friendliest cat I've ever known. She loves human company. She should have been a dog.'

Grace strokes Pomona's arched back. 'She's adorable.'

'We've had her since she was a kitten. I got her for Pelagia. When they're both in the house, they're inseparable.'

'And how is Pelagia?'

'She's becoming… very opinionated, lately.'

'You mean, she's growing up. They don't stay young for long, especially girls. At least she's not at the boyfriend stage.'

'I don't even want to think about that.'

Grace glances around the garden. There is a children's slide and a swing at the far end, a few trees and parched yellow grass. Two white butterflies investigate an array of coloured flowers housed in several pots situated next to the house.

Vasilis catches her look. 'I'm not much of a gardener, as you can see.'

'A garden should be for a child to play in, just like this one.'

He smiles with raised eyebrows. 'You approve, then?'

'I do.' She replies.

'We spend a lot of our time out here. Pelagia loves to be outside. She's even asked if she can sleep out here.'

Grace screws her face up. 'Oh! too many creepy crawlies.'

There is a blank expression on Vasili's face.

'I mean cockroaches and insects and mosquitoes. I'd be terrified.'

'Oh! I see. You're scared of them. Didn't you know we have lots of big insects?'

'I didn't really think about it. And then, I saw a huge cockroach scuttle across my bedroom floor... it was my first night here.'

Vasilis laughs. 'Did you get much sleep?'

'I did after I killed it. I wasn't going to bring any high heel shoes with me, but I'm glad I did, although, I don't think the cockroach felt the same.'

Vasilis laughs, surprised. 'I couldn't imagine you killing anything.'

She smiles. 'It's amazing what you can do when you're desperate.'

He notices her glass is empty. 'More orange juice?'

'No thanks.'

She can see him thinking.

'We've all been there,' he says, finally.

'What do you mean?'

'Desperate.'

'I suppose we have, but we're still here, you and I.'

'I had a reason to carry on with my life... if it wasn't for Pelagia... well, it might have been different. You seem to be doing well, now.'

She nods. 'I have my moments.'

'The important thing is to be true to yourself.'

'I try. My problem is there's times I'm not really sure who I am.' She looks down at the table. Why did I say that? I shouldn't have said that. She thinks for a moment that he might be frightened off or, even worse, think she's mad.

'I'm sorry, I shouldn't have said that. I didn't mean to make you feel...' she searches for the word, but fears she is making it worse. She wishes she hadn't mentioned it.

He looks at her. 'Feel like what?'

'I don't know. You might think I'm ... crazy, maybe.'

'Why would I do that, Grace? Of all the people you've got to know in Molyvos, surely I, after what I've been through, would understand.'

She averts her eyes. 'I'm sorry.'

'Don't be. You've got nothing to be sorry about. Why would I judge you? That would say more about me than it would about you.'

For the first time, there is a lull to their conversation. Vasilis can sense she is thinking.

'Do you have any regrets?'

There is a hush of anticipation. She sees a strange expression steal over his face. 'Some, I suppose,' Vasilis finally says.

'I'd like to know what they are. If you don't mind telling me?' She removes some stray hairs from her face.

'Well, when I was younger, much younger, I was a good football player. I had the opportunity to do some trials for professional clubs, but I became interested in girls and music and I played less football. I always wondered what would have happened if I had continued playing.' He points to his cigarette packet. 'That was the worst decision I ever made. I started smoking when I was eighteen, most of my friends were smoking. Back then, everyone smoked, it's different now. I worry sometimes what it's doing to me.'

'What about these new e-cigarettes. I've heard they can help people stop.'

'And they're not as bad for you?'

'Well, I'm not so sure about that. There's been no research done on them, no long-term research, so, really the jury's out on that one.'

'I would have liked to have travelled more. I've only ever been to Italy. It was the only holiday I had with Drosoula. She was pregnant, although we didn't know it at the time.' He pauses. How could he regret the choices he made that brought his daughter into his life? 'I regret some things in my time with her, but not it all. How could I? We had Pelagia together.'

'Yes, you did. She's a lovely girl. You must be proud of her?'

'I am. Sometimes I think she's well beyond her years. She has an older head on her. I worry about her. If anything was ever to happen to me, who would look after her?' He reaches for the packet of cigarettes and then withdraws his hand. He nods towards the packet. 'Maybe it's time to give these up.'

Grace smiles with satisfaction. 'Now, that's a decision you won't regret.'

'It felt good saying it.' He crumples the pack. 'I've smoked my last cigarette.'

'Going cold turkey might be hard, maybe you should try cutting down to start with.'

'No. Once I've set my mind to it, that's it.'

'I wish I had your confidence.'

'It's not about confidence.'

She looks surprised.

'I'd be doing it for Pelagia.'

'Well, that makes it different,' she agrees.

'What about you, Grace? Do you have any regrets about leaving Edinburgh?'

'Only if I end up going back.'

Vasilis looks at her curiously. 'Would that be such a bad thing? Edinburgh is your home.'

Going back to Edinburgh now. She thinks of the implications and a knot pulls at her stomach.

She looks at his dark and worried eyes. Sometimes, even she struggles to understand her own emotions, but it registers with her deeply. The thought of not seeing Vasilis again seems to suck the oxygen from her.

She has become exhausted with the difficulties of coping with her life. She fears what would have become of her if she had stayed any longer in Edinburgh. Returning was never an option, not now anyway. She is protecting herself. She is compelled to make this work.

Everyone has secrets. Will my ones, if revealed, do more harm than good?

She feels him lightly touch her arm. 'Are you all right, Grace? What's wrong?'

'Nothing. I'm fine. The thought of ever leaving Lesvos makes me sad, that's all.' Although it is true, it is also a disguise, it's a decoy.

Should I tell him?

Will it push him away from me?

Consumed with these thoughts, she is beginning to have reservations. Just then, his smartphone rings. His conversation is in Greek. After the call is finished, he looks at her. 'That was Fotini.'

'What did she say?'

'You can see the little girl, Rasha, tomorrow.'

She knows they have both felt this moment lie between them. They have been avoiding it, until now. Even before she came to visit Vasilis. In fact, the moment she opened her eyes in the morning, she knew her decision was made.

'Will you take me?'

There is a silence between them. It feels like an eternity. Vasilis scratches his chin.

'Can I persuade you not to go?'

Grace shakes her head and purses her lips. 'It's something I have to do.'

He looks at her in despair. 'Well then. It's against my better judgement... but I'm not going to try and change your mind. I don't think I could, anyway. Yes, I'll take you.'

The Present

The Most Profound Effect

Sometimes, when Vasilis meets her, even before they have said a word, he imagines kissing her. There are times when she is talking, he is mesmerised with the curve of her neck, the outline of her face, the generous shape of her lips, the way she is always touching her hair; there is a self-conscious innocence in the gesture.

He never thought he could experience love again. Since Drosoula left him, he has always felt vulnerable, apprehensive, he can't help himself. Bringing someone else into his life also means he needs Pelagia's acceptance. This will take time and persuasion. It is important to go at her pace.

He has spent years scrutinizing the reasons why Drosoula may have abandoned them. All the possibilities and the consequences have gone through his head. He has waded through them. None of that matters now. He has thought it through clearly. He can unshackle himself from the judgements of his mind. The feelings he has for Grace has relinquished the past's hold on him. He can move forward now, he can escape the past, the thoughts and memories that have ricocheted through him. He can be free of them.

He has tried to be a good father to Pelagia and bringing Grace into their lives doesn't make him in any way less of a good father.

He can feel a growing exhilaration. He knows this feels right, not wrong. If it were so, he would have doubts, but he has none. He has an unfulfilled capacity to love again and to be loved.

It doesn't matter what history Grace has. What matters to him is she has opened up to him, she has put her trust in him, and he is glad of it. It intensifies the experience of being with her. It brings them closer, they have a bond, an understanding. It brings emotions of its own. It excites him when he thinks of being with her. He has thought of little else.

He is devoted to his life with Pelagia, it is fortified with love, and a squeeze of panic has always travelled through him at the thought of their familiar life ever-changing. The thought of Grace fills him only with contentment. It is something he thought he would never have.

He can't disengage her from his mind. She is a constant presence. In recent days, he has speculated about this. It can both distract him and focus him. It has the most profound effect on him. It astonishes him.

The Present

A Silence Comprised of Humiliation, or Anger, or Both

They drive through a billowing landscape thick with forests and undulating hills. Every now and then their view is awash with ancient olive groves and picturesque villages.

'I'd love to see more of Lesvos and visit some of these villages, they're beautiful. I love the stone houses,' says Grace.

'There's nothing stopping you.'

'No. I suppose not.'

'Once you have seen the girl, why don't we have lunch in a village?'

'I'd like that. You choose.'

Soon they can see the camp fence and the tents come into view, a town of tents, and filth and rubbish. During the drive, Grace felt uplifted, the prospect of seeing Rasha again had filled her in a glow of effervescent happiness. Now, dread slithers inside her.

'I'll park over here,' Vasilis is saying as Grace constructs an image in her head of how life must be for Rasha.

'I'd forgotten how unnatural this place feels, it's no place for a child.'

'No, it isn't, but it's better than the hell she's come from. Come on, let's go.'

At the reception centre, Fotini is waiting for them. She looks pensive.

'Everything okay, Fotini? You look distracted,' Vasilis says in Greek.

'We've just heard from the hospital.' Vasilis hears a slight quiver in her voice. 'Rasha's uncle died this morning.'

'Oh! Poor little thing.'

He looks at Grace.

'What is it, Vasilis? What did she say?'

'It's not good news. The uncle has died.'

Grace's chest ignites.

'Are you okay, Grace?'

She doesn't answer him, instead, she asks Fotini, 'Does she know?'

Fotini shakes her head. 'Not yet. We're not even sure if she knew her uncle was here. She hasn't asked about him. She might not be told.'

'What will happen now?'

'We've placed her with a Syrian family for now. They also have young children. They lived in the same neighbourhood. They knew the family. They are happy to take her for the moment. We've been in touch with METAdrasi they have a facility here in Lesvos. They help children like Rasha. They move them out of detention centres and into appropriate facilities, even school. They also find suitable foster parents, but that will take time.'

'Can I still see her?'

She seems to be considering this, she looks at Vasilis and then back to Grace. 'Just for a short time, five minutes, that's all.'

Outside the tent that the family live in, a woman, her head and shoulders covered with a blue hijab, is crouched over a basin of murky water, scrubbing clothes. From inside the tent a man appears, he is about thirty, unshaven with a round face and to Grace's surprise, he smiles at them.

'This is the woman I told you about,' Fotini says, gesturing towards Grace.

He moves forward and offers his hand. 'Hello. My name is Tarek, and this is my wife Maya.'

'Hi, Tarek, I'm Grace and this is Vasilis. You speak English well.'

'I was a teacher.'

'Oh, I see.'

'One night, the school was bombed and in a second, I had no job. We used our savings to travel here. We have nothing left.'

She registers stunned disbelief, her mouth is open, but no words come out. Grace can hear children's voices coming from the tent.

'We have food, water, medicine, a doctor can visit, and my children have a dry place to sleep. It is hard, but when you live in Syria, death is guaranteed. We are alive here.'

'Yes. At least your family is safe from the war.'

'What is your interest in Rasha?'

'I saw her coming off the lifeboat. I heard about her mother and I just wanted to know she was… she was cared for.'

'I knew her father.'

'I know. Thank you for taking her into your family.'

The inside of the tent is smaller than Grace thought it would be. The floor is covered in mattresses and stacked in one corner there is a pile of clothes and sleeping bags. In the centre, cooking pots sit on a grill above a small fire.

Three young children are sitting in a corner of the tent playing with dolls. Tarek points to one of the girls. 'This is Rasha.'

On hearing her name, Rasha turns her head and looks at Grace, who remembers when she saw the little girl coming off the boat, her hair wet and stuck to her head. Now, Grace is distracted by Rasha's mass of dark curly hair and its length; it is long, very long.

Grace feels almost nervous as she takes a few steps towards Rasha. Tentatively, she crouches down beside her. The girls are pretending the dolls are talking to one another. Rasha glances at Grace, and Grace can tell she is apprehensive about her presence. She smiles at the girl whose large dark eyes can't conceal the sadness behind them.

Grace watches them play and then she asks Tarek to tell her what the girls are saying.

'They are pretending to be back home, playing outside, going to the shop to buy some sweets.'

Just then, one of the girls makes the sound of an explosion and the dolls are thrown into the air and land with contorted arms and legs. Grace doesn't need Tarek to explain this part of the game. Grace feels an immense longing to gather the girls up in her arms and embrace them, protect them. But, in that instance, she understands she can't save them from the horrors they have seen and the hell they have left which still lurks in their young minds.

Grace cannot muster the strength to dispel her despair. She breathes in the musty odour of the tent. A shiver of self-consciousness comes to her. I've been delusional. What was I thinking? She has misled herself with her own anguish, a belief that this little girl could somehow fill the void left in her life by Olivia. She feels an absurd sense of shame.

She gets to her feet and rummaging in her pocket she hands a bar of chocolate to Tarek. A little gift that now seems irrelevant and worthless.

'Give this to the girls.' She turns her head to look at Rasha for one last time and leaves the tent.

Outside, Vasilis and Fotini are waiting for her. Without a word, she brushes past them.

She tries to imagine what sort of a fool she must look. She had felt sure her decision to come here was the right thing to do. Now, all she wants to do is get as far away as she can. She feels she is drowning in her despondency and choking on her naivety.

When Vasilis meets her at the car, he can see she has been crying.

'Are you okay?'

She sniffs and wipes her eyes. 'Can we just go, please?'

Tactfully, Vasilis doesn't say anything. As he drives, Grace can feel him looking at her from time to time.

Vasilis feels awkward, but he thinks it best to wait and let Grace speak in her own time. He does not know if her silence is comprised of humiliation, or anger, or both.

She picks at a loose thread on her blouse. As time passes, she chews over what to say, but she is struggling to find the right words.

He waits. It feels like an eternity. His stomach rumbles, and he looks at his watch. 'Do you still want some lunch?'

She bites her lip and nods.

'By the way, your mascara has run.'

She searches in her handbag for a tissue and flips down the sun visor, peering at her reflection in the small mirror.

'God. I look a mess,' she says, wiping the black streaks under her eyes.

He smiles. 'We're nearly there.'

'Where are we going?'

'Skala Sikaminias. It's nice, you'll like it.'

Soon, the road drops down a steep hill. 'There it is, what do you think?' Vasilis asks.

In front of them is a picturesque harbour enclosed by a jetty. At the tip of the jetty, a whitewashed church looks out to the Aegean.

'That is the church of Panagia Gorgona, it means, Mermaid Madonna. It's also called, Panagia Ton Psaradon, Madonna of the Fishermen. The name comes from a painting of the Virgin with a mermaid's tail.'

'That would be worth seeing.'

'I've never seen it myself. I'll park over here.'

Once parked, they walk to the harbour where, outside, taverna tables line the harbour under the protective shade of imposing plane trees.

Vasilis smiles at Grace, as she settles into a chair and scans the menu.

'The fish is fresh, caught this morning. I'd recommend it.'

'I'm not that hungry, really. I think I'll just have the bread and olives.'

'I think I'll have the grilled swordfish,' Vasilis says, leaning back.

'I haven't seen you have a cigarette today.'

'That's because I was serious when I said I was giving them up.'

'Good. I'm glad. How are you finding it?'

'Mm… I missed it with my morning coffee.'

A waiter comes and takes their order.

'This is a lovely spot.'

'You should see the sunsets, they're special. Worth a photograph.'

This gives her an idea. She takes her smartphone from her bag. 'I want a photograph taken of the two of us.'

There's a couple at the next table and Grace asks if one of them would take a photograph. The male, in his late thirties with a neatly trimmed beard and round spectacles obliges her.

Vasilis leans into her and curls his arm around her shoulder. The man fires off two photographs in quick succession. 'One more, just in case those two are blurred.' He hands Grace her smartphone, who thanks him.

She looks at the photographs, switching from one to the other. She frowns in concentration as she dissects herself.

She's never liked looking at herself. She is always critical of how she looks. She scrutinises if the top she is wearing suits her. She studies her complexion, the lines at her eyes, the wrinkles on her forehead when she smiles, they always look prominent to her, even when others rebuke her concern. Then, she turns her gaze to Vasilis. He is smiling broadly. She examines the curve of his brow and the line of his jaw.

'You're smiling,' Vasilis says. 'I take it they meet with your approval.'

'You look nice. I'm not so sure about me. I never take a good photograph.'

'Let me see.' Vasilis holds out his hand. When he has her smartphone, he looks from one photograph to the other. She is smiling, her face turned towards him. Her mouth is open slightly, as she smiles, and he can see the whiteness of her teeth. Her hair brushes his hand and he remembers the feel of her, the smoothness and warmth of her skin on his fingertips.

Vasilis looks up from the smartphone and smiles at her. 'We look like a couple, don't you think?' He hands it to her, and she looks at the screen. 'We do.'

She lifts her eyes to him. He is surveying her face, and then he reaches over the table and lightly squeezes her hand. 'You can talk about it, you know.'

She looks away from him, out to the sea. It seems so calm, so gentle, as it sparkles in the sun's light.

When she turns, she catches his eye. She seems embarrassed. She combs her hand through her hair and sighs. 'You were right, after all. I shouldn't have gone. It was stupid of me, I know that now.'

'What happened?' He wonders, briefly if they should go somewhere less public.

If anyone will understand, he will. 'I realised Olivia is gone, she's not coming back. I have to accept that and try to move on. I can't replace her, Vasilis.'

'Then you needed to do this, Grace. If you hadn't, then nothing would have changed. This wouldn't have happened, and you wouldn't have realised that this little girl can't take the place of your daughter. It's a good thing. You might not see that now, but you will.'

She forces herself to smile. 'I do. In a way, I'm glad. No more pretending to myself.'

'It's okay. I still feel the pain of it. Sometimes, when I'm watching Pelagia play, it hits me like a punch to the stomach. You need to keep talking about it, you really should. Don't bury it inside yourself.'

He lifts his hand to her face and holds it there, brushing her cheek, it feels soft, like a tissue. 'I'm here for you. If you can't talk to me, who else can you talk to?'

There is a pounding in her ears and her chest feels like it is about to burst. 'I'm sorry.'

'What for?'

'I feel bad. I've dragged you through all this.'

'I want to be here, with you,' Vasilis says, betraying none of the apprehension Grace is sure he must feel.

She shakes her head. 'I'm just glad it's you who is here with me.'

He smiles. 'That makes the two of us then.' Vasilis can see the waiter approaching with their food. 'Do you still want to eat?'

She nods.

'Good. I'm starving.'

After lunch, they walk towards the church. Beyond it, there is nothing but the Aegean stretching like a turquoise blanket, as far as the eye can see. Grace watches, as the surface glistens silver, dappled with light.

'Are you alright?' There is a trace of concern in his face.

She must admit, the experience inside the tent had left her feeling weary, but now, the scents travelling on the air and the warm breeze licking her skin are soothing to her.

'I'm just enjoying this, being here, feeling the sun and the breeze, watching the sea and being with you. For the first time today, I feel content.'

He slips his hand in hers. It is a bold act. Her smile tells him she is enjoying the curled warmth of his fingers laced in hers and his heart leaps.

She turns and looks at Vasilis. She studies his fine jawbones, the curve of his mouth, the prow of his nose, his deep-set eyes, the speckles of grey in his hair; she wants to consume every little detail of him.

When they reach the church, Vasilis tries to open the door.

'It's locked.'

She looks out, over the sea, towards the shimmer of warmth on the horizon. 'Never mind. The view from here is stunning.'

He turns to face her. 'Yes. It is.'

He lowers his head and gently presses his lips to hers. Her mouth is soft and warm, as he brushes his lips against her. He wonders if she will pull away from him, but her mouth is accepting. He touches her face and runs the back of his hand down her cheek. With the tip of his finger, he touches her soft lips and whispers her name. He curls his fingers around the nape of her neck. Her breath is warm on his lips and then, ever so delicately, he kisses her longingly.

She wants to tell him everything. She feels she must. She has tried to push it to the back of her mind, but it lies on her, weighted and heavy.

He looks at her, concentrating now. 'What? What is it, Grace? Are you alright?'

I don't want to tell him, not just now, not here. I don't want to spoil this moment. I want it to last forever.

'I'm fine. More than fine. I was just wondering where this goes from here?'

He smiles. 'Wherever you want.'

The Present

A Case of Cramp and the Mythological Soulmates

'How does it feel to be seventy-four, Peter?'

'The same as yesterday when I was seventy-three.'

Sofia laughs and hands him a neatly wrapped present. 'Happy birthday.' She leans towards him and kisses Peter on the cheek.

'Thank you, Sofia. What would you like to drink? The first one's on me.'

'But it's your birthday, you shouldn't be buying the drinks.'

He waves away her concern. 'Nonsense. When did I ever succumb to convention?'

'Well, in that case, I'll have a gin.'

'Perfect. Take a seat and I'll bring it over.'

The restaurant has a sweeping view. Below them, the setting sun gilds the rooftops of the town and levels itself across the Aegean. Around the table, a group of Peter's friends have assembled to celebrate his birthday.

Sofia takes a seat and smiles at Grace. 'It's a beautiful evening.'

Grace wants to clear the air and awkwardly touches Sofia on the arm. 'I'm sorry for the other day.'

'Oh, don't be. I've forgotten all about it already.'

'That's a relief. It's been playing on my mind and I... well, I've been embarrassed about it.'

'Is that why I've not seen you lately? I did wonder.'

Grace nods.

Peter returns with Sofia's drink. 'Right then, is everyone ready to order?'

'Is Vasilis coming?' Sofia asks Grace.

'Later. One of his staff phoned in sick at short notice, so he's having to cover for them.'

'That's a shame.'

Peter smiles. 'I can recommend the beef stifado. I had it the other day, the beef was so tender it just melted in my mouth.'

Grace surveys the menu. 'I think I'll have the chicken souvlaki,'

'What about a starter?' Peter asks heartily.

'Not for me, thanks,' says Grace.

Sofia looks up from her menu. 'I'm just going to have the chicken souvlaki as well.'

'Well then, I'm having a starter, we'll just have the starters and the mains all together, shall we? that way, everyone's is eating together.'

During the meal, a waiter arrives with a surprise cake, with seven candles, each for every decade. The whole restaurant sings 'happy birthday,' and Peter makes an impromptu speech that receives rapturous applause from everyone. They order coffee and liquors and gradually people start to slip away, thanking Peter for inviting them and saying their goodbyes with firm handshakes and tipsy embraces.

Peter heads off to the toilet, leaving Grace and Sofia to finish their coffee.

'So, you went to the camp?'

'I did, Vasilis took me, grudgingly.'

'And did you meet with the little girl?'

Sofia's question brings reverberations of the anguish she felt. 'It was a mistake. I really thought I could help her. I even deliberated on taking her out of the camp and looking after her. I know you don't have to look at me in that way, it became very apparent that was not going to happen.'

'What happened then?'

'I changed. Being in that tent and watching the girls play, speaking in a language that sounded exotic, but I didn't understand, seeing her as she really is, just a little girl. But now, she has a family, she has others to play with who are just like her, who have had their homes and everything they knew taken from them. She wasn't amongst strangers, she was loved and cared for. And... she wasn't Olivia... she was never going to be Olivia.

'When I lost Olivia, nothing could ever prepare me for the pain. For a long time, it felt like my heart was drowning. Every part of me ached with grief. Seeing Rasha reminded me of what I'd lost, but I can't replace Olivia, she's gone. I accept that now.'

Sofia takes her hand and gently squeezes it. 'You're such a brave girl. I can't imagine what it must have been like for you. You've turned a corner now and that can only be a good thing.'

Grace seems to be considering this when Peter returns to the table. 'If you ladies don't mind, I think I'll say my goodbyes and head off to bed while I can still stand. I think I'll be needing some Paracetamol in the morning. I'm not used to overindulging these days.'

He leans forward and kisses both women on the cheek. 'Goodnight ladies, sleep tight.'

They watch Peter weave around tables and chairs, swerve a waiter holding a tray of food, and then stumble down a step. He turns towards them and, in a theatrical manner, waves his Panama hat and heads off along the serpentine cobbled lanes.

'I'm always last to leave,' Sofia says, tipping the remains of her drink into her mouth. 'I'll walk you home.'

On an impulse, Grace says, 'I think I'll go and see Vasilis. Would you mind?'

'Of course not. Off you go. In fact, I might just have another one of these.' Sofia lifts her glass and grins.

Grace sheds her shoes and walks barefoot along the sand towards the gentle whisper of the sea. At the water's edge, she gazes out over the dark undulating surface and lets the surf wash over her feet. She luxuriates in it. Behind her, the soft yellow glow from Vasilis' taverna radiates a sense of calmness across the sand. The moon hangs like a silver disc, sending a beam of light over the sea and, around Grace, the air is still and warm.

These last few days she has felt unnerved, inside she has been disturbed with her thoughts, her mind has been swimming with questions. Was it love? It was love. We did love each other, she is sure of it. But it changed. Jamie changed. The erosion of their love is complete.

She has an image of him, the last time she saw him, leaving her, leaving her life with his accusations and the sting of threats. It was to be the last humiliation.

She can see him now for what he is, more clearly than she ever did, perhaps because she did not permit herself to see it before.

She closes her eyes and, at that moment, grief washes over her. She can barely breathe.

What she did, sending the photograph to Jayne, she did for self-preservation. Jamie's threat of going to the police compromised her situation, her stability, it had become unbearable.

What Jamie did to her, after that, was even worse, and she has been running away from it ever since.

She knows now, she must tell Vasilis and soon, but first, she must wait for the appropriate moment. She will convince him she had no choice.

Grace wraps her arms around her stomach and bends forward, as though she has taken a strike to the core of her being. There are still unfinished consequences at play.

Consumed with these thoughts, Grace is unaware that Vasilis has seen her from the taverna and, as he approaches, he calls her name, bewildered by her appearance.

She turns to face him.

'What are you doing out here?' he asks disconcertedly.

She tries to compose herself. 'It's such a beautiful night, I felt like a walk. Everyone at the meal has gone home.'

'How did it go?'

'It was lovely. Peter had a good time, which was the main thing. Have you been busy tonight?'

'We were. It's quiet now... What's wrong?' he asks.

Grace shakes her head. 'Nothing's wrong, you just startled me, that's all, I'm fine, honestly.' She speaks without stopping herself, it is a lie. She can tell he is not convinced and, even though she tries, she can't mask the strain in her voice. Grace turns towards the sea. 'Have you ever swum at night?'

He blinks, taken by surprise. 'Not in a long time.'

'What was it like?'

He shrugs. 'I can't remember.'

'I haven't, but I want to.' Grace slides the straps from her shoulders and steps out of her dress, throwing it onto the sand. Vasilis looks at her in alarm and turns towards the taverna in a panic. When he looks back at her again, she is walking into the sea in her bra and pants.

'Grace, what are you doing? Someone might see you.'

'Let them, I don't care.'

'Have you gone mad?'

'If I have, then it's a wonderful feeling.'

Astonished, Vasilis watches as Grace slips into the dark oily surface. Above the water, he can see only the curved shape of her shoulders and wet hair as she swims away from him. He scoops her dress from the sand and lifting it to his face he brings the fabric to his nose and inhales her familiar scent as if she was standing right next to him.

'Be careful, don't go too far,' he whispers.

When she turns to head for the shore, Vasilis can see that she is smiling. Suddenly, she is frozen with panic, and then her arms flay around her in a frantic attempt to keep herself buoyant. She swallows some seawater and spits the salty taste from her mouth. She cries out his name. He runs into the sea, the deeper he gets the heavier his legs feel against the weight of the water. He dives into the surf. She has gone. This is unthinkable, this should not be happening. She breaks the surface, gasping for air. He is close now, so close. He can see the fear in her eyes. Her arm reaches out, she is slipping under again, the space between them is like a cavern. The weight of the water is slowing him down, dragging him. Her face contorts in pain. He calls to her. He is desperate now. And then, he is close to her. He clutches her arm and pulls her towards him. The relief is instant. He instructs her to hold onto him. As he swims to the shore, her mouth fills with seawater, she is still coughing and grimacing in pain.

Grace has a discernible limp as they both stagger onto the sand. Gently, Vasilis eases her into a sitting position. She takes hold of her calf and massages the muscle.

'Are you okay?'

'I'll live, thanks to you.'

'What happened?'

'Cramp! In my leg. I couldn't do anything about it, it came on so quickly.' She can hear a near hysteria in her voice and she tries to calm herself. 'Oh Vasilis, thank God you were here.' A sense of shame and foolishness consumes her, as she looks at Vasilis dripping with seawater, soaking wet.

'I'm sorry. I don't know what came over me. It was an impulse. I wanted to feel the water around me. I wanted it to carry me. I wanted to feel weightless. What's wrong with me?'

'Can you walk?'

'I'm not sure, I think so.'

'Just stay here. I'll get a towel. You can't put your dress on until you're dry.'

When he returns, she is sitting with her arms wrapped around her knees. She looks up and smiles as he hands her a towel.

'Thank you.' She is surprised to see he is carrying a flask.

'I thought you needed a hot drink.'

She dries herself off. When she is done, she slips her dress on and ties her hair into a bun.

They sit sharing the coffee. Her brow is strained with concentration. How extraordinary, she thinks, even now, against the night sky, the castle above the village looks serene, shimmering like a gold crown.

'This is not just coffee, is it?'

'I put some whisky in it, to warm you inside.'

'I'm sorry. I'm such an idiot. I don't know why I do things like that.'

She feels it build inside her, it comes from deep in her stomach and when it overflows, she starts to shake and then she cries. She clings to him, her shoulders heaving with sobs. He holds her tightly to stop her shaking. She feels anger and grief and a love for this man that hurts. He touches her face with his hand, puts his hand to her chin and tilting it ever so slightly, he says something to her in Greek.

Her eyes are red and between sobs, she asks, 'What did you say?'

He smiles. 'I love you.'

'I know.'

He leans forward, he finds her mouth, it is open, and her lips are soft as he caresses them.

'I don't know if I can do this again.'

'I'm not like him, Grace.'

'I know.'

'You're beautiful.'

'I'm flawed.'

'We all are.'

She sighs.

For a moment there is a silence between them.

'Do you know much about Greek mythology?'

Grace shakes her head, bewildered. 'Not really. Why?'

'Well… the first humans were created with four arms, legs and eyes, and two noses and mouths. Now Zeus… you've heard of him, haven't you? Well, Zeus was afraid that these humans might be very powerful, so he split them in half. Each half had to find the other half of itself. Today, this is what we call our soulmates and I've found mine in you, Grace. I can't imagine not loving you.'

The Present

The Melting Pelagia and Secrets that Need to be Told

Vasilis is with Pelagia. She is, for the first time, wearing a satchel on her back while walking to school. Vasilis thinks it makes his daughter look older, like a caterpillar that has transformed itself into a butterfly, a thought that, if spoken, would please her.

They make their way through familiar cobbled lanes that join, like unattached ends of rope. They pass the ceramic shop where handmade cups and vases are displayed in wicker baskets and decorated plates hang like paintings outside on the stone wall.

Pelagia points to a docile dog, lounging on a step and she can't keep a smile from her mouth as she notices the bright red bow tied on top of its head.

They greet old Maria, sitting outside her daughter's shop, amongst a display of handbags and satchels, leather sandals and shoes, and railings with lines of linen and silk. Overhead, they are shaded by creeping vines that conceal miniscule birds, that dozing cats, who stretch lethargic limbs, keep an interested eye on.

Unwilling to reach the school so soon, Pelagia wishes she could step inside the doorways they pass and browse through the beads and bracelets, necklaces and bands.

Further ahead, they will pass Stella's shop, with its grown-up shirts and blouses, skirts and dresses, and an assortment of hats and scarfs. She likes looking at the ornaments and pictures in the shop next to Stella's but, this morning, they are running late, and even though she walks with deliberate slow steps, Vasilis is already pulling on her hand and striding purposefully.

Even amongst the tangible presence of the patterned pots, and flowering plants that splash the ledges above

them in vivid red and purple petals, Pelagia looks
crestfallen, and she can't dislocate herself from this mood.
Despite Pelagia's remonstrations, Vasilis takes the winding
stone steps two at a time, then strides through an archway
and a small dimly lit passageway.

Pelagia often likes to feel the bark of the trees, with the
corkscrew trunks sprouting branches that interweave with
the climbers above them. This morning all she can achieve,
for the briefest of moments, is to run her hand along their
rough bark, as she and Vasilis hurry by.

Soon we'll pass that woman's house with the weird
name, Pelagia thinks, then we'll see who's in a hurry.

She starts to quicken her pace. From the corner of her
eye, she knows her father is examining her as he follows.

'Oh! Suddenly, someone wants to go to school.'

'Well, you don't want me to be late, do you?'

They turn a corner and Pelagia is immediately
apprehensive. She sighs heavily. Across from them, sitting
on her small balcony is Grace.

Vasilis catches her by the arm. 'Slow down, it's not a
race.'

Grace stands, resting her hands on the railings.
'Kalimeri.'

Pelagia rolls her eyes.

Vasilis raises his hand and waves. 'Good morning,
Grace. Say good morning, Pelagia... Pelagia,' he says
again, more audible this time.

'Do I have to?'

'Where are your manners?'

She bites her lip.

'I'm not going to ask you again. You're embarrassing me
and yourself.'

'Kailmera, Grace,' she mumbles.

She waits, unsettled, shifting from foot to foot, while her
father speaks to Grace.

'Are you free this lunchtime?'

'It might be difficult, there's a bug going around my staff, the flu, I think.'

'Are they all men?'

'Yes, why do you ask?'

She smiles. 'So, they've got a cold, then. Back in Scotland, we call it *man flu*.'

'What do you mean?'

'It means you're the weaker sex.'

Vasilis laughs.

Pelagia snorts. Why can't she speak in Greek? She starts to fidget with the buttons of her school shirt. 'Baba!'(Dad) Pelagia pleads.

'I'd better get going. Why don't you drop by later for a coffee?'

'I'd like that. See you soon.' Grace looks at Pelagia, 'Antio, Pelagia. Kalee sou mera.' (Bye, Have a nice day).

Pelagia looks at her in astonishment. 'Efharisto.'

'Your Greek is improving,' Vasilis says, impressed.

'I've downloaded an App.'

'I'll test you later and see how good you are.' He blows her a kiss.

When they get to the school, Vasilis crouches down, so his face is opposite Pelagia. 'This is about your mother, isn't it?'

She shrugs.

'She will always be your mother. No one can replace her, no one is going to replace her. Do you understand, Pelagia?'

'I can't help feeling the way I do.'

'I know. Grace is a nice person. You would like her, honestly, you would if you gave her a chance.'

She stares at her feet and notices her shoes are scuffed at the toe.

'Do you think you could? It would make me happy, and you want me to be happy, right?'

'I suppose so.' She glances at him and then looks away.

'You better get to class. Off you go.' He kisses her on the forehead and her face brightens.

On his way to the restaurant, Vasilis looks at his watch and picks up his pace. He ponders how his life has changed since Grace arrived. He is aware she is troubled, part of her has been damaged, he knows that. Even so, she has a certain grace and determination about her. He wonders if this is what attracted him to her in the first place.

Images of Grace smiling and laughing interweave themselves with his recent encounters with Pelagia, who feels that Grace's presence has threatened her safe and secure world. She has become fragile. It hadn't occurred to him Pelagia would react like this. She had previously restrained her utterances of disapproval to subtle hints, now she is openly expressing them. He thought he knew his daughter, she tended to over-dramatize, but he wasn't prepared for her vulnerability. Her happiness depends on him. He knows he must exercise patience with her and tread with caution.

He has tried to decipher his feelings and each time he comes to the same conclusion, the same thoughts. He has had his doubts but, with each day he has spent in Grace's company, they are soothed and shrink from him. A continual oceanic wave of wanting to be near her and touch her crashes over him, whenever he speaks to her, walks with her or is close to her. He is enfolded in an inward rapture. Even after this short time, he thinks, I can't imagine not loving her.

Just then, the ring tone on his smartphone goes off. He answers it. Even before he has ended the call, he turns around and runs towards the harbour and the lifeboat.

She slides her sunglasses from her eyes, now that she is shaded from the white glare of the afternoon heat. Vasilis waves at her. He is coming out of the kitchen with a plate and places it on a table in front of a man who nods in appreciation.

Grace takes a seat with an unobstructed view of the sea.

'I heard more refugees arrived. How was it?' she asks Vasilis, as he sits opposite her.

'As it always is, except no one died this time.'

'Thank God for that. Were there any children?'

'There's always children. There was a lot this time, cold, hungry and wet.'

'Do you think this will end, one day?'

'If that was to be so, then all the wars, religious intolerance and political fanaticism would have to end. There have always been these things, throughout history, so no, I don't think it will end soon.'

'At least they're safe now.'

'This is just another stage in their journey. Even if the war ended in Syria tomorrow, how many of them would return home? I'm not so sure they would.'

'No. What would they be going back to? I can't imagine how that must feel.'

'Some of these people have lost wives, husbands and children. How does a person bear that pain and live out each day, one after the other?'

'I can't imagine how desperate they have to be. They must feel betrayed and angry when they get here.'

'Where is the world's outrage at this human misery? I wish the world could see what I'm seeing; capsized rubber boats, lifejackets and bodies scattered and floating in the sea, eyes full of fear, children in shock, terrified.'

She presses her hand into his. It is a wordless acknowledgement of her concern.

He frowns. 'I've heard from some of the refugees, they've become so desperate to escape the war, they're selling their organs to fund the journey to Europe. Can you imagine that, to have lost all hope and dignity that they would go to such lengths?'

'It's just disgusting that people are making money out of other people's suffering, it's dehumanizing.'

Vasilis scratches his jaw. 'I'm worried, Grace. There have been fights in the camp and protests around the island. If you stretch an elastic band, at some point, it's going to snap.'

Grace has a passing memory of Rasha and pushes it from her thoughts.

A metallic clang comes from the kitchen, a saucepan or a bowl.

'Remember the other day, after we visited the camp and we went for lunch? You said there was something you wanted to tell me.'

'Yes. But that wasn't the right time.'

'And is this the right time?'

'I've thought about nothing else.'

'Then tell me.'

'It's not as easy as that.'

'Why not?'

'I haven't told anyone. I haven't been ready, until now, until this... me and you. If what we have together means anything to me, then I can't carry this weight any longer. I need to tell you. You need to hear about it. You need to understand. At least, I hope you'll understand.'

'Then take all the time you need,' he suggests.

The Past

A Releasing and an Invitation

How extraordinary it was that I was not as surprised as I might have been by my actions, that I did not falter, that I had only one thought.

Did I regret what I did? Did I feel shame? I had a conscience.

A part of me regretted the harm I'd caused.

I thought I had been so clever. The nightmare would now finally end. I had reasoned that Jamie had forced me into sending that photograph, therefore my action had been legitimate.

I believed I would be finally rid of him and, indeed, his threats stopped and, as time passed, the violation I felt no longer stained me. It began to melt from me, like the thawing of snow.

My contentment was soon to be repressed. I hadn't anticipated what would happen next. It was incomprehensible.

It started with the messages, again. Twenty, thirty a day. This time he texted, he emailed and even messaged me on Facebook.

And then I understood what I'd done. I had compromised Jamie. I had compromised Jayne and their son's future. I realised, irrevocably, I had compromised myself.

The day it happened, I had lunch with a friend. I took a taxi home. I stood at the front door, enjoying the sun on my back. I turned the key in the lock and reached for the door handle, pushing it open. Then, a shudder ran down my spine. I became aware of a shape, someone behind me.

He was taller than me, physically stronger. Before I knew what was happening, he had pushed me in the small of my back. My heart was like a drum as he grabbed a clump of my hair and dragged me across the hallway. The pain was agonising, piercing my scalp. I screamed, and he spat at me to *shut the fuck up*. I remember the word *bitch* being thrown at me.

When it stopped, I was lying on the living room floor. Jamie was standing over me, and to my horror, I saw a tuft of hair in his hand, my hair. White shards of pain stabbed my skull. My gaze swept around the living room. I reached out, stretching for something, anything solid, anything I could hit him with.

Within an instant, he had straddled me, his fingers clamped around my throat, crushing my windpipe. His eyes strained with hate. And then, I saw a flash of silver and felt another type of pressure on my throat, cold and sharp. It pressed into my skin and I could sense rivulets of blood trickling down my neck. With his free hand, he ripped at my blouse, hoisted my skirt above my thighs and pulled at my underwear. His eyes never left mine. He told me if I struggled, it would mean nothing to him to slit my throat; he was going to do this either way.

He glared at me, unrepentant. He hissed at me that I had brought this on myself. I was responsible, it was what I deserved. There was so much malevolence in his words, they paralysed me.

I lay on the floor until it was dark. A cold sweat stained my brow and I felt sick. I held on to a chair, and with an effort, heaved myself to my feet, my head faint, as the room spun around me.

I realised I couldn't talk. I didn't want to report to the police. I didn't want that ordeal, and anyway, how could I? I was suffocating. I was crushed.

I felt dirty. I stood in the shower for a long time, scrubbing him from my skin, my pores, erasing any trace of him. I felt worthless, ashamed that I had let this happen. I did try to stop him. He was too strong and that look of hatred on his face when he held the knife and pressed it against my throat shocked me to my core.

I struggled with the flashbacks, they were horrendous. Often, they were triggered by a sound or a smell. I didn't think I'd ever be able to cleanse it from my mind.

I felt like a pendulum, swinging between believing nothing had really happened, to knowing, it had.

The impact was dramatic. At its worse, I struggled to eat, to sleep, to work. I lost weight, I was exhausted.

Looking back, I was in shock. I went through every emotion. I felt numb. At times, I was unemotional. I cried. I laughed. I was even physically sick.

I was finding it difficult to cope with day-to-day situations. Even going out to shop was an ordeal. My resolve would often collapse, and I'd be tearful a lot of the time.

I read somewhere survivors can often experience suicidal thoughts or self-harm. At one point, during the very low days, if I'm honest, my mind slipped into that dark place.

I remember when I was younger when, as a family, we celebrated Halloween. It had become a tradition to find the biggest pumpkin we could buy. Mum would slice off the top of the pumpkin so that I could scrape out the seeds with a spoon.

After that day, I felt like that pumpkin, scraped raw, until there was nothing left inside me.

The thing I feared most was being alone. When I closed that front door, I was alone, in my house, with its overgrown garden and driveway that was busy cultivating every weed known to man. Everyday living in that house was a constant reminder of what happened to me.

It didn't go unnoticed, my wilting persona. Friends did their best to engage me with social outings. The more they tried, the more I retreated into myself, until the offers became fewer and eventually, they just stopped inviting me.

It sounds stupid, I know, but I often wondered if I was to blame? Was I responsible for what happened? Every morning, I awoke with a jolt, experiencing again, not the actual physicality of what he did to me, but the moments before, the days that led up to it. I played them in slow motion, rewinding them, reeling backwards, and always I'm taking back to that very moment. I pressed the send button on my smartphone and sent the photograph. It never occurred to me I was sealing my own fate.

I was signed off work with anxiety and stress. I told no one the real reason for my absence. It was my secret and it would stay that way. I learnt to focus on the positives and the things I enjoyed. That's how I dealt with it.

I was seeing my GP every two weeks. She was monitoring me physically, as well as mentally, and adjusting the dose of Sertraline that had now become part of my bloodstream, as much as the plasma and cells.

I needed to leave the place I loved. I could no longer stay in that house. My memories had become soiled with the nightmare Jamie had visited upon me.

For several days, my mind rolled over the practicalities. My passport was in date, it was renewed the year before. Would I need it? Maybe not, it depended on where I was going to go. London? Maybe.

I had an aunt in Berwick. When we were young, my sister and I always visited for two weeks in the summer. I remembered the windy coastal walks, the driving rain coming off the North Sea. No. Too cold. Too small. I felt suffocated at the thought.

Then, unsuspectingly, I was given an opportunity that set my mind. I was walking through The Meadows on my way to hand in another sick line at the university. Normally, I just posted them, but I was now making a concerted effort to get outside and walk.

My phone rang. It was Monica. I hadn't seen or heard from her in ages. I was staggered at how time had slipped past, undetected and unnoticed.

'Monica, how are you? It's been like… well, forever, it feels. It's wonderful to hear from you.' It was a relief hearing her voice. I felt like laughing and crying at the same time.

'I know. I'm fine. I should have phoned you sooner. Where does the time go? I've heard all about Jamie swanning off with that woman, and they have a baby. My God, the nerve of the man. What a bastard he turned out to be. I can't believe what he has done to you, poor soul. How are you?'

I was taken aback by the intensity of her words. I stumbled, searching for something to say. 'I'm getting there.' I nodded, reassuring myself.

'I'm glad. It's good to hear. Listen, you don't need to tell me, I mean about Jamie, so don't feel you need to talk about that.'

'That's kind of you, Monica. I'm getting over it, I think, slowly.' What I was trying to get over was an entirely different beast to what Monica inferred.

'These things take as long as they take, there's no hard or fast rule. As long as you're coping, that's the main thing.'

'Are you still living on that island of yours? What is it called again?'

'Lesvos. Yes, I'm still here. I'm almost a native now.'

We both laughed, and I realised it had been a long time since I'd done so. It felt good, refreshing.

'Look, the reason I'm phoning is, I've got an apartment here that I don't use now. I've moved to a bigger house, but I've kept it for friends if they want to come out and have a little holiday.'

'Oh, that's nice,' I said, not sure where this was going.

'Anyway, I just thought, well, it's lying empty now and if you felt you ever needed to get away from it all, you know, recharge the batteries, or just be somewhere different for a while, then you can use it. It's yours. What do you say?'

The truth was, I didn't know what to say.

'Grace are you still there?'

'Sorry, Monica, yes, I'm still here.'

'Well then, what do you think? I'm not expecting you to come tomorrow, so don't worry.'

'I don't even know where Lesvos is.'

'You don't have to. You just need to get on a plane.'

'Well, that should be easy.'

'Look, I know I've surprised you with this, but it would really mean a lot to me that you know you've got the option, if you need it, that is.'

'Thank you, Monica. I'm not sure. It seems a dramatic thing to do. It's quite far away.'

'I know. That's my point.'

'Look, thanks for the offer, but…'

'Just think about it, Grace. Take your time. As I said, it's an option and it would be good to see you again. I'm not going to be in Edinburgh anytime soon, am I?'

'I suppose not.'

Monica was my mum's best friend. When she married, Arthur, her husband, set up a property development company in Edinburgh that became successful. She remained close to my mum, and I grew up with Monica being a constant presence in my life, my adoptive mother.

As I grew older, she became more of a friend and confidant. When Monica's Arthur's health began to fail, they decided they no longer wanted the stress and strains of running a business, so they sold it. Monica and Arthur left Edinburgh for London but soon moved to Lesvos. Not long after that, Arthur died, and Monica had lived in Lesvos ever since.

'So, you have my number. As I said, the apartments yours if you want it. Whenever you want. It would be good to see you again, Grace. I miss you, honey.'

'I miss you too, Monica.' A rock lodged in my throat.

'It pains me to think what you've gone through. I wish I'd been there for you, you know that, don't you?'

'Of course, I do.' I said, reassuring her.

'Well, I'm sending you big hugs and kisses, and nothing would please me more than to be able to do it for real.'

By now, the tears were rolling down my cheeks and, up until that point, I hadn't realised how much I'd missed her.

'You take care, honey. Love you.'

'I love you too, Monica.'

The Present

A Promise

Throughout Grace's narration and her detailed descriptions, Vasilis has listened intently. When she has finished, he sits speechless and rakes his hands through his hair. It is a shock to him, she can see this straight away. A quiver of uncertainty passes through her. Have I done the right thing?

'Grace I…' He hesitates not quite sure what to say. 'I can't believe…' He flounders slightly. 'I mean, it's horrific. You've been through so much and now this has happened. Have you told the police?'

Grace exhales and presses her fingernails into her palm. 'I've never spoken of this to anyone. I thought that somehow it was all my fault. Could I have done anything differently?'

'Why would you say such a thing? Listen, this doesn't reflect who you are, it shows who he really is, it tells me, he is insecure, he has no respect for you, or himself. Men like him should have their balls cut off. I'd gladly do it for you.'

She looks away from him. Regret begins to slither in her stomach.

'I'm sorry, I know… this is not helping.'

'I don't need your anger, Vasilis. I don't have enough room in my world for any more anger.'

He reaches over and squeezes her hand. 'I'm sorry. It's just, of all the things you could have said, I wasn't expecting that.'

'No. I don't suppose you were.'

'Grace he's committed a crime, the worst kind.' His voice is softer.

She bites her lip.

'Did you get help?'

'I've only spoken to my GP. She wanted to refer me to a psychologist, but I wasn't ready for that. We spoke about Olivia, Jamie and his baby, my anxiety, but nothing else. This has been a closed book for me up until now.'

'How did you cope?'

'I used my imagination. In my head, I created a different world, one which Jamie couldn't penetrate. I had control over it. It was the only thing in my life I felt I had control over. I still grapple with and anguish over the ghosts of my past. But, gradually, I'm getting them out of my system, well... most of them. I think I'll always be living in an eternal white-knuckled calm.' She smiles, but Vasilis can see the sadness there.

'When Monica offered me the apartment, I was given an opportunity. A chance to escape the hell my life had become, an opportunity to leave behind everything that reminded me of it. That's what I thought, anyway.'

Grace swivels her gaze towards the sea, its colour reminds her of a turquoise dress she used to wear. 'You haven't ordered anything yet,' she says without taking her eyes from the water.

'No. I'm not that hungry now.'

When she pulls her gaze from the sea his expression is apprehensive. No. Troubled, maybe? She can't decide. It almost makes her want to cry.

'I was just trying to decide how you looked. I haven't scared you off, have I?'

'Do I look scared?'

'I'm not sure. You tell me.'

Vasilis thinks for a moment. 'I've got the best job in the world, and do you know how I know this because life is sacred, it's cherished and a precious thing. When I wake every morning, I know, on that day, I may have to go out to a sea, a sea that might be angry or calm, it doesn't matter, because I know I may save a few precious lives. But that doesn't stop me from feeling scared every time I leave the harbour.'

She crinkles her nose. 'So, you still want to see me, but I've scared you? Did I get that right?'

He smiles at her. 'I love you, but that doesn't stop me being concerned about you.'

'There's something else I must tell you.'

'What? What is it, Grace? Are you ill?'

'No. They don't call what I've got being ill.'

She looks at him fearing his reaction, fearing she might lose him. Her heart pounds in her chest and she braces herself.

'What is it then?'

There is a strained silence. 'I'm pregnant!'

The word sounds shocking to him, knowing who the father will be. It feels like he has been stung. His chest feels crushed.

'Pregnant!' He is racked between an instinct to comfort her and a desire to stand up and walk away.

She can see he looks disorientated. 'Vasilis?'

His mouth has suddenly gone dry. He takes a deep breath. Already, he has questions he needs answering. Has she prepared for this?

'It's his child? You're carrying his child?' He asks the question but knows the answer.

'You're stunned. I still am, too.'

'How long have you known?'

She tucks a strand of hair behind her ear. Briefly, she closes her eyes. 'I'm nearly eleven weeks. I've known for some time.' She presses her fingertips to her forehead. 'I was terrified, I still am. How ironic is it? I can't keep it. I just can't. I can't have a part of him inside me.'

'I wouldn't expect you to,' Vasilis says gently.

'I don't know what to do.'

Below the fan of eyelashes, Vasilis can see Grace's eyes glisten with tears.

'You can only do what is best for you.'

'I'm in Greece for Christ sake, what will I say? I was raped by my ex-partner and now I'm pregnant, take it out of me.'

'I don't know how these things work but I can find out if you want me to if that's what you really want?'

She wipes her eyes with a napkin. 'I promised myself, I wouldn't do this… cry. What now, Vasilis? Surely this changes everything between us?'

They sit in an uneasy silence.

'Maybe I should go back to Edinburgh?'

Vasilis is taken aback. 'No. I don't want you to.'

'What do you want, Vasilis? What do you want now, after this?' She looks away from him, sullen. 'Would this be too much for you? Too much… for us?' She turns to face him and looks at Vasilis anxiously.

'It doesn't change how I feel about you.'

'How can you say that? I have his seed inside me, growing each day. It's like he's still punishing me.'

The raw nature of her words startles him, he recoils from the change in her tone.

'I'm frightened, Vasilis.'

'You don't have to be. I'll be here for you, whatever you decide.'

'I'm frightened of myself.'

Vasilis holds her face in both hands and pulls it close to his. 'You're an extraordinary woman, Grace. You will find the strength to get through this and you won't be doing it on your own. I'll be with you, every step. I promise.'

She is crying now. She tries to blink her tears away. In this moment, he is astonished by his intense desire for her. He wants to take her pain from her. If he could, he would gladly suffer it for her. It gives him a physical, burning ache. He presses his lips to hers and it feels like he is pouring his essence and his soul into her.

The Present

A Decision Made

Vasilis has met her at the harbour. The restaurants are close to the water's edge and busy serving lunch, the air rich with the smells of cooking.

'I've made some enquiries, discreetly of course. The hospital in Mytilini performs these... terminations. Since you won't have insurance, it will cost probably in the region of 500 euros, and you will have to wait, you can't get it done immediately unless it is done privately, in which case, it will be done straight away.'

Grace is shocked at how clinical this sounds as if it is just a normal everyday procedure. There is a hesitation about her. It is no longer just a thought in her mind that she thinks constantly about, it is real now. She cannot imagine this baby in her world. There will be procedures, forms to fill out, money exchanged, a consultation, consent to be given. She tries not to elaborate on the fundamentals, the practicalities. She is afraid, but mostly, she is ashamed.

'The hospital will answer all your questions. I have their number.'

He hands her a piece of paper.

'Thank you.'

'If you want, I'll go with you of course.'

She hasn't thought about this. Does she think it best to be on her own? Will they speak English? Her Greek is not adequate, and it will be essential to communicate with and to understand the health professionals.

He touches her on the shoulder. 'You shouldn't be alone.'

'What about Pelagia?'

'I'll get someone to watch her.'

'I'm sorry,'

'For what?'

'For causing you all this trouble. You don't have to do all this.'

'I want to do it. I want to help.'

Grace is momentarily lifted by his offer. She looks towards the cobbled road with its steep gradient that leads to sprawling stone houses layered like a tiered cake, rising towards the castle. For a moment she is gripped by the scene that warrants a brief smile.

She studies the number Vasilis has written on the piece of paper. For a time, they both think about the phone call, not speaking. Around them, the light on the water is dazzling, the harbour, with its small flotilla of boats and picturesque frontage, is temporarily irrelevant.

'You will need to phone today,' Vasilis urges. He can tell by the expression on her face she doesn't want to hear this.

Grace rubs her hand across her face. 'I know.' Despite this, she wants to put it off. She finds herself thinking of Olivia and the life she never had, it is a shard her mind keeps getting snagged on. She welcomed her into this world and with the same breath said goodbye. The bitterness inside draws in her breath.

He's right. She can't put this off.

'I'll give you some privacy.' Vasilis walks away.

When he returns, Grace is watching fish weave in and out of rocks in the clear shallow water of the harbour.

'Are you okay?'

She turns to face him. 'I think so.'

'It's all done then. Have you a date?'

The words punch through her. She nods and draws in her breath. 'Friday.'

He touches her arm. 'That's quick.'

She gazes at the fish again. 'They had a cancellation.'

'Oh!'

'Obviously, someone has changed their mind.'

'Possibly. You don't know that for sure.'

'No. I don't.' She finds with alarm that she is near to tears.

The Present

Guilt and Relief

Grace is sitting in her small kitchen, ticking off a list she has made in her mind. She wonders how other women cope once they have gone through with the procedure. She makes the decision to search the internet. She opens her laptop. For a long time, Grace just sits there, staring at the dark screen and wondering if this is the right thing to do. For a moment, she is about to abandon the idea, but something inside her urges her on, and she cannot ignore it. She switches the laptop on and waits for it to start up. Her hand moves over the keyboard. With the touch of a key, Google loads. She waits impatiently.

This is my choice; this decision is mine alone. It gives me control over my life and my body.

She pours over the articles her search has found. Her mind highlighting words that jump out at her: *emotional, severe anxiety, drop in hormones, a huge relief.*

She hopes she will feel a sense of relief once this over? Relieved that she has got her life back. She wants to feel a resolution, a sense of closure.

She wonders if she will suffer a loss and if that loss will be intolerable? She knows how it feels to bear such extraordinary emotion, and it scares her. She can't imagine the pain of grief again, its veil is so thin.

At times, she has felt immeasurable guilt and shame that she let this happen.

Her reasons for choosing to terminate the pregnancy hold true, they are not unresolved. She asks if she is judging herself by the standards of others, by the values of others. Is this what she fears?

She hopes she can forgive herself. Without it, she is certain her life will be intolerable. She wonders if there will be regret? Perhaps for years.

Words jump from the screen: *numbness, feeling dirty, worthless, simple relief, overwhelming loss, anger.*

She peers at a quote taken from a woman who was raped. The violence of the rape made much less of an impact on the woman than the abortion. Grace finds this inconceivable. She is consumed with anger, she wants to scream.

Grace straightens her spine, she rubs the ache in her back. She hopes that Vasilis will understand. She trusts he will have the courage to be silent, to listen, and to support her. Otherwise, she will be alone. She thinks Sofia will not be able to overcome her beliefs and personal views on motherhood and the virtues of the family, so Grace has decided it is best not to tell her.

Suddenly, Grace is incredibly tired. She places her hands over her stomach, she isn't showing yet and she has convinced herself that's a good thing. She thinks that if her stomach had begun to round, such a physical change would represent the baby inside her. As it is, it is only represented by the thoughts in her mind and, in some way, this makes it easier.

Grace closes the laptop and pours herself a glass of wine, hesitating as it sits on the kitchen top.

Should she be drinking? What difference will it make now that I've made my decision?

She takes the glass and raises it to her lips. She inhales the wood aroma. She tilts the glass and lets the wine slip over her tongue. The taste is instant and gratifying. And then, unsuspectingly, Grace is overcome by a surge of guilt. She turns on the tap and lets the wine fall into the flow of water. She watches its deep colour dilute and run down the plug hole, and she is astounded at how profound her sense of relief is.

The Present

Someone to Walk With

They drive along the coastal road leaving Molyvos behind.
To her right, Grace has a clear view of the Aegean, calm in
the early morning light. At the horizon the sky is pink.
Once they reach Petra, they swing inland. Olive groves,
bordered by stone walls, straddle the road and, further
inland, rolling hills are clothed in a swathe of trees, and
vegetation dominates their view.

They climb in altitude, across prodigious hills, passing
the occasional house, and the small town of Kalloni, and
the even smaller Arisivi. When the road becomes flat and
wider, it encourages Vasilis to increase his speed.

The journey has been made in relative silence with just
the occasional comment. Vasilis finds the ability to
summon the appropriate words difficult and, since Grace
seems content to be alone with her thoughts, he gives up
the struggle. Again, they skirt the coast, before heading left
and inland once more.

'Not long now.' His words induce a palpable tension.

Soon they are passing through the environs of the capital,
Mytilene.

Grace reaches across and touches his arm. 'Once we get
there what will you do?'

'There's a little place near the hospital that serves nice
coffee. I'll wait there.'

He parks in a space in the hospital car park and applies
the handbrake.

'Do you want me to go in with you?'

Her voice is soft but steel. 'No. I've had my hand held
long enough. I'll go by myself.'

He walks her to the front of the hospital. At the entrance,
Vasilis glances around. Several people come and go, it all

feels normal, ordinary even, but Vasilis feels the world is falling in on itself.

He reaches out and lightly touches her face with his fingertips. 'I won't stop thinking about you. You're in my heart.'

Grace takes his hand and kisses it. He pulls her towards him, and they embrace. Her thick hair is wiry around his face. He can feel her drawing in a long breath, and he curses the God he has prayed to all his life.

Grace pulls away from him. 'I should go.'

He kisses her forehead. Every cell in his body is screaming for him to stay with her, but the decision is taken from him, as Grace turns and walks into the hospital.

It has only been half an hour, but it feels an eternity. Vasilis' coffee is untouched and cold. The wait is unendurable. He tries to read a paper, but his brain won't process the words on the page. He closes his eyes and a nervousness squeezes him. He opens his eyes and examines the print again. It's pointless, he can't concentrate.

For the first time in weeks, he craves a cigarette, and he thinks of buying a packet. Surely, one won't hurt? But he can already hear the disappointment in Grace's voice.

He takes his smartphone from his pocket and checks his text messages and emails. There are none. He clicks the photos icon and scrolls through the photographs until he comes to the one he is looking for. It is of Grace. He had taken it a few days after they first met. Chestnut hair curls across her face. Blue irises sparkle like the sea, shielded by luxuriant and silky lashes. Her red lips, flawlessly shaped, smile at him. He has viewed it many times, but not with the intensity he does today.

She stands behind him, like a shadow. He feels a hand touch his shoulder and, startled, he turns. Vasilis is momentarily stunned and then permeated with an inexplicable fusion of joy and trepidation.

'Grace! Sit down.' He stands and guides her to a chair.

His eyes search her face. He braces himself and at the same time feels a rush of affection for her.

'I couldn't do it. I just couldn't go through with it.'

He sighs, not sure if it is relief, or because she is finally sitting opposite him. 'What happened?'

'I was in a room. I spoke with a nurse and then a doctor. He went over the procedure, what it would entail, my recovery... his English was good with a pleasant manner. I suddenly realised I wanted this baby. It has my DNA, it has my genes. It's a part of me, just as much as Olivia was. I was aware that something inside me had changed. I didn't want to lose another baby. I wasn't confused anymore, there was no hesitation about me. I was keeping this baby and I walked out.'

'Are you sure you're okay?'

'I'm fine.' It is an incongruous answer. Her face has gone pale. 'There's something else I need to tell you,' her voice quivers.

He forces a smile. 'You better tell me, then.'

'When I was pregnant with Olivia, I was offered a screening test at fourteen weeks, which is normal, all pregnant woman can have one. Naturally, I was anxious. Anyway, they found I had a higher risk of having a baby with Patau's syndrome.'

Vasilis looks quizzical. 'I've never heard of it. I'm assuming that's not good for the baby.'

'Neither had we. It's a rare condition. So, I had a diagnostic test. Olivia had an additional copy of chromosome 3. We were told the chances of miscarrying were high and if I did go full term, the baby might be stillborn or only survive a few days or weeks. Not many reach their first birthday.'

Vasilis can feel her grief.

'Our hopes of having a healthy baby, and a normal family life, disappeared in a second. I was referred to a specialist centre for a repeat scan and some other tests. In those weeks, I prayed for the first time in years. I still held on to the slimmest of hopes; it was all a mistake, and everything would be all right. Jamie spent his time Googling, Patau's syndrome, and everything the consultant told him was there in black and white. Our baby would have congenital abnormalities, severe physical disabilities and learning disabilities.'

Vasilis is struck by the ease with which Grace is telling him this. Her voice is firm. He forces himself not to ask what she will do now that she is keeping the baby. It is enough to know she is here with him; it can wait.

'The consultant told us we had a choice, but we didn't have to decide right away. We could go home and talk about it and come to a decision we both agreed on. I'm not against abortion in principle, but I knew I would struggle in the years to come if I didn't give our baby a chance. We wanted to give her the best chance we could. We had to try and reclaim something from what was our own nightmare.

'We spent a whole weekend talking about it and, once we finally decided, that night was the deepest sleep I'd had in a long time. A heaviness had lifted from the both of us… we had a purpose. I needed to know there would be no, 'what ifs.' I couldn't face how I'd feel, otherwise.'

'I don't know what to say. I can't imagine what you must have been through.'

'Sometimes, I wonder how we did. I think at that point, it brought us closer, for a time. I really do believe that. We had to adjust. We grieved for the baby we thought we were going to have. I knew she was a girl and we were going to call her Olivia. How can you ever get used to knowing you will never see your child smile, crawl, or take their first steps, you'll never hear their first words, experience birthdays and Christmas?

'It was so brutal. And then… we grieved for her when she was born and died a few minutes later.

'I found it hard seeing other women who were pregnant. I remember the consultant telling us that we were quite unique; most couples opted for a termination.

'We were able to plan. We wanted Olivia to have some dignity. I didn't want them to rush her away and do whatever it is they do. What was the point in that? We knew that wouldn't make a difference. So, they gave her a little oxygen, massaged her chest… and her breathing just faded. They handed her to us and in that moment, she was our baby, our Olivia, and she was loved. That's all she knew, being loved and being cherished, and that's all that mattered.'

'There were times when I wondered if I was the one who carried the extra chromosome or Jamie? I was haunted by that for a long time. You see, we went for genetic testing to find out the likelihood of it occurring again, but they couldn't tell us for definite. I can't go through any more remorse or regret. I'm tired.'

'You look exhausted.'

'This has come as a shock to you,' Grace says.

'I'd be lying if I said it hadn't.'

'I've just changed what will be the rest of my life,' she says as if the realisation has just struck her. 'I feel like I've just created a new world for myself… and I need someone to help me walk through it.' Her words infuse the air around them.

The Past

Leaving

Edinburgh was my home. I'd spent my entire life there. I went to school there. Over the years, I'd made lifelong friends, and most of my family still lived in and around the city. I studied at university and embarked on my working life, all within the confines of that tightly compact space that was my city, my world. Every building resonated the past and every street seamlessly blended the old with the new. The thought of ever leaving never entered my mind, it would have been unthinkable. Yet, the morning after I spoke with Monica, I awoke knowing that was precisely what I was going to do.

It would be like a kind of holiday, I tried to convince myself, even though, deep down, I knew it wouldn't. I would be going alone.

My happiness depended on it. My sanity was threatened, and it hung on me leaving. I had to go, I told myself. If not, I might lose my grip on life, it was that simple.

I stepped out of the bedroom and plodded barefoot downstairs. In the kitchen, I leaned my shoulder against the wall and sighed. I turned my gaze to the sink which struggled to contain a pile of dirty dishes. I made myself a coffee and a slice of toast. I switched on Sky News and watched a report on Israeli soldiers wounding Palestinian children in Gaza with live ammunition. My heart sunk at how the so-called civilised countries of the developed world could stand by, and with their lack of condemnation, condone such hideous acts against defenceless children.

I showered and dressed, washed and put away the dishes, and made a list of what I would pack. That morning, I booked my flight to Lesvos.

I looked over my travel documentation and verified again, for the umpteenth time, I had my passport along with my sunglasses, lipstick and keys, safely stored in my handbag. I went around the house confirming I'd closed all the windows, locked all the doors and switched off and unplugged all the appliances that were electrical. Satisfied with my efforts, for a long moment, I gazed around the house that used to feel like home. The familiarity of every room no longer sat comfortably with me. I told myself, I was making this easy for Jamie and when I thought about what he did to me, that's all I needed for the tears to well in my eyes.

Leaving should have felt like a punishment, but strangely, it felt good. I took a deep breath. I could do this, I told myself, reaching for my suitcase and heading out the front door.

I took a tram to the airport. There was no direct flight to Lesvos, so I had arranged to fly to Manchester and get my connecting flight.

In the departure lounge at Manchester, I was conscious of being on my own. The departure lounge was full of families and couples, heading off on their holiday to the sun. I must have looked a lonesome figure and I tortured myself that they would all know I was running away from someone, or something. Of course, I knew this wasn't true, because what happened to me had been so awful, I hadn't been able to tell another soul.

Periodically, I glanced at the information screen, waiting on my gate to be announced, when a man sat down opposite me. I tried to calculate his age, probably mid-thirties. He was well dressed, not the typical attire for a going on a holiday. His short-styled hair suited his cheekbone and the curve of his chin. His copper complexion and deep-set eyes emitted an appeal I had always found eye-catching.

He looked up from his smartphone and smiled. Obviously, I'd been caught observing him. I returned, what was an embarrassed smile, and looked down at my shoes.

'My phone's about to die on me, I knew I should have charged it this morning.'

'I think there's charging points somewhere around here,' I offered.

'There's probably not enough time now, it's my own fault.'

I turned and surveyed the other passengers and then gave an impatient glance at the departure screen.

'Are you off on holiday? Somewhere nice?' he asked.

'I'm going to Lesvos.'

'Me too. I'm going to a family wedding. My parents, they live in Mytilene. Have you been before?'

'No.' I glanced away from him towards the screen. I felt a tenseness in my shoulders. I wondered if he sensed my apprehension, as he looked down at his dead smartphone.

'I'm sorry, you must think I'm being really rude.'

'No. Not at all.'

'I've not been before, this will be my first time. I'm not keen on flying.' I offered this as an apology, in a way, to justify my behaviour, but it wasn't true, and I felt bad about it.

'Did you know it's safer to fly than to cross the road?'

'That's good to know.' I tried to sound convincing.

'I'm Petros, by the way.'

'I'm Grace.'

'I hope you're okay on the flight.'

'I'm sure I will be,' I said, aware that I had to choose my words carefully and that I was getting deeper into the deception I had created. 'Do you work in Manchester?'

'Yes. Not very glamorous though. I'm in management consultancy. And you? That's not an accent from around here.'

'No. I live in Edinburgh.'

'I've always wanted to go there, but never managed it. What is it that you do?'

'I'm a researcher at Edinburgh University.'

'Oh, that sounds interesting. What do you research?'

'That depends on what the university wants me to research.'

'Is that why you're going to Lesvos?'

'No. I'm visiting a friend.' I was aware of a pressure building in my chest. I left unsaid the real reason.

'Does she stay in Mytilene?'

'If I remember correctly, she stays in a place called Molyvos.'

'Ah, it's beautiful there. You'll like it.'

'I hope so.'

He looked up at the screen. 'Gate 12.'

For a second, I'm confused.

'It's just gone up. We're boarding at Gate 12. It's down that way.'

We both stood, feeling awkward. 'Well, since you know where you're going, I'll just follow you.'

We stood together, waiting for our turn to board. Gradually, we neared the two smiling women checking boarding passes and passports.

I wondered if we looked like any ordinary couple. If people assumed, we were. I didn't feel alone anymore, nor was I preoccupied with my own vulnerabilities. I checked the others around me. No one was staring, in fact, they weren't even looking at me. I could feel my body and nerves relax, and the tension in my muscles slipping from me. We were standing so close to each other I could smell his aftershave. I fingered the smooth edges of my passport. This was really happening, I was about to step onto a plane and leave everything behind.

'What seat number are you?' Petros asked.

I checked my boarding pass. '23 B.'
A smile creased his mouth. 'What a coincidence.'
'Why? What seat number are you?'
'22 A.'

During the flight, I learned that Petros was divorced and
had a three-year-old son he saw most weekends. He spoke
about growing up in Lesvos and eventually moving to
Thessalonica on the Greek mainland where he went to
university. He moved to London, working in the city, and
then Manchester, where he met his future wife. His biggest
passion was cooking, and he joked he'd missed his
vocation in life, he'd even considered applying for *Master
Chef* but didn't think he was good enough.

I gave him an edited version of my life's history,
omitting the sordid details of recent events. I wasn't in the
habit of being that open with someone I'd just met.
Whether it was because we were sitting together in the
intimacy of a plane, or I simply just connected with him on
some level, he made me feel like me again. Someone was
interested in me, even if it was just for a short time.

In the baggage hall at Mytilene airport, Petros offered to
buy me something to eat. I was eager to get to Molyvos, but
I was hungry. I'd enjoyed his company on the plane and for
once, I felt relaxed, due to his dreamy nature, which I found
endearing.

He said he knew of a nice little taverna he always went
to when he was visiting his parents. He enthused it served
the best souvlaki in Mytilene; the portions so large, there
was enough for two.

I was concerned I'd have to trail my luggage with me
however, Petros explained he'd hired a car for his stay and
was about to pick it up.

When we arrived at the taverna, it was busy but, once the waiter recognised Petros, with a wide smile, he ushered us to a table in the corner.

Petros was right about the portions; the souvlaki was delicious but too much.

'I can't eat anymore,' I said, wiping the sides of my mouth with a napkin.

'They can box it up and you can take it away with you if you want?'

'Oh, no. I won't be able to eat another thing, today.'

'Would you like a coffee?'

'Yes. And some more water, I think.'

Over coffee, Petros offered to drive me to Molyvos. My first reaction was to decline his offer. The second was to say I'd take a taxi, even though I had no idea how far it was. We made a compromise. In that case, Petros insisted, he would pay for the meal. He was very persistent so, reluctantly, I agreed.

He showed me photographs of his daughter on his smartphone. She was beautiful, with thick natural curls and shining eyes. He said he often thought of moving back to Lesvos, but he needed his daughter more than he needed the island.

We talked about Brexit and the deep schism it had evoked in Britain. Petros likened it to the recent austerity measures in Greece, lamenting that you don't always get what you vote for.

'I don't see what has really changed? Greece is further in debt. We just have more time now to pay it back. The governments broke, people have become poorer, companies are going bankrupt. Everybody owes money to everybody else, and nobody has the money to pay it back.'

'But what about tourism, surely with millions of people visiting every year that must have an impact on the economy?'

'Now, we're way overtaxed in Greece. Did you know small businesses, even the self-employed, pay 75 percent to the state? Young people, especially entrepreneurs, are being hit the most. Why would they want to stay when in countries like Bulgaria, business tax is only ten percent? And you're right, tourism is booming, there's been an incredible push over the past years, but the infrastructure hasn't caught up with it. It needs investments, but where would the money come from?

'Have you heard of the Greek politician, Yanis Varoufakis? Well, he was right when he said, it will take more than tourism to lift the sunken ship from the bottom of the sea.'

Petros excused himself and visited the toilet.

There was something underlying in those exchanges that evoked an undercurrent of strange emotional agitation in me that I couldn't quite figure out. It was a mild transition, a slight irritation that was inextricably linked to a deeper trouble. It was not his fault; poor benevolent Petros, the problem lay with me. I was damaged. It was my struggle.

By now, I knew the warnings: a single word, a noise, a smell was all it needed to set it in motion. My recall of what happened to me, the violation, passed through me relentlessly. I experienced it then, as I had done that day. It went over and over, again and again. The flashback plunged me into an overwhelming sense of shame, it exposed me to a visceral fear, the shadows of my inadequacies falling across me. I felt disconnected and it shook me.

I knew why I'd left Edinburgh, but why was I here in Lesvos? Would it ease my torment? Would a better life come into view? Would it be just somewhere to hide?

I looked down at the table and ran my hand over its surface. I glanced at the toilet door. Just then, a taxi drew up outside. It sparked an urgency about me.

Petros had left his car keys on the table. The hire car was parked opposite the taverna. I picked up the keys, pointed it in the direction of the car and pressed the fob. To my relief, its lights flashed, once, twice. I grabbed my handbag and rushed outside. The sun on my back was hot as I struggled with the suitcase. I cursed its weight and stubbornness, eventually hauling it from the boot.

The taxi driver watched me, uninterested until, dragging my case, I trudged towards him.

The Present

Vasilis' Struggles

Sitting in his garden, the onset of night closes around him.
Vasilis drains the last of his beer and opens another bottle.
It is still, all is quiet. Behind him, bougainvillea scrambles
along the wall of his house; in other places amongst the
garden, it spills like laughter. In the daylight, it projects a
riotous blood red, stark against the stone wall and shine of
the windows.

He tilts his head and gazes at the stars. He can feel a
tension in his neck. He closes his eyes, but he can't hide. A
body floats like wreckage in the sea. He has fought to get
the image out of his mind, it haunts him, his mind is
scarred. Will it ever heal? It recedes from him, for now.

She has Jamie's baby inside her.

Now, he has had time to consider this, the implications
have gradually eaten at him.

It changes everything. Or does it?

He is confused.

He is struggling to accept what she has done.

He is struggling to believe it.

It feels as if she has chosen Jamie over him. Does she
want to keep the baby because it is Jamie's child? This
thought crushes him. And then guilt floods through him.

He sees her face; she beamed with happiness when she
revealed she was keeping the baby.

It was right for her, that's all that matters. What gives
him the right to judge her? How can he possibly have any
understanding of how such a decision is made? It has made
her happy.

And it strikes him that he has never seen her glow with
such certainty, such assuredness. She doesn't need his
approval. She wasn't looking for his approval, just his

understanding, his unequivocal support. And this is what shames him, this is his struggle.

Her decision was instant, it was determined by one simple thing, she wants to be a mother. He told her that having another baby may bring all the pain back again, that she didn't really know how she would react, and she said plainly, it had never gone away.

This has irritated him, it scrapes at him. This feeling unsettles him, and it is made difficult by his enduring desire for her. He is now confronted with the accountability for her happiness. She has put her trust in him, and she needs him to be there for her, whatever that may entail. He feels a little dazed by this prospect, the responsibility of it.

It astonishes him the effect she has had on his life. Her presence has covered such a short span, yet remarkably, he feels he has known her all his life. When he is not with her, he misses her.

'Baba!'

Her voice catches him by surprise. He turns to see Pelagia standing half asleep, rubbing her eyes and Vasilis smiles at the sight of her ruffled hair. 'What are you doing up?'

'I had a bad dream.'

'Come here.' He stretches out his arm and she climbs into his lap, nestling her face into his chest.

'You smell of beer.'

'I'm sorry.'

'That's okay.' She yawns.

'You left me.'

'When? I'd never do that.'

'In my dream. You went out in your boat. It was night time, and it was dark, and you disappeared into the blackness to help the people on the small boats, but you never came back.' She presses herself closer to him.

'It was just a dream. I'm still here.'

She nods. 'I don't want you to go out in your boat again. Please say you won't.'

'I'm staying right here with you.' He holds her tightly.

'Why do adults always say things they don't mean? Why do they lie?'

'I'd never lie to you, Pelagia.'

'Mummy said she loved me. How could she have loved me?'

Vasilis feels uneasy. How can he soothe his daughter with words of reassurance when even he struggles to understand why she walked out of their lives? He stares at the blackness that engulfs the garden. He tries to gather himself and refocus.

'Remember last year when you fell and broke your arm?'

'Yes, it was really sore.'

'Well, I think that's what happened to mummy. Instead of her arm being broken, her mind was broken, so she couldn't be the person she was, the mummy we knew.' He's not sure if he has confused her even more.

She screws up her eyes and Vasilis can tell she is thinking. 'So, that means she will get better just like my arm.'

'I hope so.'

'And then she will come home.' Her voice lifts.

Vasilis sighs. In his eyes, as opposed to his daughter's, his wife is dead to him. He kisses the top of Pelagia's head, he hasn't the heart to deflate her hopefulness.

He feels her breathing becoming deeper and her warm body expels the tension in her limbs as she becomes heavy against him.

Once he has put her back to bed, he removes a piece of paper from deep within the drawer of his desk in his makeshift office and slumps into his chair. He unfolds the paper and reads the words, that for years his eyes have burned into and his mind has absorbed and always, he is left persistently troubled.   Scrawled along its surface, she has written:

I'm sorry. If you can find it in your heart, please forgive me, although I don't deserve it. This decision has made me happy, something of great significance has lifted from me. I know you will hate me. I would hate me. Please don't let that hate pass to Pelagia. If I could, I'd take her with me, but she will be better off with you, at home, safe and secure. I won't be able to offer her these things. That is my only regret. Tell her mummy loves her, and always will.

Vasilis breathes in deeply and folds the piece of paper. He rubs the tension from his eyes. He knows there will never be a relief from the tormenting presence of Drosoula in his thoughts. He has wondered, countless times, if he should destroy the letter? But, each time, he has found it impossible to carry out, and he tells himself, when the time is right and Pelagia is old enough, he will show it to her. She deserves that, at least.

The Present

The Start of Something

'We were both suffering from our own demons, we were in the same boat, as it were, but he was steering it his way, which wasn't mine. That became a problem.'

They are sitting in the garden, it is late. Around them, Vasilis has lit candles whose small flames flicker in the silver beam of the full moon.

'What did you do?' Vasilis asks.

Grace smiles. 'Like I always do. I ignored it for days, and then weeks, months even.'

'Jamie must have done the same?'

'As a couple, by then, we'd both lost our way, our identity. I think what happened to us, it transformed us, but obviously, as it turned out, in different ways. Olivia's death affected me more than it did Jamie. For me, there was no getting over, just getting through.'

'How long were you together?'

'Um, nearly four years. Yes, two months off four years. God, when I think about it, I've had shoes that lasted longer than that.'

Grace wonders if she should speak freely, but then, what if he takes things out of context? I could censor myself, tell him what I want him to know. No. I don't want us to be like that. I want us to be open with each other.

She ponders if Vasilis thinks the same and if so, what will he tell her? 'Does it worry you, you know, the things I've done to Jamie?'

'You did what you had to do at that time. I can't judge you on that. I wasn't there.'

'But I had a choice. It was my free will. I didn't have to send that photograph, or steal his child... what does that make me?'

With deliberate slow movement, Vasilis reaches for her hand. 'Of course, you had a *will*, but the liberal in me won't let me think it was free.'

'What do you mean by that?'

'Well, how can you decide what emotions or desires you have? People don't decide to be happy or sad, to be easy to get on with, or to be anxious. People don't just wake up one morning and decide to be straight or gay. You said you had a choice, and yes, you're right, you made that choice to do those things. My point is this, was it an independent choice?'

'What! What does that mean?'

'You. Me. Everyone's choices are determined by biological, social and personal conditions that we have no control over. Think of it this way. I can decide what to have for lunch, what book I want to read, who I'm attracted to. All these things, in some way, are dependent on my genes, my gender, my background, my nationality and culture. I didn't choose any of these. As a person, I don't think or feel freely. Do you see what I mean?'

'I think so. But, is all that just an intellectual way of excusing what I've done, making it all right, acceptable even?'

'No. For me, it makes sense of what you did. Don't you see that?'

'I want to, but all I can think about is the pain I've caused. I did it because I could, that's the truth of it.'

'You're so frustrating, do you know that?'

'I'm inadequate you mean. I've done terrible things.'

He tightens his fingers around her hand, a sudden anger straightens his back. 'Don't say that. That's not true.'

'It's what you're thinking, isn't it?'

Vasilis sighs. 'I'm thinking how much I love you.'

'You love me? The crazy woman who is capable of crossing a line without even realising it?'

'Of course, I love you.'

'I've hardly been here in Molyvos for five minutes. How can you say you love me?'

'Time isn't important. You can't tell me what I feel.'

'You only know the me you see here, you don't know the other me, the one I struggle with. Life for me has never been a happy ever after. It's never worked out that way, so what makes this any different?'

He is struggling to answer her. *Say something. Say anything.* 'Isn't love enough?'

'You have to know the person you love. How can you say you know me when I feel lost... lost in here?' She prods her temple with a finger. All I seem to do is lose the people I love. It must be in my DNA.'

He reaches out for her. He feels it is the right thing to do. She steps backwards. 'No.'

'I love you, even if you don't feel loved.'

'But is it enough?

'Why would you want to bring all that pain back?'

She bends her head forward. 'I've told you before, it's never gone away.'

He takes another step towards her. She raises a hand half-heartedly. With a finger, he brushes stray strands of hair from her face. He leans into her and kisses her on the mouth. It is soft and papery. He smooths her hair with his hand, and it is enough to know she wants this.

She takes a long breath. 'I've never said I didn't feel loved.'

He pushes open the door and holds it, as she slides passed him. She tries to take in the room which is lit only by the moon, outlining a bed and an ornate wardrobe. She can just make out a dressing table, the feminine touches long disappeared. She hears the door close behind her and feels his breath on her neck.

'Are you sure about this? This is what you want?' His voice is but a whisper.

'If it wasn't, I wouldn't be here.'

As she has anticipated, her words offer him clarity which is recognised by the touch of his mouth on her neck. It slackens the tension in her bones. She moves her head to the side, and he trails his lips along her shoulder. How long has it been since he has made love to his wife in this room? It is a thought she casts from her. She turns to face him and places her hand on his chest. She can feel a warm sensation stirring, a craving she is thankful has not left her.

Vasilis is astonished she is here with him. He holds her face in his hands and peppers her skin in feathered kisses, and then yearning for her, he seeks her open mouth.

Disposing of any sense of modesty, they undress each other with deliberate movements, unhurried and savoured. The unspoken condition between them is trust, they are bound up in their surrender to physical passion, the freedom she allows him, to taste and stroke and kiss, is a confirmation she willingly wants this. He knows what this means to her, he appreciates the enormity of it, and he is relieved because he wants all of her and it is a revelation that she wants this too.

Grace opens her eyes to catch a prism of sunlight spill into the room. She takes in the walls and window, and the furniture that was dark and shapeless the night before, now washed in sudden light and new to her.

She moves and the sheet slides from her exposing their nakedness, the musk of their bodies blending with the warmth of the air around her. Vasilis stirs, his breath on her neck, his arm resting across her stomach. Her mind swings back to their lovemaking and the pleasure of it. He makes her feel secure and wanted, physically weakening the pain and grief which has tormented her recent life. She feels a sensation of being alive, and an unexpected calmness follows it.

She is allowing herself to love again. She turns her head and takes in the features of Vasilis' face, half-submerged in the pillow. She often just listens to the way he speaks, as he unravels a line of thought. She focuses on the texture of his voice, immersing herself in its pace and rhythm, its masculine tone. She is aware of her own feelings, how she savours his voice and how totally absorbed she is, as his words calcify into sense and meaning. She is often amused by the exaggerated gestures that accompany his words.

She wants to lie here, with him, all morning. She is conscious of the short time they have, and she wishes she could suspend its movement and halt the spinning of the earth.

Quite suddenly, she is alerted to faint padding coming from outside the bedroom, bare feet on the floor, and then she can hear movement behind the door, a muffling sound. She grabs the sheet and pulls it up to her chin, holding her breath.

The residue of sleep slides from Pelagia's face as she stares at Grace. Grace digs her elbow into Vasilis' side who groans and croaks a 'Good morning.'

'Vasilis!' Grace urges.

He lifts his head from the pillow and, seeing the panic on Grace's face, he turns towards the opened bedroom door.

'Pelagia, honey. Kalimera.'

'Why is she here? Why is she in your bed, baba?'

'Eh, it was late, so I asked Grace to stay the night.'

'I don't want her in the house.'

Bravely, Pelagia is like a dam, forcing her tears away and Grace feels sympathy, but also respect for the little girl's fortitude.

Grace doesn't have to understand Greek to know the thread of the conversation. Pelagia is upset, bordering on crying and Vasilis is trying to remain calm and in control.

'Why don't you get yourself washed and I'll make us all some breakfast.'

'Tell her to go away.' Pelagia turns, her hair flowing around her shoulders, as she runs down the hallway and into her bedroom, slamming the door behind her. The sound is like a bomb echoing through the hallway, its aftershock slamming into Grace.

'That didn't go too well,' Vasilis says, scratching his head.

'Poor girl. I'd better go.' Grace swings her legs over the side of the bed and sits on the edge of the mattress. The serenity of the last few minutes obliterated, her sense of modesty returns, and she covers herself with the sheet.

'Stay.'

'No, I can't. Not now.'

'Have some breakfast, at least.'

'How can I? I don't want to cause any more upset to Pelagia. I feel bad enough as it is.'

Once she has on her bra and underwear, Grace drops the sheet back onto the bed and hikes her jeans over her legs. Fastening the buttons on her blouse she can feel Vasilis' eyes upon her. 'I'm sorry, but it's better that I go.'

'I'll talk to her. Give her time, she'll come round. I know her. It won't be long until you're her best friend.'

Vasilis stands up and, naked he walks around the side of the bed and stands before her. Grace looks away self-consciously, but also afraid of her own desires. Vasilis pulls her towards him and traces the shape of her breast with a finger.

'Don't go.'

'I have to.'

'Aren't you hungry?'

She smiles. 'That's not the point.'

'I know.' He kisses her then. 'I love you.'

'I know.' She rests her head on his chest. 'What have we started?'

He strokes her hair. 'Something we can't deny.'

Grace raises her face to him and brushes Vasilis' cheek with the back of her hand. She murmurs his name and makes herself walk away.

The Present

Neos

The phone call from Natasha is unexpected, to say the least, as is her request. She wants to meet with Grace, who detects a tension and pressure to her voice.

The day is hot with only a whisper of a breeze when Grace finds the café in Mytilini, on the waterfront. She orders a coffee and water, checks her watch and waits.

She doesn't see Natasha approach her. Once they have embraced, and Natasha is finally sitting opposite her, Grace is relieved that she has come. Natasha lights a cigarette, inhaling deeply. She smiles at Grace; it is forced, and Grace knows it.

'Thanks for coming. I wasn't sure you would.'

Grace smiles. 'Of course, I was coming. I've heard the shopping's good.'

They laugh, and it is a relief of tension. Whatever it is that is troubling Natasha, it seems to subside for a moment.

'Do you want anything to eat?'

'I'll just have a water.'

Grace beckons over the waiter and Natasha orders a bottle of water and takes another long drag on her cigarette.

'Did you get in touch with dad?'

'Yes. I did.'

Natasha purses her lips. 'How was he?'

'Upset. Bewildered. Confused. Do you want me to go on?'

Natasha turns her gaze to the sea.

Grace can see Natasha is not so self-assured as she was when they last met. She watches her expression as she speaks. She can see Natasha's mouth constrict.

'I'm grateful for what you did. It couldn't have been easy for you.'

'No, it wasn't, but your parents had a right to know.' She wonders if Natasha feels guilty?

'Yes. They did and, as I said, I'm grateful.'

'Do you miss them? They certainly miss you.'

There is a tense pause.

'So, Natasha, why am I here?'

Natasha turns her head and looks along the street. Grace follows her gaze. 'He doesn't know I'm here, with you.'

'Who?'

'Neos.'

'The man you live with?'

'Yes.'

'And is that a problem?'

'For him, yes.'

'Why? Why would that be?'

Natasha stubs her cigarette out in an ashtray, and Grace can see the effort of control collapsing in her expression to something more fearful.

'Natasha, is everything all right?'

She sighs heavily. 'No. Not really.'

'What is it then? What's happened?' Grace feels a surge of anguish churning in her stomach.

'Can I stay with you?' Her voice is frightened and urgent.

Suddenly, Grace is scared for Natasha. She can feel the warm caress of sunshine on her forearm and such a sensation feels out of place, a contradiction at a moment such as this. She looks at Natasha's hopeless face. Her eyes are pleading.

'Of course, you can.' Grace lays her hand on Natasha's arm. 'Whatever has happened, don't worry, you're safe now. All right?'

Natasha nods, momentarily calmed by Grace's assurance.

'I've no choice. He's taken my phone now. I'm frightened, really frightened. He wants to keep me locked up in the house all day. He doesn't want me seeing anyone. He has taken my key, but I found a spare one. That's how I'm here, now. He said I don't need anyone, just him. I'm scared Grace, I don't know what he'll do next.'

'We need to get you out of there, now. How far is it?'

'A few streets away.'

'And where is Neos?'

'He visits his mother today, always on a Wednesday at one o'clock. He locked me in the house.'

'How much time do we have?'

She checks her watch. 'Half an hour, maybe less.'

'We need to get your things, we don't have a lot of time. My car is parked not far from here.'

Grace stops the car a few metres from the apartment, her heart pounding. 'You need to be quick.'

She watches as Natasha hurries along the path, puts her key in the lock and disappears through the doorway. Grace takes a deep breath. She checks her rear-view mirror, a side street and scans beyond the door Natasha has just entered.

She sees a man lurking in a doorway, another crossing the street. Nervously, she taps the steering wheel. It hadn't crossed her mind, until now, that she has no idea what Neos looks like.

Five minutes pass and Natasha has still not reappeared.

'Come on, come on,' Grace urges. She starts to have misgivings, *we shouldn't have come here.* Her foot taps the clutch pedal continuously.

After a few further fretful minutes, she can't take the uncertainty any longer.

Standing at the door, Grace breathes deeply to calm the hammering in her chest. She pushes the door with the palm of her hand. Inside it is quiet, not a single sound penetrates the air around her. She finds the silence excruciating. She steps into the hallway and swallows. She is aware her teeth are clenched, and a fine film of perspiration coats her brow. The hallway is an L shape, the light dull. She strains her eyes, waiting for her vision to accommodate this new environment. She inches closer to the corner, one hand on the wall. She must force herself to take a further step.

To her immediate relief, Natasha is sitting on a sofa, her hands clasped in her lap. When Grace tries to read Natasha's face, she has a sudden fear that something is wrong, terribly wrong. She moves into the room, her hands shaking.

'You must be Grace.'

Her heart leaps as if an electric shock has passed through her. She turns to see a man, standing in the corner of the room. He is tall and slim with short hair.

Natasha flinches at the sound of Neos' voice but says nothing.

'Natasha has changed. She is happy here. She has been feeling ill lately, but she is better now. Her head is much clearer.'

Grace looks at Natasha. 'Natasha, come with me. You don't have to stay here.'

'She stays.' There is a menace to his voice.

Natasha says nothing but stares at her feet.

'I would normally offer you a drink of something, tea or coffee, but I'm going to be rude and ask you to leave, Grace.'

'Not without Natasha. I'm not going anywhere.' Grace can hear the voice but doesn't recognise it as her own.

'I can persuade you to go. I'd prefer if you went voluntarily.'

'That's a threat.'

'Only if you want it to be.' He smiles, and it vanishes as quickly as it came.

Then, Natasha lifts her head and tucks a stray hair behind her ear. 'Everything's fine. I'm fine. I'll phone you some time, honest, I will.'

'I don't believe you.'

Neos takes a step towards Grace. 'I want you to leave, now.' His voice is controlled but intimidating.

'Natasha,' Grace says, one last time.

'Go! I'm alright. I'll phone you. I promise.'

Grace is forced to face the fact; although she is frightened for Natasha, she has no idea what to do about it. She has considered going to the police, but the more she thinks about this, what would they do? Where is the evidence that Natasha is being held against her will? Neos can easily convince the police a crime has not been committed, because Grace knows, for whatever reason, when Natasha is in Neos' company, her resolve is weakened. He has a controlling hold on her, one that is dominant and prevailing.

There is a clutch of panic in her stomach.

Leaving Natasha is unbearable, there is a sense of separation about it. She has no doubt Neos would have physically removed her from the house, so, reluctantly, she left.

She drives around Mytilene in a daze, her hands shaking as they grip the steering wheel. She can't get Natasha's face out of her mind. Grace's mind plays her encounter with Neos in a continuous loop. She feels detached from the world around her and dislocated from her own body. Eventually, she heads back home, exhausted.

In the kitchen, Grace pours herself a glass of water. She feels unsteady on her feet and, immediately, she thinks of the new life forming inside her. She slumps into a chair and takes a long drink, the water draining the dry taste in her mouth. She puts her head in her hands and begins to sob.

Suddenly, there is a knock at the door. Grace closes her eyes for a moment, shutting the world out. She wants to stay in the darkness. Nothing happens in the darkness. She becomes untouched. There it is again, louder this time. It pushes her back into the kitchen. She dries her eyes and makes her way down the narrow hall. The light is blinding as she opens the door. She squints her eyes. 'Sofia.'

'Grace, something has happened.'

'What... what is it?'

'There's been a terrible accident.'

The Present

Fragile

The coffin is abnormally small and impoverished. Around a
bleak hole in the ground, Moustafa, the body washer,
stands next to his wife and reads, in a solemn voice, a verse
from the Koran. His words float amongst a handful of
mourners, huddled together, stone-faced, heads bowed.

A woman in a headscarf wails uncontrollably, her head
rests on her husband's shoulder. He supports her with a
cradling arm. He looks broken, his eyes sunken in dark
skeletal sockets, lost, devoid of hope, staring at his feet.
There is only one certainty in his life; around him, death
has followed. It does not discriminate between the young
and the old, the healthy or the sick. It waits in the shadows.

A single rose slips through Grace's fingers, landing on
the coffin. She sobs like a child and leans into Vasilis who
swallows the rock in his throat and shudders to take a
breath.

How can this have happened? It feels like a violation, an
end to innocence. The world is a Godless place. Grace
breathes in tightly. Reluctantly, she knows they will have to
leave. She is weary and tired. Belief and idealism are now
insignificant. She tries to regain her composure and, in
doing so, she looks at Moustafa and thinks he once would
have been handsome in another life.

Vasilis surprises Grace by saying a short prayer and then
indicates they should leave. Grace looks at him with red
eyes and nods, noticing two men hovering by a plane tree,
spades in hand, impatient to finish their task.

They turn to leave. Grace looks at Tarak and his wife
Maya. The intense reality of their grief is crippling, and
Grace's heart shrinks inside her with despair. All Grace can

do is embrace Maya and feel the depletion of the life Maya has hoped for.

Rasha had been playing with the other children when it happened. A group of Afghanistan men had gotten into a disagreement with some Syrians over one of them owing another money regarding cigarettes. At the onset, it became violent. A running battle ensued, hand to hand fighting, knives were the chosen form of weapons, stones and bottles were thrown. Some of the Afghans had catapults and it was a stone from one that struck Rasha's head, as she and the other children tried to run to safety. The stone, travelling like a bullet, killed her instantly.

Once the camp's security and the police finally regained order, without detaining anyone, medics had tried to revive Rasha, but it quickly became apparent their efforts were in vain. This was not the first time such fights had occurred in the camp, but now, fear and unrest swept through the camp like a cyclone.

The news of Rasha's murder was reported by the mass media, bringing to the world's attention the conditions the residents of the camp had to endure daily.

Grace's hope is that Rasha's death will not be in vain, but mobilize international condemnation amongst the other European nations and instil a will to help the Greek government in its time of need.

Grace stands staring at the two cemetery workers, as they shovel earth into the grave. She cannot disentangle herself from the belief that if only she had insisted Rasha stayed with her she wouldn't be dead; Rasha would still have the rest of her life in front of her. She had been convinced by others that it was the right thing to do, it was the way it was done. Children who lost their parents stayed within the camp until a relative was found, or the adoption process took its course. Both options had been unavailable to Grace, she did not meet the criteria. She had believed one thing, that Rasha was safe but, to her cost, it turned out to be another.

She has failed Rasha. Her thoughts and impulses demand that Rasha's life should mean something. She can't be forgotten, abandoned in the corner of a graveyard, as if her life has no meaning, no worth, no value.

She is crying now.

'Grace!' Vasilis prompts, touching her gently on her elbow. 'We should go now.'

Reluctantly, Grace lets Vasilis guide her away from the grave.

'How can this have happened, it feels... it feels like a dream, a nightmare that we'll all wake up from.' Grace leans in against Vasilis as they walk.

He says nothing, and she wonders what he is thinking? He probably just wants to get home and hug Pelagia. She touches her stomach and already she is feeling connected, bonded to the life, the fragile life growing inside her.

Grace closes her eyes and tries to sleep.

Natasha has not been in touch, and she is not answering Grace's text messages. This worries her. Maybe she should return to the house with Vasilis and insist that Natasha returns with her to Molyvos? And then, there is little Pelagia. Grace can understand the girl's mistrust in her. Is she holding on to the possibility that one day, her mother will return, and they can be a family again, and Grace's presence in their lives, somehow, makes this less likely? She can feel the tears fill her eyes.

Rasha, poor Rasha. She had so much to live for. Her life was just beginning. Who knows where it would have taken her? The aspirations she would have had and the dreams she could have made and fulfilled? All of this is gone, brutally ended. People will hear about her as they watch the news in their warm and clean houses. They will say how dreadful it is that a little girl who fled a war that destroyed her home and everything she cherished became an orphan who died in a camp that was meant to shelter and protect her. It is a tragedy they will say and carry on their lives with little care or thought for the others still in that world. This brings upon her a feeling of despair.

Grace sighs heavily, frustrated. She tosses and turns. After a while, the sheet feels like a constraint and she abandons her attempt to find sleep.

She makes a cup of coffee in the small kitchen and steps outside into the perfect solitude of her compact balcony. Grace sits back against the wicker chair and cradles her cup. She stretches her legs and savours the taste of her coffee. Although the lamps illuminate the deserted streets below, Grace can still make out pinpricks of light against the night sky. She has grown accustomed to life in Molyvos and acquired a tranquil routine. She is even trying to converse in the little Greek she knows, up to a point, to the delight of those she speaks to.

Lately, Grace's thoughts have been clouded. But one thread is clear, she decides she will phone Natasha again and, if unsuccessful, she will return to Mytilene tomorrow, and she will not leave until Natasha agrees to accompany her back to Molyvos.

Her determination solidifies into tenacity. She must do something. It matters to her. It's important. She believes this fervently.

Grace has a sudden pang of panic, but then, she assures herself, Vasilis will want to come with her. After she had told him how controlling Neos was with Natasha, Vasilis forcefully expressed his concern, implying Grace should not have gone without him. In retrospect and, considering what had happened, she agreed, he had a point.

She thinks it too late to phone, so she sends Vasilis a text. Grace yawns and the pull of her bed is now irresistible.

The next morning, Grace awakes early, showers and is eating breakfast by seven o'clock. She checks her phone. There is a reply from Vasilis. He will pick her up in his car once he drops Pelagia off at school. She exhales deeply.

The Present

A Plan of Sorts

'Are you sure she will be in the house when we get there?'

'I don't know. If the house is locked, she will be inside. If she's not there, then she'll be with him. I'm sure of that.'

'This Neos, he sounds like he'll get violent if pushed too far.'

'I know. That worries me.'

'Grace, promise me if that does happen, you'll get out of the house and let me deal with him.'

'No! I won't do that. I can't do that.'

'You don't have a choice. Tell me you will, or I'll turn this car around and take you back to Molyvos. I mean it.'

She knows by the look he gives her that he is serious. She sighs and reluctantly agrees. Vasilis' face softens. 'Good.'

He parks the car a few streets away from the house. He reaches into the glove compartment and pulls out an object wrapped in a towel.

'What's that?'

'Don't get worried. It's a gun.'

'What!'

'I know, I know. It was my father's. It's old. It should be in a museum, but I thought it might come in handy. Did you see what I did there? Handy... it's a handgun.'

'How can you joke at a time like this? You can't use that thing.'

'Hopefully, I won't have to. There are no bullets in it anyway. It's real, that's all that matters. It can't shoot him, but I can threaten him with it if I have to.'

'Isn't there a law against this?'

'I don't know. I've never done *this* before.'

'Now that we're here, I'm not sure that just knocking on the door is going to get us in the house.'

'Can we get around the back of the house?'

'I don't know.' She nods towards the gun. 'If you must take that, you'll need to hide it.'

They unfold themselves from the car and walk briskly along the street. They work their way around parked cars and a children's play area to a street leading to the house.

A pulse of trepidation jerks at Grace's throat. Around them, nothing much moves. A disinterested dog sniffs at a clump of burnt grass in the playground, cocks a leg and urinates on the trunk of a tree.

They stop at the corner of the street. A man emerges from a doorway and walks by them. As he passes, he glances at Grace, who thinks he eyes her owlishly. She catches her breath. *Pull yourself together.*

'The front of the house is too open. If he's in there he'll see us approach the house. I think we can get around the back,' Vasilis says, pulling on her arm.

They enter a small lane that takes them to a courtyard. They hear footsteps, spin around and duck into an archway. An old man passes the entrance to the courtyard, oblivious to their presence. They can hear music that sounds like it is coming from a radio. Vasilis' eyes dart from one window to the next. He slides along the wall of the house and tries the door. Unsurprisingly, it's locked. Grace bites her lip. She still can't believe Vasilis has a gun tucked into his jeans and covered by his t-shirt.

An image of Natasha flashes before her. *She must be terrified. What if he has hit her?* She feels a determined sensation enter her. She looks at Vasilis who is grinning to himself.

'What is it?'

He turns to her. 'I think I know how we're going to get in the house.'

The rectangle-shaped window is only twelve inches in height and a foot off the ground. It is being held open by a wedged coaster. Grace removes the coaster and opens the window as far as it will go.

'I think I can squeeze through it.'

Vasilis crouches and peers into the darkness beyond the window.

'What is it?' Grace whispers anxiously.

'It looks like a basement. There's a bit of a drop.'

Grace slides herself, legs first, through the opening. Her back scrapes the wooden frame. Slowly and with effort, she manoeuvres herself further into the room. 'I can't feel the floor.'

'I'll take your hands.' Vasilis grips her hands and lowers Grace. He feels her weight lessen.

'There, I've made it.'

'Find the door.'

The air is dim and musky, and it catches Grace's throat. She stumbles against a table. She climbs several steps and grips the door handle. She takes a deep breath, closes her eyes and applies pressure to the handle. To her relief, the door opens, and a streak of light covers the floor at her feet. Grace tenses as her ears strain, listening for any sound that might alert her.

'Try and open the front door, if you can,' Vasilis says in a hushed voice.

She pokes out her head and steps carefully on the floor tiles, forcing herself, one foot after the other, and makes her way along a narrow hallway to the front door. She scans the area for a key but knows there won't be one. She slips into a room and tries the window; it too is locked. She peers through the window and scans the empty street. Where is Vasilis? His face appears on the other side of the glass, just like in a horror movie and Grace jumps backwards her heart racing. 'Jesus, Vasilis you almost killed me!'

There is something wrong. Why is he so frantic? Vasilis'
voice is inaudible. 'I can't hear you. What's happened?'
But she doesn't need an explanation, it is written all over
his face. She is in impending danger. She thinks for a
moment, he looks vulnerable. Then, Vasilis is waving his
arms like he has suddenly gone mad. Exasperated, he has
gone. Grace presses her palms against the window. She
tries to peer down the street. She turns and shrinks into the
wall. Her knees feel weak and she feels faint. The room is
warm and a wave of nausea breaks over her. Her head
begins to throb. What if Neos is here? She remembers his
voice, it sounds like an incantation inside her head. A hot
panic fills her chest.

She finds herself once more in the hallway. She makes
her way to the door at the top of the small basement. It is
closed. She can't remember closing it. In fact, she knows
she didn't, but someone did. She grips the handle. The door
stays firm, it is stuck fast. Someone has locked it. She can't
get to Vasilis. She feels a heaviness inside her. She is
sweating. She wants to shout out for Vasilis, but fear has
taken her voice. Where is Vasilis? Where is he? Her legs
begin to shake. She feels a strong urge to urinate.

It happens so fast. Grace has made her way to the end of
the hallway when a hand grips her arm and spins her
around. She screams and feels his breath on her neck, as he
pushes her towards the stairs. Grace stumbles. Another
hand pushes on her lower back forcing her to climb the
stairs with difficulty. She is finding it hard to breathe. The
stairs turn to her left and she uses her hand to steady herself
against the wall. At the top of the stairs she is pushed
against a wall, her cheek flush on its surface. She can hear
the rattle of keys, then a turning and a click. Grace is crying
now. He grabs her hair and drags her through the opened
door. Her mind flashes back to her kitchen in Edinburgh,

the searing pain in her head, the fear of what might happen, Jamie pressing down on her.

Grace is thrown, like a toy doll, across the floor. As well as the aching in her scalp, she is aware of the pain in her arm. She lifts herself up on her elbows and finally she can see his face. With his eyes fixed on her, he scratches his unshaven chin. There is the sound of whimpering. Grace is shocked to see Natasha cowering in the corner, reminding her of a frightened animal trapped and snared. At the sight of Natasha, Grace feels like her heart has stopped before it thuds back to life again. She turns, and Neos' eyes are staring fixedly at her.

'I knew you'd come back. I've been waiting for you.'

'What have you done to her?'

'Nothing. She brought this on herself.' He hisses the words with sudden fury.

Grace tries to inch away from him.

'You see, this is how it always ends. They're never strong enough, just weak, insignificant, worthless. Even an insect has more worth.' There is something irrational now, unbalanced, in his voice. 'Although, you are different, Grace. That's how I knew you'd come back.'

'You're wrong.'

'Oh, that would be so disappointing.'

Grace crawls towards Natasha. She wraps an arm around her, and Natasha buries her face into Grace's neck.

'It was you who kept the window open, wasn't it?'

Neos grins.

Though Grace is frightened, she feels disgust and anger towards him. She studies his face. What is he going to do with us?

His eyes are wide and wild looking. 'You were like a little fly caught in my web, and what do spiders do with the little flies they catch?'

She flinches but doesn't answer him, as Natasha tries to bury her head deeper into Grace.

From downstairs there is an unsettling sound of glass smashing. They are silent. Neos cocks his head and his face darkens. Grace and Natasha hold onto each other tightly.

Neos spins round, steps out of the room and locks the door behind him.

Vasilis watches Grace disappear into the darkness of the basement. He calls to her to try and open the door and immediately he regrets letting her go into the house on her own. He looks around him and then gets up from the small window. He hears the basement door close, a click and the sound of a key turn in a lock. Someone has locked the door! Grace is trapped! He had not foreseen this; so preoccupied had he been with entering the house, it had not occurred to him that Grace might be in danger. He runs to a window and presses his face against the glass. He scans what he can make out of the spacious room. She's not there. He moves to another window, another room.

She recoils when Vasilis appears suddenly at the window. He sees he has frightened her, for a second. With vigorous hand gestures, he shouts at Grace, urging her to find a way out. Across her face run successive expressions of astonishment, shock and panic. His heart hammers in his chest. He feels the shape of the gun underneath his shirt and he knows what he must do.

His heart hammers in his chest as he runs to the rear of the house. He picks up a small rock and throws it at a window. The glass shatters into large pieces. He kicks at the segments that are still in place within the frame. As he climbs through, he feels a searing pain in his hand. A piece of glass has lodged itself in his palm. He tenses himself and pulls the projecting fragment from his skin, where immediately, rivulets of blood pump over his palm.

Neos will know he is here. Vasilis feels suddenly vulnerable, exposed, and there is no time to conceal himself, as Neos appears in the doorway, his fists balled. Neos lunges at Vasilis and even though there are eight feet between them, he covers the distance easily to Vasilis' alarm. Neos's shoulder crashes into Vasilis' and pain stabs through his chest as he stumbles backwards with the momentum. He falls like a felled tree, glass crunching around him. A fist pummels his cheekbone. He raises his arm to fend off the blows, but they continue to rain down on him. Somehow, Vasilis manages to land a punch into Neos' stomach, who groans with the impact and doubles over. It's all the distraction Vasilis needs. Neos is momentarily unbalanced, and Vasilis grabs a handful of hair and heaves Neos from him. Vasilis tries to stand, his legs shake, and he slips. Neos grabs Vasilis' leg and pulls it towards him. In his other hand, to Vasilis' alarm, Neos is wielding a knife-shaped shard of glass. Vasilis shuts his eyes and behind them, Grace's face emerges through silver specks of light.

Natasha is biting her lip so hard it is bleeding. Her eyes are squeezed shut and she is trembling. She begins to cry desperately. Grace holds onto her, brushing her fingers through Natasha's hair, as they huddle in the corner of the room.

She knows it is Vasilis who is downstairs and, in this moment, she fears for him more than herself. The locked door has muffled the sounds that emanate from the lower part of the house.

'What's happening, Grace? Who's in the house?'

'A friend. His name is Vasilis and I love him.'

Natasha looks at her. 'Will he get us out of here?'

Grace can feel the desperation in Natasha's look as if it scalds her face. Her voice wavers. 'I hope so.'

Grace adjusts her leg, numb with tingling pins and needles. She cocks her head. 'Listen.'

'I can't hear anything.'

'Something has happened.' Grace is struck with the silence around them and then they hear footsteps on the stairs, spiralling towards them.

Tears are spilling down Natasha's face, which she covers with her hands. Grace clasps her arm around Natasha. She wants to close her eyes, but a strength inside her forces her to stare at the door, as if not to hold the sight of whoever appears would be a weakness, a sign of vulnerability.

Grace drags herself upright. She can't stop thinking that something dreadful has happened to Vasilis. It feels like a nightmare, it is a nightmare, but it is the kind you don't wake up from. Muscle fibres twitch, and an electric current crackles through nerve endings. She holds her breath.

She hears the jangling of keys and footsteps coming closer to the room. Suddenly, the footsteps stop.

Then nothing but silence except the thudding of her heart. She is certain he is still there.

Please be him. God, make it be Vasilis.

A key slides into the lock and the door opens.

She braces herself.

She holds her breath. The air in her lungs escapes in a cry of relief that nearly bends her in half. As he steps into the room, she propels herself against him, calling his name and nearly knocking him off balance. Vasilis gathers her in his arms, her tears against his chest and the scent of her hair leaves him almost hysterical in a release of emotion.

It is him and it is not. She meets his eyes and a sensation not unlike a tremor passes through her.

Then she sees the blood. 'Vasilis you're bleeding!'

'Never mind me, it's not as bad as it looks.'

'Where is he?'

Vasilis raises the gun. 'Still feeling the effects of this, I hope. It might not have any bullets, but if it smacks you in the face, it hurts. We need to get out of here, now!'

The Present

In This Moment This Is What Matters

'How is she?'

'Sleeping.'

'Good. Do you think she will be alright?'

'Eventually.'

'What now?'

'She can stay with me for as long as she likes.'

Vasilis nods in approval.

'I'll phone her dad. I won't tell him what's happened. Telling the truth would be disastrous. I'll just say she's staying with me.'

'That would be wise.'

'At least she's safe, for now. Neos doesn't know where she is.'

'He knows where Natasha works,' Vasilis suggests. 'The camp will be the first place he'll look. Will she go to the police? She should. You do know that?'

'I don't think she has a choice. I'll persuade her if need be.'

Grace raises her hand and puts her finger to his lips. She slides it along his face and around the shallow cut on his neck. 'I'm sorry.'

'What for?'

'Look what's happened to you. He could have killed you.'

'He grazed me, that's all.'

She holds his hand and inspects the small cuts on his palm. 'There could still be glass in there. I'll clean them.' She goes into the kitchen. 'There's a first aid box in the cupboard.'

When she returns, Vasilis is sitting down. She sits beside him and opens the box and inspects its contents. 'Good.

There's some sterile wound dressing, cleaning wipes, bandages and I've got tweezers in the bathroom.' She begins to clean the dried blood. 'You should have gone to the hospital.'

'It was more important to bring Natasha here.'

As Grace gently removes pieces of small glass from his hand, Vasilis looks at her intently. She lifts her head from her work. 'What?'

'You would have made a good nurse.'

'You're obviously delirious.' She inserts the tweezers into a cut and Vasilis flinches. 'Sorry.'

Once all the glass is removed and the wounds clean, she dresses his hand with a bandage.

'There. How does that feel?'

'Much better, thank you.'

She runs the tip of a finger lightly over the bandage. 'No. It's me who should be thanking you. If it wasn't for you, Natasha wouldn't be here.'

Vasilis moves a curtain of hair from her face. Grace moves her face to the side, and he brushes her neck with his lips. He can smell her hair, the scent of her skin. He slowly laces his fingers around her neck. She turns her head and he pulls her mouth towards him. She is so close, he gazes into her eyes, transfixed. He can feel his love for her run through him like the rapids of a torrential river. Eagerly he kisses her.

'I love you.'

'I know.'

'You are the most important thing in my world. I wouldn't know what I would have done if anything had happened to you.' Her eyes search his. 'Sometimes, I feel I've been cursed, but meeting you has lifted it.' She hesitates. 'Does that sound too weird?'

'Stop talking.' He leans into her and she feels his breath on her skin. He kisses her throat and is astonished at how profound the feeling of his onrushing desire is.

Her breath comes unevenly, her mind disarrayed as she thinks of Natasha in the other room.

'Not here.'

He takes her hand. 'The bedroom?'

She nods, and with this gesture, he has her consent. It is all the encouragement he needs, as he holds her hand, she makes no attempt to release it and in silence, they move towards the bedroom.

Grace goes over to the window and closes the shutters, extinguishing the brightness of the day and blunting the sharp details of furniture, as if a veil has just passed across their eyes.

She embraces him, circling his neck with her arms. She pulls his mouth to her lips and feels his hands fan over her back and down her spine. He fumbles with the buttons on the back of her dress and in hushed unison, they remove each other's clothes.

They lie back on the bed, sliding against each other. He rests his cheek on the flat of her stomach and traces the small white scarring across her skin. He adjusts himself and begins to kiss with deliberate slow motions her inner thigh, touching with the tip of his tongue a cluster of freckles. A mild panic forces her modesty to summon unwanted images of her imperfections, the spare flesh on her waist and the stubborn but slight roundness of her belly. Nevertheless, knowing what he can see, she does not feel embarrassed, such feelings she has of herself are now erased, her insecurities no longer matter. In this moment, there is only what is between them, now. Love? Passion? This is what matters, everything else has devalued.

He traces his fingers over that most sensitive part of her, and her breathing quickens in a flame of indulgence.

The Present

Going Home

'Am I really here? Did it really happen?' Natasha is standing in the doorway of the room she has slept in. Her head feels tight like a twisting knot, as the reality of the situation hits her.

'You're safe now.' Grace assures her.

'Are you okay about me being here?'

'Of course. It's nice to have the company. Did you sleep well?'

Natasha sits beside Grace. 'I did, for the first time in ages. How long have I slept?'

'A few hours. Would you like a shower?'

'I'd love one.'

'I put a fresh towel in your room.'

'Thank you.' She rubs the side of her head. 'I've no real collection of the past few days, how strange is that?'

'The mind has ways of protecting itself.'

'I suppose.' Natasha says, unconvincingly.

'Did he...' Grace pauses and clears her throat. 'I mean...' She runs her fingers through her hair and looks down.

Natasha smiles vaguely. 'No. He didn't.'

'Oh. That's a relief.'

'I keep seeing his face. It's like my brain's stuck on pause.' Natasha stands and walks to the window, looking down into the street below. She sighs. She can hardly believe what has happened to her. 'I can barely remember how it feels to laugh, to be happy, to be able to smile without wearing a mask and pretending. It would feel extraordinary.'

'Are you sure you're okay? We can eat here. I'll make you something. It's no trouble, honest.'

'It'll be good to get out and walk. I just want to feel… normal again.'

This expression unnerves Grace. It is connected to her own life and the choices she's made. *Normal again, there is no normal. She'll learn that, but for now, I won't disturb the state of her ignorance. What she will discover is, understanding more about herself, who she has become.'*

'I've made a decision, Grace.'

'A good one, I hope.'

'I think you'll agree with it. I'm going home, back to see mum and dad.'

Grace nods in agreement. 'They'll be so relieved. I think it's the right thing to do.'

'I need to get as far away from Neos as I can.'

'Did you tell him where I lived?'

'No. He won't know where I am. Not yet, anyway.'

'When will you go?'

'I'll check the flights, but if I can, I'll go tomorrow.'

'So soon.'

'I know. If it wasn't for you and Vasilis, I don't know what would have happened to me. I owe you my life. That's why I must go. I don't want to put you in any danger, and anyway, I've got a lot of making up to do. I need to see mum and dad… and make things right between us.'

'Have you been in touch with them?'

'Not yet, but I'll phone them.'

'You seem hesitant.'

'What if they don't want to see me? It's possible, after what I've put them through.'

'Of course, they'll want to see you. They'll be ecstatic. You're their daughter and nothing you've done is going to change that.'

'Are you sure? I mean, I wouldn't blame them if they hated me.'

'Believe me, that's not going to happen.'

'I wish I had your confidence.'

Grace smiles. 'You'll become the daughter you're meant to be.'

'Are you sure you don't mind me being here? I could go to a hotel.'

Grace shakes her head. 'Don't be silly. You can stay as long as you like, even if you decide not to go home. Which I hope you don't.' Grace raises her eyebrows.

'I won't. The more we talk about it, it feels right. The prospect is making me excited.' Natasha moves across the room and sits back down. 'Is this your own place?' She asks curiously.

'It's a friend's apartment. She's letting me stay awhile.'

'A nice friend to have.'

'Yes. She is.' Grace feels a growing pressure in her heart and inhales tightly.

'I can't believe how hungry I am.'

'I could make you something to eat, or we could go out if you want? It's up to you. Only if you're up for it?'

Natasha thinks for a moment and before the certainty deserts her says, 'I'd like to go out after I've showered.'

Grace smiles. 'I know the perfect place.'

The Present

Accusations and Honesty

The next morning, Grace makes breakfast for two, a departure from her normal routine and it is a reminder that recent events have turned her world on its head. She makes coffee and toast, sets the table with milk, sugar, Sofia's home-made jam, a selection of cheeses and a jug of orange. Once she has finished, she observes her work and wonders if Natasha would prefer eating on the balcony instead. Grace can hear water running, a wardrobe door opening and the soft thud of feet on the floor. It occurs to her that such morning activity is unfamiliar, it's a novelty for her to hear another's physical presence in this space she regards as home. It is an odd mixture of welcoming the companionship and not quite being ready to let go of the thread that connects her to the life she has made for herself in this apartment she now has an affection for, a contentment that each day brings. Am I ready to share it? She had no idea she would feel like this. She feels a weight of anguish and uncertainty and then she is agitated with herself for even thinking like this. Soon, Natasha will be going home within the next day or two. Grace feels ashamed of herself. Natasha needs her, and Grace has a personal and moral obligation towards her that she must carry out.

'Something smells nice.'

Grace looks up. 'Good Morning, Natasha. It's just some toast.'

'I love the smell of toast in the morning, don't you? Although, I think it smells much better when someone else has made it.'

'You're probably right.'

Natasha smiles and sits at the table. Grace joins her and pours them both a coffee.

'I really enjoyed last night. It's been quite some time since I had an evening out. I need to tell Vasilis how good the food is at his place.'

'You did, several times.'

'Oh! I did have a bit to drink, didn't I? More than I usually do.'

'Vasilis enjoyed your company.'

'So, I gave a good impression of myself?'

Grace smiles. 'You did.'

'Thank God for that.'

'Try the jam, it's home-made.'

'I didn't know you made jam.' She looks at Grace quizzically.

'Oh no! I don't. It's a friend of a friend who makes it. I'm addicted to the stuff. Make sure you put a lot of it on your toast. I've got another four jars in the cupboard.'

'I couldn't help notice… you know, you and Vasilis, you're suited to each other, there's a… certain chemistry there. Am I right?'

Grace nods.

'I knew it. You're seeing him. So, he's obviously not married, or is he?'

'He is.'

'Really! Grace. I never thought you'd have an affair with a married man.'

'Really?'

'Well, yes.'

'Why not?'

'I don't know. I just never had you down as that sort of woman, I suppose.'

'I'm not, really.'

'You're not?'

'It's complicated, I suppose.'

'How?'

'Vasilis' wife left him. She just walked out and never came back.'

'But she has a daughter.'

'I know. He's never heard a thing from her since that day.'

'So, technically he's still married.'

'Yes. I suppose he is.'

'Poor man. For all he knows, she could be dead. I take it the police knew?'

'He had to report her missing. She must have left Lesvos. I'm sure someone would have seen her otherwise. Anyway, how are you this morning?'

'I'm fine.'

'Are you sure? You've been through a lot.'

Natasha pulls her hand through her hair. 'I'm free of him now, both physically and mentally.'

Grace looks interrogatory at her. 'You should see someone, a doctor maybe.'

'You mean a psychologist or counsellor. I don't need that.'

'It would help. At least give it some thought.'

'I won't let the bastard win. I want to punish him. I want him to suffer.'

'It's not a sign of weakness, in fact, it's healthy.'

'What would you know about it, Grace? How could you possibly know?' Natasha rebukes her, more forcefully than she intends.

Natasha's accusations provoke an unguarded response. 'That it could get worse... the feelings, the anxiety, the pain, the loneliness, the blaming yourself, the loathing. Do you want me to go on?' She can feel the pull of that world dragging her back.

Natasha gazes at her, and her jaw drops. She appears horrified, as her hand covers her mouth. 'I'm sorry. I didn't know.'

'We don't need each other's sympathy, it's irrelevant.' She surprises herself with the harshness of her voice.

'Would you tell me about it?'

Grace hesitates, but the temptation is too strong. As she talks, it occurs to her, she still carries the weight of what happened and, when she feels the emotions swell up, she recognises the ache that still lurks in the shadows of her mind.

Natasha is shocked by Grace's discarded discretion. Tears begin to fill Natasha's eyes. When Grace is finished there is a long silence. Natasha is looking down into her lap, her hands clasped together so tightly that her knuckles are white. 'I hope I can become as strong as you.'

'Fortunately, my outward appearance doesn't reflect what's going on inside me. I'm not that strong. Just promise me, when you get back home, you'll see your GP.'

Natasha nods her head. She takes a drink of coffee and composes herself. 'I've booked a flight.'

'That was quick. When do you go?'

'Today. The only one I could get was to Athens, then to London. I've not told mum and dad yet. I want to surprise them.'

'You'll certainly do that. What time is your flight?'

'Five o'clock.'

'Are you sure you want to go so soon?'

'I have to. I need to get as far from Neos as I can and anyway, it's time I put things right between mum and dad.'

Natasha reaches over the table and holds Grace's hand. 'I can never thank you and Vasilis enough.'

'Just do the right thing.'

'I intend to. I wish I'd met you sooner,' says Natasha regretfully. 'We'd have made good friends.'

'There's nothing stopping us staying in touch. In fact, I'd like that,' Grace says, encouragingly.

Natasha's face brightens, as though Grace's words have fanned the dying embers of a fire. 'I would too.'

Grace drives Natasha to the airport and they say their farewells through tears and promises to meet up again.

Even then, Natasha reveals she still feels Neos eyes on her. Grace assures her, given time, this will fade, and her voice betrays her personal experience that this is not entirely true.

Grace watches Natasha disappear into the airport and gives her one final wave.

On the drive to Molyvos, Grace steers the car into a small clearing by the side of the road. She gets out and stands, staring at the sea. In the distance, she can see the unmistakable shape of a cruise ship.

Grace shuts her eyes for a moment. She cannot regret what has passed between them, even if she wants to. She cannot shut off her feelings for Vasilis. She has confronted the complexities of her past and with this, she has found independence, a confidence that has matured and swelled inside her. Yet, a strange sense of guilt momentarily constricts her breathing.

When she thinks of Vasilis and what has happened between them, she wonders what is probable and what she dares imagine is possible with the time they have left.

An ache inside her intensifies. Will she ever be able to submit to it? She shivers at the entirety of Vasilis' trust in her, she feels undeserving of it, especially for what she is about to do.

The Past

Retribution

From the moment I walked into the upstairs apartment, I was suffused in a warm glow that filled my chest. It had Monica's touch and influence. The furniture was modern, but classy, with a minimalist feel. It was simple, but it appealed to me. I had an image in my mind of what it would look like, but it was smaller than I'd anticipated, and I realised that was its charm. It was compact, bright and clean. I wandered from room to room, inspecting the contents in the kitchen cupboards, tracing my hand along the sheets of the bed, before trying out the mattress that wasn't too soft or too hard, just as I liked it. There was another bedroom, smaller than the first with just a single bed and wardrobe. To my surprise, in the bathroom, I found a bath, as well as a shower and fluffy white towels, draped over a railing. In the living room, I opened the shutters and light streamed in. I walked out onto the balcony, with just enough room for a table and two chairs and I marvelled at the view. I could hardly take my eyes from the sun glistening off rooftops, capping stone buildings that sloped towards the sea. I craned my head and to my right, I noticed a harbour, bordered by restaurants, where tables spilt onto cobbled paving. I wondered how it would look and sound at night. The sea had an iridescent turquoise sheen, a sight I would always remember and marvel at.

If it was at all possible, I thought I could be genuinely happy here. I inhaled the air around me and imagined it purifying my lungs. Mostly, I felt an overpowering relief that I'd arrived.

I spent the first few days getting to know the geography of the streets and lanes. Shopfronts and doorways became familiar and recognisable, landmarks that solidified the mental map I held in my mind. I started to see the same faces, acknowledge the occasional greeting and took coffee in the same cafe. Once I found a good coffee, I stuck with it.

I met Monica for lunch. I knew she was looking out for me; even in Lesvos, her motherly instinct was like a blanket she wrapped around me. I was grateful. I could understand her concern. She had been shredded with worry and she told me she was overwhelmed with relief that I was finally with her. She promised me she wouldn't turn up at my door unannounced. She wanted me to recover, become myself again and, to do so, I needed space and time, and that was what she was giving me.

I wondered what she meant by, *recover* and I thought of the phrase, 'recovering alcoholic' where the assumption is you are only one drink away from relapse. Would I always be damaged? I couldn't imagine how that would feel. It scared me, it was unimaginable.

No one really knew why I had to leave Edinburgh. I banished myself. In the end, I had no choice. I wasn't breaking free, it was an abandonment, that was all it was. I was walking away from the past, but it would always be there, waiting for me.

The more I got to know my way around and my eyes became accustomed to the nuances of buildings, shop fronts, houses and each winding lane, it seemed I had been in Molyvos before. I hadn't, of course. Maybe, this is just the mind's way of adapting to new environments and experiences? On some level, it helped. Mostly, during the day, Jamie was kept perfectly intact to the back of my mind. Jayne, on the other hand...

One morning, as I sat eating breakfast on the balcony, an incredible feeling of nauseating guilt swept over me. I asked myself, how do I live with it? How do I live with the guilt? It was all a mistake, I placated myself, like a motherly hug absolving my sin. But then, pressing its way through my guilt, arose another emotion… shame.

Many times, I wanted the memory of it to evaporate like steam, but the narrative persisted, and I can still recall the damp smell of rain rising from her clothes.

When I opened the front door and saw her standing there, a heaviness began to drag inside me. I think it was because I wasn't invisible to her anymore.

My smile must have faded, and I almost felt sorry for her. It had been raining and her hair seemed glued to her head, a limp umbrella dangled from her hand, bent and broken by the wind. Rain dripped from the end of her nose.

As she spoke, she looked at the ground, as if speaking to her sodden shoes. 'We need to speak.'

'Come in.'

She crossed the threshold and followed me as I walked into the kitchen. She stood there, shaking her arms free of her coat. I offered my hand. 'I'll hang it up if you like and let it dry.'

I went and fetched a towel. When I returned, Jayne was sitting at the kitchen table, one leg crossed over the other. I glanced at the floor. Just a foot away from her, I had lain on my back, humiliated, while Jamie rolled off me. My mind objected and resisted, and I pushed the image from me.

We sat opposite each other, a long note of silence between us. Jayne's skin looked painfully white.

'This is… unexpected and a bit weird. Does Jamie know you're here?'

Jayne shook her head. 'No. I don't need his permission.'

'I didn't mean it like that.' I was becoming increasingly nervous.

'I know you didn't.'

'Why are you here?'

'You might not believe me, but I admire you. If I was in your position, I'm not sure I could've done what you did, in fact, I know I couldn't. I understand why you did it.'

For a moment, I was confused. What did, *it* mean? There could be several *its*.

'In a funny kind of way, I should be thanking you.'

'Thanking me?'

'Yes. I've left him. You see, Grace, you opened my eyes to the man he is. God, he fucked you, here, in this house of all places. Did you do it on purpose? Did you plan it, so that you could trap him?'

'You mean the photograph I sent? No. I just took advantage of the situation. I realised I was being used. I didn't know what I was going to do with it, well, not at the time, anyway. That came later. I'm not proud of myself that I slept with him. I suppose I was vulnerable in a way and he took advantage of that.'

'So, you absolved yourself. That would make it easier, I suppose.'

At the time, I thought, *absolve* was a peculiar word to use.

It made it easier to hate them both. I believed they got what they deserved. But she was sitting in front of me and I could see the devastation I'd caused, her blue eyes, the thick, dark lashes, strained and troubled. I was still trying to work out if she knew it was me who stole her child, or that Jamie had threatened me with a knife and raped me. If she did, she was not letting on. Was she shielding what she knew in the hope that I would disclose it?

'I've always wondered how it happened… you and him.'

'We met at work. I had just started, and Jamie was responsible for my induction. We fell in love.'

Four simple words that drove a knife through me. They created a tremor in the air, a friction that quaked between us.

'Before or after Olivia?'

Jayne rubbed her temple, she drew a long breath. 'Does it matter?'

'To me, yes, it matters. I need to know. After all, you knew about me, I didn't know about you.'

'We started seeing each other before the baby...'

'When?'

'I can't remember. A few months, perhaps.' She looked away and I thought I saw a flicker of embarrassment; a slight flush rose on her face.

Had I driven Jamie from me? Had I excluded him with my grief? Had I not been enough? No. that's no excuse. I couldn't accept that. Even when I was pregnant, I remembered him being distracted, sometimes stiffening when I touched him. He said, at the time, it was the pressure of work, he felt stressed. I grew cold just thinking about it.

'I suppose that makes us even, we both fucked him without the other knowing.'

I was taken aback by the abruptness of her voice and then I contemplated her rationale. It was an infuriating fact that said more about Jamie than it did about Jayne and me. I wanted to feel angry towards her, but there was no rage inside me, maybe a slight irritation, but that was all.

I tilted my head to the ceiling. We had more in common than we knew. I felt stifled sitting in the chair. I stood up and stared out of the window, at my tired and overgrown garden. 'Are you staying in the house, or is he?'

'I'm staying at my mother's, for now. There's more than enough room for us all. I think she's enjoying having us around, though she'd never admit it. She's always been the independent type.'

I tried to remember those days before Olivia was born. When did Jamie go out? Where did he say he was going?

I turned and looked at her. 'When did you see him? Where did you go?'

'It doesn't matter, now, does it?'

'I need to know.' For the first time, my voice was raised. Jayne flinched. She reminded me of a timid bird, trapped in a cage.

'Sometimes, after work. We'd go for a drink, or we'd go back to my place. I'm sorry... so sorry. You must hate me.'

I could feel a muscle twitch on my face. This time, something hardened inside me. I could feel the whole force of a rage that swelled at the thought of their deception. Not only was he unfaithful to me, even worse, and uncomprehendingly, he betrayed his own flesh and blood, yet to be born.

'I've stopped blaming you. I want us to forgive each other. Any wrong you've done me and what I've done to you. We can't go back and change the beginning, but we can start from where we are today to change the ending.' Jayne's voice was pleading and vulnerable

She didn't know. She really didn't know. Jamie hadn't told her. He lied to me. He had used me all along. She had no idea it was me who stole her child.

He raped me. I wanted to scream at her. He put a knife to my throat. The image appeared, like electricity crackling in my mind.

I breathed deeply. There was a look behind her eyes I connected with. She was a victim, just as much as I was. I was overcome by a climactic rush of attachment. I heaved my shoulders straight and felt grateful to her. There was no need for retribution. She had offered me a truce between us, the least I could do was to offer minor reassurance. I had a sudden rush that this was the right thing to do. Sometimes, the truth is better left unsaid, its complications outweighing its benefits. I managed to find it in me, and with elaborate care, I persuaded her I too, forgave her. I was surprised to hear myself say it.

Jayne stood up, no doubt encouraged by my words. 'I'm so relieved, Grace. This is the right thing to do. It's the right way. It is. Maybe, after this has all settled, we can become friends. I'd like that. Wouldn't you?'

It was not the response I'd anticipated. I shifted my weight, fearing she was going to embrace me, such was her enthusiasm. And then it came out. A spontaneous impulse that shattered her expression.

'He raped me. He held a knife to my throat and raped me. I was nothing to him.' I raised my hand, my palm held towards her, fending her off. Jayne opened her mouth and then closed it. I saw it, in a second, spread over her face. She could now see Jamie for what he was. And had been.

The Present

The Dragonfly

She sees the white hat first, and then the man standing outside a shop speaking to a woman. He is holding a decorative plate and they are deep in discussion. As she nears them, they disappear into the shop. A moment later, Peter reappears.

'Peter, Hello. How are you?'

'Grace, my dear. I haven't seen you in a while.' He tilts his hat.

'I've been… busy.'

'We've missed you at the cleanups on the beach.'

'How's it going?'

'Very successful. And we've branched out. Diversified. I've taken our model around the island; most of the beaches are now being cleaned.'

'I heard about that. That's great, Peter. It really is.'

'And you, are you well?'

She hesitates. 'I'm fine. And you?'

'I'm seeing the doctor for a sensitive issue.'

'Oh! Nothing serious I hope?'

'Not exactly. Haemorrhoids. Painful buggers. Some days, I can hardly sit down. It's better if I walk.'

'It sounds nasty.'

'I wouldn't wish them on my worst enemy.'

'What's that you've been buying?'

'I've had my eye on this for ages. It's a decorative plate to go on my wall. Similar to these ones.' He points to a row.

She stares at them, not really taking them in. 'Nice. I wouldn't mind a few for the apartment.'

'Why don't you then?'

Her throat tightens. She tries to formulate an answer.

'Are you sure everything is all right dear?'

'No. Not really.' She puts out her hand to steady herself and Peter grabs it.

'I think we need to get you somewhere you can sit down.'

They sit on a spacious veranda that overlooks roofs and out to the sea. Grace can see the harbour where several boats are berthed alongside the restaurants that hug the quayside.

Peter orders a bottle of water for Grace and a coffee for himself.

'Do you want anything to eat?'

'No. Thank you.' Grace runs her fingers through her hair.

'Are you ill?'

'No. I wouldn't call it being ill.'

Peter puts his hand on hers. 'What then? Do you want to talk about it?'

The waiter brings their drinks and Grace eagerly drinks from the bottle. The sun is still high and aches with heat. The waiter leans over and hoists the umbrella in the middle of their table until it is fully expanded and covers them in its shade. Grace can smell a smoky scent in the air. Surprisingly, they are the only people seated outside. It will make it easier for Grace to talk. And she does. This time, she tells Peter everything. There are moments when she pauses, collects herself and takes a deep breath before starting again. She is sure Peter will understand. When she has finally finished, her bottle of water is empty.

Peter nods towards the bottle. 'Would you like another one?'

She shakes her head.

Peter scratches his neck. As well as his concern, he feels awe at her composure. She has put her trust in him, and he feels it as a great responsibility, his duty even, to honour that faith she has consigned in him.

'My word, my dear. You have been through so much in your short life. I almost find it beyond imagination. You're like the dragonfly.'

'The what?'

'The dragonfly. In almost every part of the world, it symbolizes change and transformation. Change, such as self-realisation and emotional maturity, and in some cultures, it signifies an understanding of a deeper meaning of life.'

'How do you know all this?'

'It was an interest of mine, years ago, I studied mythology.'

Grace laughs. 'So, you think I'm a dragonfly?'

'I think you, my dear, have lived through experiences that don't touch many lives and the important thing is, who you have become because of it. And even in the short time I've known you, I've seen you absorb the elements of a new life, that has made you the person you are now. It's a transformation that is enviable.

'We all need to live in the moment without regrets and live life to the full. Look at you now, you are becoming aware of who you are, what you want and what you don't want.

'You are discovering what you are capable of by getting rid of the things that limit your growth and ability to change. You are uncovering the real you and in doing so, removing the doubts you have about your sense of identity.

'The dragonfly is a symbol of happiness, a new beginning; it means hope, it means embracing change and, most importantly, being able to love. I've seen all of these in you, my dear.' Peter shrugs opened palm. 'So, yes, you are a dragonfly.'

'I love the way you think, Peter. I could never have put it like that.'

'Ah, finally evidence that all that money my parents spent on sending me off to boarding school wasn't wasted.' There is a glint in his eye.

Grace smiles at him. 'I'm not too keen on your sense of humour, though.'

They both laugh, and Grace feels a simple elation and she is grateful for it.

'So, my dear, what now? You're carrying the burden that you can't give birth to your baby here in Lesvos. At some point, you will have to return to Edinburgh.'

'I know, I can't stay. I need to take the test again. I've no choice. I must give this baby the chance I gave Olivia.'

'You haven't told Vasilis yet, have you?'

'No. But I will. What was it you said…? About having the ability to live life without any regrets. Well, this dragonfly still has a few.'

The Present

The Telling Time

She has been dreading this.

It has kept her awake most of the night, tossing and turning, her legs tangled in the sheet, the heat in the room oppressive. It hasn't been the ideal way to prepare herself, to summon the courage she knows she will need. It is what it is, and she can't change that. If there was another option, which she is sure there isn't, it has eluded her.

As she walks the cobbled lane, overhead she notes how striking the vines are against the sky's deep hue of blue. It has been her favoured colour for as long as she can remember often filling her with a sensation of great warmth. This doesn't transpire today, for today is different. Even the dozing cats can't transform her mood.

An image comes to her.

She can feel the tender curl of his fingers, the soft touch of his lips, his breath warm in her ears, the rapturous sensation of his gentleness, the soft intrusion of his tongue, that begins the melting in her stomach and the arousal burning between her legs. She runs her fingers up and down his spine, recalling the subtle tremor in his body and the realisation of blissful abandonment.

She stops walking and leans her back against the stone wall of a shop front.

She will not allow herself to believe this is not necessary, but still, she hesitates. She does not have the luxury of indecision. Even in the growing heat of the morning, she feels chilled. She finds herself wild with panic. She can't protect him from this and, at that thought, her throat tightens. Instinctively, she knows she cannot endure another day of this, and she can feel it begin to swallow her.

She winds her way down the lanes, replying to the occasional, '*Kalimera,*' that is offered by a passer-by or familiar face. One of these is an old woman who always sits outside her daughter's shop. She often smiles as Grace passes, displaying a wide gap in her teeth. Grace wonders how many times she has passed this way wearing an expression of pleasure and contentment. Today, she can feel the old woman's scrutiny and she is conscious of how she must look, her face branded with her pain.

She is amazed by the love she feels for him and this makes the disloyalty even more intense. She draws in a much-needed long breath.

She observes him, as he drinks his coffee. She can feel her arms and legs grow tense. Impulsively, she reaches over the table and takes his hand. 'Let's go for a walk, along the beach.'

Her bare feet sink into the wet sand and she can feel it squish between her toes. A timid wave brushes her feet just above the bone of her ankle.

'Are you alright? You've been very quiet.'

She shrugs. She doesn't want to answer him, but she can no longer prolong this. 'I thought this was going to be complicated, but really, it's not.' She turns towards the sea.

'When I told you about Olivia, I wanted to tell you then, but couldn't. You see, I need to go back home.' She pauses, only slightly and not long enough to give him time to respond. 'Remember, I told you about the test, the one we took before Olivia was born and we found out about Patau's syndrome?'

He nods.

'I need to go back to Edinburgh. I need to know.'

'But why? You can get scanned at the hospital here.'

'That's not the point. If my baby has Patau's syndrome, I can't give birth to her in Lesvos. I need to be home.'

'We're not a third world country, Grace.'

'You don't get it, Vasilis. It's not about that. I might not go the full term, my baby may die in labour or, even if I give birth and it is alive, the chances of it living are...'

'I will be here for you. You won't be alone.'

Grace feels suddenly fearful. 'I know you would, but I can't stay.'

'Then I will come with you. You will need me.'

'Pelagia will need you more.'

'You can't go.'

'I have to.'

'When?'

'As quickly as possible.' She turns from him, back to the sea.

'When?'

'Tomorrow.'

He sighs, and she can hear the frustration behind it.

'This is not easy for me, Vasilis. Do you think I would have chosen this? This is not what I want; it's what I have to do.'

'That day, at the hospital, you asked me to help you walk through this. Do you remember?'

She nods.

'You knew then, didn't you?'

'I wanted you to understand. I needed you to. Just like I do now.'

'You had no intention of staying. You led me on. I thought we... had a future.'

'We still do.'

'You lied to me.'

'It wasn't like that. It's not like that.'

'How do you think I felt, knowing what had happened? You were carrying his child. I fought with that, so much, but I was able to push it from me, for you, for what I felt for you, and now, you are throwing it in my face.'

'Vasilis! Why are you being like this? I want to stay. I want to be with you. But I can't. This is not what I want either.'

'Pelagia comes first, she always will. I will live my life as I always have done.'

She screws her eyes shut. Her head begins to ache. When she opens her eyes, she reaches for him. Vasilis draws away from her instantly. Her breath comes in quick short bursts and she cries out, 'I love you. Please don't do this.'

'How is this love? How can love hurt so much? If you loved me, you wouldn't be leaving. We could go through this together. I would have given you all that I could. I was prepared to be there for you. To suffer with you if I had to. I would have absorbed your pain, your grief. That is what love is. Not this. Not leaving.'

'You're being irrational, you're not thinking. You're hurt. I get that. I still need you, Vasilis. You can't give up on us.'

'One of us already has. What will I tell Pelagia? She is just beginning to accept you. Do you know how hard that has been for her? For me?'

He turns and walks away.

'Where are you going?'

'I don't know. I don't know anything anymore.'

Grace falls to her knees. The sand is hot on her skin. Her chest heaves and it feels like her heart has been ripped from her. She can hardly move, scarcely breathing. She feels she has lost the feeling in her arms and legs. Her hair tumbles around her face. She begins to sob, and her nose runs.

Sofia hands Grace a glass. 'Here, take this.'

Grace is thirsty and gulps the water until there is almost none left.

Sofia flips the 'Open' sign on the back of the door to 'Closed' and turns the key. 'Let's go through to the back of the shop.'

Grace follows her and sits on a chair next to a table. Grace can see the room is obviously used as a storeroom for Sofia's shop and as a small office. There is no window, so Sofia flicks a light switch and waits until Grace composes herself. 'Do you want to talk about it?'

Above them, the strip light hums. 'I must look a mess.' Grace's eyes are red and puffy, and Vasilis' voice swims in her head. She finishes the remnants of water in her glass.

'Would you like another one?'

'No. I'm fine. Thanks. I didn't mean to barge in like that, I'm sorry.'

'Don't worry, but I think old Mrs Kafatos almost had a heart attack. She couldn't get out of the shop quick enough. By now, half of her friends will know.'

'Was I that bad?'

'You did me a favour, really.' Sofia says with a grimace. 'Mrs Kafatos had spent the last ten minutes telling me about her grandson's wedding in London. Every detail was pored over. She's just got back and probably told half the population of Lesvos. I was losing the will to live. So, yes, you were a… welcomed distraction.' Sofia smiles. 'What's happened, Grace?'

'It's all gone horribly wrong…' Grace tails off.

'What has?'

She tilts her head back and closes her eyes. 'Vasilis and me.' She feels suffocated and, behind her eyes, she can feel a dull ache.

'What! How?'

Grace is uncertain where to begin. Only two people know she is pregnant, and the events that led to it. Vasilis and Peter. She knows she must tell Sofia, after all, she has been a good friend. Slowly, Grace forms her response and, with a great effort, she begins. She is exhausted from this constant recycling of her past.

When finally, she is finished, she takes a deep intake of air at the memory of it all.

'Oh, Grace! You have kept this inside you all this time. I can't imagine what you have been through.' She steps forward quickly to her and wraps her arms around Grace. When they part, Sofia asks if anyone else knows.

'Obviously, Vasilis knows... and Peter.' Grace's mouth trembles a little.

'Can I ask you something about you and Vasilis?' she says with complete seriousness. 'When Vasilis told you about the time his wife left, did he mention anything else about her? Did he mention her condition?'

'He said her mind was unstable, she may have been depressed?'

'And that's all?'

'Yes. What else could there be?'

'I think I know why he reacted so badly.'

'What do you mean?' Grace is struggling to understand.

There is a quick intake of breath and then Sofia looks at Grace and says, 'When she left Vasilis that day, it was not just his wife that left him... she was seven months pregnant. So, you see, you're not the first pregnant woman to leave him.'

There is a pause, as Grace takes this in. She covers her mouth with her hand. 'Oh, God! I never knew. He didn't tell me. Why did he not tell me?'

'You'll have to ask him that question.'

'But this is not his baby.'

'Does it matter? He obviously loves you enough that he feels his past is repeating itself.'

'I'm not like that...I'm not like her. Surely he knows that?'

'Then tell him.'

The Present

Returning

Edinburgh in December turns into a giant Christmas tree. At night, the streets glow in a kaleidoscope of light. The buildings glimmer in a decorative fusion of colour and ornamentation, spreading a pervasive sense of wonderment and delight amongst the shoppers, visitors and revellers that fill the streets.

It is against this winter postcard that Grace is slumped, sitting on the pavement, her back leaning against wrought iron railings that stop her from falling onto the road. A young man looks on concerned, his hand still clutching the smartphone he used to call the ambulance.

Three women crouch beside Grace. One of them tells her to take deep breaths and resist the urge to push. Grace's brow is lacquered in a fine coating of perspiration, while around her the women's breath turns to condensation, rolling out of their mouths, like little clouds of fog in the wind chilled air.

Curious pedestrians crane their necks, attempting to catch a glimpse of the heavily pregnant young lady with the ashen complexion.

Grace tries to concentrate on the voice of the woman, whose face is leaning into her, so close that Grace is immediately aware the woman is wearing a top set of ill-fitting dentures. The woman's face melts from her as the pain hits Grace again, and her knuckles turn an anaemic white, as her fingers clamp around the icy railings. Grace muffles her screams and catches the unmistakable trace of garlic on the woman's breath, who assures her the ambulance will arrive soon.

It wasn't supposed to be like this. She can't give birth here, on the street. She does not want to think of this, as another surge of pain grips her.

***

She stands naked in front of the mirror. Her fingertips brush the stretch marks on her stomach and descend to the short wiry hair below her bellybutton, a silken feeling under her touch.

She has always wondered if she would feel the same burst of love she experienced with Olivia. At the time she could never decide definitely, but when she laid her eyes on him for that first time, she experienced an unequivocal love that was the same, yet different, but still just as overwhelming.

She rests her eyes on the reflection in the unsympathetic mirror. She has lost so much weight her appearance is gaunt, her features sharp. She should have been the mother of two children, instead, she is on her own in this empty house whose rooms feel unfamiliar to her.

She scrutinises herself, raises her chin and studies the angle of her jaw, the shape of her lips and the curve of her eyes. Her hair falls limp and unwashed around her shoulders. She stares at her eyebrows, they need plucking. She needs to do a lot of things.

She decides she has neglected herself since that night when the contractions came and she slipped on the ice. Through each wave of cramping pain, she knew then, soon, this was not going to be the only pain that would visit her that night.

Strangely, she thought she would cope this time. She knew what to expect. She leaned heavily against the hurt; the sudden intensity brought unimaginable pain and even now, her breath catches in her throat. She thinks of the emotions that reverberate around her and throb in her head. The strangest thing about this is, sometimes, she feels quite the opposite, overcome by a tranquillizing numbness to the world around her. Again, the grief has been incredible and quite astonishing at times.

She named him, Jack. When he was born, she held him in her arms and her eyes filled with tears. She spoke to him and told him he had a sister and her name was Olivia. She told him how much she loved him and how beautiful he was. Her eyes remained fixed on him as she watched him slip away. She was stunned at how peaceful he looked as if he had just fallen into a deep sleep. And then her body began to shake, and she cried for her dead baby. She wanted it all to end. She wanted to die.

She has not seen Jamie since her return, such an encounter would be unimaginable.

There are days when she feels a weight on her shoulders, but lately, she is aware of it gradually sliding from her.

She has promised herself that, like cuts on her skin that have turned to hardened scabs, she will peel the anger, the grief and her abandonment from her mind, leaving her healed and new.

She turns and walks to the mirror fronted wardrobe, opening its door. As she considers what to wear, Grace is momentarily distracted from a noise in the garden. Birds are singing, and this elicits a picture in her mind… sitting with Vasilis in his garden. At the memory of this, she smiles for the first time in what seems an eternity. She is filled with a mixture of rapture and sadness. She knows she is about to cry and unlike recently, this time, she struggles to stop herself. She shuts her eyes and remembers…

The Past

Leaving

She has grown fond of her little apartment, especially her morning coffees on the balcony, observing the comings and goings of those who are no longer strangers to her, but friends and acquaintances. She doesn't want to stain the happy memories of this place with what she is now feeling.

She has not slept. The rooms are full of a heavy silence, a perfect metaphor for what has passed between Vasilis and herself. She has not seen Vasilis since he left her on the beach. She knows she can't leave Lesvos without seeing him. She needs to put things right. The thought of having this between them, unresolved and unchallenged, is a torment that is unthinkable, it leaves a hole in her stomach. Every new day is an opportunity for a fresh start, she tells herself. She has made up her mind.

'I don't believe you,'

'I'm sorry Grace, but it's true.' Theodore the waiter says, as he gestures with his hand to emphasise his point. 'Why would I lie? Vasilis has left.'

'Oh Vasilis,' she murmurs.

'The boat was called out over an hour ago.'

'When will he be back?'

He shrugs. 'It takes as long as it takes.'

'But I'm leaving for the airport soon.'

'I'm sorry. I need to get back to work, we're very busy.'

'Of course.' She turns and, exasperated, she glances at her watch. She has an hour to spare. In desperation, she tries phoning Vasilis. She hears his voice asking to leave a message.

Inarticulate with worry, she struggles to form her thoughts. Seized by the urge, part of her wants to say, *it has all been a mistake, and I will stay, and my baby will be born in Lesvos, and...* 'Vasilis... It's me, Grace. I went to the taverna and was told you were called out. It's a comfort to know you're rescuing people who find themselves in a situation, so dreadful I can't even imagine what that must be like. That's what I love about you. I love you, Vasilis. Please find it within you to understand why I must do this. Your reaction yesterday left me confused and I've been trying to work it out. I knew you had your reasons, but now I know why. I know your wife was pregnant when she left you, Sofia told me. I'm not leaving you. Even if we are apart, we will still be together in our hearts. Please understand that. This is hard for me too. This whole thing is completely out of my control. If I could, I would stay here with you. You must believe that. You have to believe in me, Vasilis. I don't know any other way to convince you. I don't know how I will bear it if I don't see you. When you get this message, phone me... remember my darling, I love you. We can get through this and be together, again. Please, please phone. I don't have long.'

As she speaks, she has been walking with no purpose and she finds herself advancing along the sand on the beach.

She wants to feel a sense of stillness. She is tired of worrying about what other people will think of her; they don't live her life. Vasilis is all that matters, what he thinks, what he feels, and he is not here.

When she first arrived in Molyvos and the days and weeks passed, she felt a transformation build in her chest. It seemed like everyone around her was listening to the same radio station. They were all on the same frequency and she could see things more clearly. ... and then there was Vasilis. In her mind, it was a universe of its own. She could feel herself relax, and this, in turn, yielded a comfort and for the first time, a sense of relief seeped through her body.

Now, she feels on the verge of tears. Her shoulders stiffen as she sucks in the sea air and wonders how it has come to this.

Along the beach, she watches the figure of Peter and the others gradually combing the sand and cleansing it of plastic and discarded rubbish. She remembers her first foray into clearing up the beach, it was then she laid eyes on Vasilis and the enthusiasm in his smile told her all she needed to know.

Sofia goes with her to the airport. Once her bags are checked in, Grace looks at her smartphone.

'Nothing.'

Sofia squeezes Grace's hand. 'That doesn't necessarily mean what you're thinking,' she says soothingly.

'I don't know what to think anymore.'

'I know Vasilis. I've known him since we were children. He will be simmering, he can be stubborn, but not like this, he would not want to hurt you. That's not the Vasilis I know.'

'I hope you're right... I need to go now.' Grace's voice is tight.

Sofia opens her arms and Grace falls into them. 'I love him, but I feel crushed by the weight of it.'

'Do what you have to do. Be true to yourself. Leave Vasilis to me. Once this is over, Vasilis will still be here. He'll be waiting for you. I promise.'

Grace tries to smile but she can't. All she can do is nod, with a film of torment across her face.

'Go, before you change your mind. This is the best you can do for your baby. Remember that.'

Sofia watches, as Grace turns and waves and then, with the greatest reluctance, disappears into the departure lounge.

Suddenly, she realises. 'Grace! Grace! I don't have your phone number.'

The Present

The Return of the Dragonfly

She has tried to contact him, by phone, but always, there is silence. She has stopped leaving messages because she can no longer get through to his number. Has he changed it? Why does he maintain his silence? Grace wonders what this means, what any of it means? It feels like Vasilis has disappeared from the face of the earth. She is tormented by his absence, an absence she feels like a wound. It presses at her, surge after surge of her past life. Her uncertainty rises in front of her like a tidal wave. Has she hurt him that much that he has erased her from his mind? She trembles at the thought. She can't accept it is over. She needs to see him. She needs a kind of clarification. To stay in Edinburgh would be like giving up.

She had expected to return to Lesvos, to resume her life with Vasilis and the life she had grown into, her apartment, her friends, Pelagia...

In a corner of her mind, Vasilis is waiting for her. She frantically assures herself this is still a possibility, otherwise, she cannot fathom the brutality of his silence.

She taps the buy button on the laptop. It is done. The gratification it brings clears her head. Grace opens a cupboard door and reaches for her suitcase; there is a compelling urgency about her. In a few days' time, she will be on a flight, back to Lesvos.

In the days that follow, Grace paces around the house willing time to pass quickly. She works in the garden, cutting back shrubs and weeding the flower beds and stone paving. She goes into the city centre and meets Monica for lunch. She luxuriates in Monica's welcoming hug. Monica

tells Grace she can stay in the apartment for as long as she
likes, as she won't be returning to Lesvos. Enthusiastically,
Monica explains her life is settled in Edinburgh and she
likes it that way. She is enjoying her new beginning and it
is long overdue. She hasn't been this happy for years.

It occurs to Grace that Monica may be able to contact
someone in Lesvos and enquire about Vasilis. It troubles
Grace that she hasn't thought of this until now. To her
disappointment, Monica has deleted all the numbers in her
contact list from those she knew in Lesvos. Incredulously,
Grace asks why would she do such a thing? Monica
explains she is finished with her past, it is behind her. It is
today that matters, it is the present that is important to her
now.

After lunch, Grace walks around the city. She finds
herself on Calton Hill, with its grassy slopes and sweeping
views of the city skyline, the old town, the Balmoral,
Princes Street and Edinburgh Castle. She ambles around
the prominent Neoclassical monuments, and the unfinished
replica of the Parthenon in Athens, pulling her collar up
against the unforgiving and biting wind. She steadies her
eyes on the uncompleted structure of the Parthenon, a
landmark she is familiar with, which now initiates a
longing for the surroundings of Molyvos and Vasilis, as
well as spurring a recognition of the depths of her
loneliness.

***

She instructs the taxi driver to drop her off on the outskirts
of Molyvos, preferring to walk. It feels like she has never
been away. She inhales the smell of the sea and fixes her
eyes on the castle. The wheels of her suitcase rumble over
the cobbled streets as she makes her way towards the
apartment. As she walks, she pauses. Should she go to
Vasilis' house? She is desperate to resolve the

misunderstanding between them. Her answer shows itself by an instinct to listen to the inner voice that urges her to visit the apartment.

She turns the key in the lock, steps inside and the door closes behind her. She stands for a moment, not quite believing she is finally here. She scans each inch of space, every detail. She absorbs the scent of musty air, the concentrated silence that amplifies her breathing and her pulsing heart against her ribcage. She moves further into the hallway, the living space and bedroom, brushing her hand over surfaces of furniture and the sheets on the bed. She wasn't sure how she would feel and, even now, it is like she has never left. Everything is how she remembers it, a capsule in time, undisturbed, uninhabited. She feels she has arrived, no, she feels she has returned; this is a more fitting way to phrase it, she concludes.

Finally, she steps out onto the balcony and immediately this stirs an unyielding warmth in her stomach more than she expected. It fills her with a rising elation. At the same time, it endorses a wash of strength and comfort that consumes her, a confirmation that prompts an unshakable feeling that this is the right thing to do. It is what her circumstances demand.

She sinks into the chair where she has spent so many mornings watching Vasilis walk Pelagia to school. So much has happened and so much has changed since then.

If only she had made Vasilis believe she would return to him? If only she had seen him before she left? If only?

Vasilis shuns social media, it is not for him. She remembers his insistence it was breeding a generation that didn't know how to communicate or socialise with one another, their world existed only within the parameters of a small screen. He called it absurd, an epidemic on such a vast scale, people had forgotten what it meant to be human. Would things have worked out differently if she could have contacted him on Facebook or Twitter? It doesn't matter anymore, not now that she is here.

After a time, back in Edinburgh, to clear her head from distractions, Grace deleted her social media accounts to make herself absent and, in a way, to make herself vanish.

She takes a deep breath and sighs, and for an instant, she is hesitant, what if he refuses to see her? She has gone over the possibility of this and it disturbs her because this admits doubt, scepticism in the faith she has in him, and in what she believes they still have.

It is time. She stands up and is strangely moved by the sky which is grey and low, and the sea which is shifting with rough and angry waves. She doesn't know what she is more surprised by?

She can still feel the chilled air through her jacket. It is the first time she has seen it like this. This is a different Lesvos. It has affected her judgement. It has altered her assumption of the way things are and how they once looked. She has to adjust to this changed reality in front of her. It is a new impression that challenges her past experience, but she finds no comfort in it, only a sense that what was once an experienced reality can ultimately be altered. She feels a profound fear that maybe the Vasilis she finds will not be the Vasilis she knows.

The Present

A Familiar Face

Should she go to his house first or the taverna? She checks her watch. They'll be busy serving lunches and Vasilis often helps. She decides the taverna.

Grace walks with her hands deep in her coat pockets. She is glad she brought some long-sleeved flannel shirts and sweatshirts as she hunches her shoulders against the chill in the air.

Grace notices a man standing in a shop doorway, studying her intensively while smoking a cigarette. She tries to hold her hair from spilling over her face, but in the autumnal light, it is difficult to make out his face. From what she can see, she doesn't recognise him.

His attention is unsettling, but then, the sudden thought that it is out of season and probably unusual to see someone he does not know at this time of year compensates for his interest in her. And then, another reason presents itself. What if he recognises her? Grace glances at him. He drops his cigarette, stamps on the butt with a mud-stained boot, and to her relief, disappears into the shop.

Grace is uncomfortably aware, she may quickly become the centre of attention. She was a known face and always keen to practise her Greek whenever the opportunity presented itself. Vasilis may already know she has returned, Grace rationalises.

As she walks, Grace hears her name being called. She turns to see the owner of the voice. He is wearing a white Panama Hat and, this time, she recognises straight away who it is. 'Peter!'

'My dear, it really is you. What a wonderful surprise, Grace.' He hugs her and when he pulls away, she can see his eyes have glazed over with tears. 'You're back.'

'Yes. I am.'

Peter looks away, towards the direction of the taverna, and then back again.

'I just arrived this morning. I'm on my way to see Vasilis, that's if he'll still speak to me.'

There is a short silence and Grace can see Peter's face vividly change, as its colour drains from him.

'Are you alright, Peter?'

He looks at her and Grace can tell he wants to say something.

'I'm fine, my dear,' he says quietly. 'Can we go somewhere to talk?'

'We could go to Vasilis' if you like?'

'I was thinking of somewhere more intimate. You can tell me all about Edinburgh.'

They sit at an outside table, overlooking terracotta roofs that slope towards the Aegean. Grace tells Peter everything. She had a boy and named him Jack. Peter smiles briefly at the mention of the name. She mentions her exasperation at Vasilis' silence that turned to torment with each week that passed. She was relieved that Monica was an ever-present source of support and constant shoulder to lean on. 'I don't know what I would have done without her.' She divulges that she doesn't know what a normal life is anymore. 'The closest I got to it was living here.' She pulls her fingers through her hair. Peter lets her talk, waiting for the right moment.

'There's something I have to tell you.' Peter stiffens. He hesitates and then he reaches over the table and takes her hand.

She looks at him, not quite understanding what this could mean.

'What? Is it Vasilis? Does he not want to see me? Is there someone else? That's it, isn't it? He's seeing someone?'

He shakes his head. 'No. It's not that.'

'What then?'

'There was an accident.'

'An accident?' she repeats. 'What do you mean? Is Vasilis alright?'

Peter gathers himself. 'Vasilis was closing up the taverna, everyone had gone home. The police said it was a robbery. There was money stolen and Vasilis was beaten up, badly. He spent a long time in the hospital.'

'When was this?'

'It was the night you left.'

'That was months ago. I have to go and see him. Where is he, Peter?'

'I'm sorry, Grace.' He squeezes her hand. 'He didn't recover. He went into a coma. There was nothing the doctors could do for him. Vasilis passed away.'

'He's dead? No. Vasilis can't be dead. He's waiting for me.'

'They still haven't found any suspects. The security camera was tampered with. I'm so sorry, Grace.'

Grace brings a hand to her mouth. She stares for a long time at her coffee cup. Then she is trembling, her hands are shaking. 'He is waiting for me.' She hears the words reverberate in her head. There is a tightening in her chest. She covers her face with her hands. 'He walked away from me on the beach. It was the last time I saw him...' The image echoes through her mind and a cry rises in her stomach, and escapes as an imperceptible moan, shuddering into an animalistic shriek, a horrible sound that takes Peter by surprise.

He stands swiftly and is by her side. He crouches beside her and cradles her head in his hands. 'Oh, my dear. My little dragonfly.'

She presses into his chest and sobs uncontrollably. She lifts her head, her eyes bright with tears. 'Why didn't anyone get in touch with me? It's been months?'

'We tried. Sofia doesn't have your number, nor I. When you were here, there was no need for it. We saw each other almost every day.'

'My number was in Vasilis' phone,' she blurts out, almost incomprehensibly.

'That day you left, and Vasilis was on the lifeboat, his phone fell into the sea. Yiannis was with Vasilis when he lost it. It happened just before they reached the dinghy. Yiannis said that Vasilis knew you were trying to contact him. It was always his rule that no one used their phone when they were on duty. He was about to break that rule, but it slipped from his hand and fell into the sea.'

'That's why he didn't answer my calls. I went to the taverna, but he was already gone. I phoned him… I kept phoning.'

Her pain is unbearable, she senses it with every instinct she owns.

'Always remember, Vasilis loved you. I've never seen him look so happy when he was with you. You transformed him, Grace. Come now. Let's get you out of here. I'll take you home, Grace.'

Grace grabs Peter's arm. 'Pelagia! What's happened to Pelagia?'

The Present

A Secret Revealed

The next morning, Grace is sitting on the bed, her dressing gown wrapped tightly around her. She can hear running water, the clunk of cutlery and the padding of feet coming from the kitchen. She glances at the window. The sky is heavy with dark cloud and droplets of rain run down the glass. On her way to the kitchen, she passes through the living room. Last night's debris: two glasses and an empty wine bottle remain where they were left.

Grace doesn't need to look into a mirror to know her eyes are blotchy and puffed. She rakes a hand through her hair, as she stands at the doorway to the kitchen. Sofia is buttering toast and looks up. Sofia moves towards her and gives her a gentle hug. 'I didn't want to wake you. I've made some breakfast.'

'I'm not hungry. Coffee will be fine.'

'You should try to eat something, Grace.'

'Maybe later.' Grace sits at the table and rubs her eyes. She looks at Sofia. 'Thank you, for last night. It was good of you to stay.'

'Did you get much sleep?'

'Not really.'

'Why don't you get a shower and we can go for a walk. I think we can both do with some fresh air.'

'I haven't unpacked yet.'

'Well, you do that while I clean up in here.'

Grace looks away and her tears well up. 'I loved him.' She is conscious she has said this in the past tense, and she is profoundly aware of how different this feels when she thinks of Olivia and Jack. It doesn't matter what name she gives the feeling, it is complicated, dissociated from her normal senses, it has an astonishing intensity, yet she knows it has undeniably changed everything.

For the first time, she wonders where he is. She looks up at Sofia. 'Where is he?'

'The cemetery is not far from here. We can go if you want?'

'Yes. I've come a long way to see him. I owe him that.'

As they walk, Grace sniffs and rummages through her bag for a tissue. She is near to tears again. 'I'd like to see Pelagia. How is she? If there's a God, he's so fucking cruel.'

'She's staying with Vasilis' sister. I think you've met her.'

Grace nods.

'I could ask her for you. I'm sure it would be fine.'

Grace frowns. 'She might not want to see me.'

'And then again, she might.'

Grace clasps her hands together. The thought of not seeing Pelagia again is too much to endure. She clenches her hands harder, trying to stop the tears.

In the months that follow, Grace pushes back the tide of grief and self-pity. It arouses in her a feeling that she is not beyond redemption. Gradually, and to Sofia's relief, Grace's appetite returns, and they often eat out, usually in one of the restaurants at the harbour.

During the day, Grace is now venturing out, buying bread at the bakers, cheese and pasta from Sofia's Deli, and getting reacquainted with the homemade jam she loves.

When talking with others, she only speaks Greek, and often, she is met with a kind word of appreciation and praise, as others are impressed by her progress in their language.

She visits Vasilis' grave every morning, replacing flowers and speaks to him as if he is still with her.

The memory of the happiness Vasilis brought into her life is never lost. She thanks him for melting the sense of vulnerability she possessed, purging the troubles in her life with his gentleness, his encouragement, his passion and his persuasive force that was always effective in removing self-doubt from her thoughts and replacing it with a feeling of ecstasy.

Mostly, she loves him for making her feel safe and wanted.

He saved her from herself.

He believed in her.

He liberated her from her past and walked with her towards a future that promised possibilities.

It was an exultant feeling. It still is.

Most mornings, she walks Pelagia to school, continuing the routine Pelagia had with her father. It helps Grace get through the day in front of her. They have spent this time getting to know one another again.

Pelagia is worried her father will fade from her thoughts, so she asks a lot of questions about him and Grace tries to answer them, as honestly as she can. It is an integral part of the healing process for them both.

It was not always like this. At first, Pelagia refused to see Grace. However, Grace's gentle and friendly persistence gradually breached Pelagia's resistance to her. It helped that, by now, Grace's Greek was improving by the day, and this eased Pelagia into a sense of security and familiarity.

The days fall away. They take walks to Petra and have lunch at a taverna that always involves ice cream, and bicycle rides that last well into the late afternoon.

On one day, Pelagia is reserved and unusually quiet and, when Grace enquires why, Pelagia replies she is scared

Grace is going to leave her because everyone she has loved
has done so.

'Oh, Pelagia. You don't have to worry anymore. I'm not
going anywhere. I couldn't stay away. I had to come back.'

'Why did you want to come back?'

'I had to because… really, I had no choice. You see, I
loved your father and I couldn't bear another second
without him.'

Pelagia lowers her head. 'He is not here now. You don't
have to stay.'

'When I first came to Lesvos, I was looking for
something, something I had lost. Somehow, I thought I
would find it here. The more I tried, the further it seemed to
move away from me. Then, when I met your father, he
made me feel happy again, a feeling I had never felt for
such a long time. He turned a beautiful light on inside me
that glowed and became stronger with each day I spent with
him. My life was worth living, after all. He made me want
to love again. And I thought I'd found what I'd lost.'

Grace strokes Pelagia's hair. 'And when he was taken
away from me, that bright light inside me faded and the
darkness returned. I thought my life had ended as well…
But I was wrong.'

'You were, how?'

Grace draws a long breath. 'The light was always here. I
didn't find it, it found me. The reason I will never leave is
because it was here after all. It is you, Pelagia.'

She is caught in the warmth of her eyes and then Pelagia
buries her head into Grace's chest. 'I miss him so much.'

'I know you do. I do too.' Grace kisses the top of
Pelagia's head.

Pelagia looks up, her soft face awash in soft light.

'Can you keep a secret?'

'I'd like to think so if I have to. Why?'

Pelagia looks at her with satisfaction across her face.

'Yesterday, after school, a man met me. He said he was daddy's friend. He told me if anything ever happened to daddy, he was to look after me.'

'Do you know this man? What did he look like?'

'I've never seen him before. He said it was our secret and daddy wouldn't want anyone to know. He said he had a present daddy gave him to give to me. I could only get it if I promised not to tell anyone about him. He said he would come back again, in three days' time. I can tell you, Grace, can't I? I can tell you anything.'

'I'm so glad you did.'

'I haven't seen him before, but I've heard his voice.'

'What do you mean?'

'It was late, and I was woken by shouting. I could hear my daddy and he sounded angry. He was talking to someone downstairs. I heard the voice of the man who met me at school. I started to get scared because the man was also angry.'

'Did you hear his name?'

'No.'

'When was this?'

'A few days before daddy was hurt and went to hospital. Have I done anything wrong?'

Grace holds Pelagia close to her. 'You've done the right thing, Pelagia. This man is a very bad person. Do you know what he was talking to your dad about?'

She shakes her head; the world of adults is confusing.

Grace looks into the big eyes placed on her and she tries not to show her worry and fear.

'What will happen?'

'Don't worry. I know what to do.' Grace holds Pelagia tightly to her.

The Present

A sense of Survival

She is dreading this moment, for a while Grace has considered abandoning her plan. She ponders the risk. She has gone through it, chewing it over in her head. She has nursed it and now the time has come.

Grace hears the engine before she sees the 4x4. She is sitting across from the school in the shade, she hasn't touched her coffee. Some of the tables around her are occupied and she blends in inconspicuously. Grace checks her watch, it is nearly time. The 4x4 comes to a stop across from the school gate.

There is the smell of cigarettes in the air and the sound of normal conversations. Her heart is pounding inside her chest. She can't make out the occupant of the vehicle, but she knows it is him. She has been here for the last few days, watching, observing the patterns, the parents picking up their children from school, on foot and in cars. At first, a trickle of children exits the school and within a minute they are like a swarm of bees, spilling out into the playground and heading for home.

Grace is already walking. She stops abruptly and looks over to the 4x4. The door has opened, and a man steps out, a tall man, skinny with sharp features. He leans into the 4x4 as if he has just forgotten something. For a moment, she imagines Vasilis, she forces herself to walk and it feels like she is walking through cement.

He is standing with his back to her as she nears him, he turns to face to her. She recognises him immediately through his badger toned stubble.

'Neos!'

'Hello, Grace.'

'She's not here.'

'I haven't come for the girl. It's you I want. I've been waiting patiently for you. I've been watching you. I know where Pelagia is. She's being watched, and one call from me, and the girl and your friend, the Deli lady, will get a visitor. So, Grace, it's up to you to keep them safe.'

He grabs her arm, she feels the clench of his fingers, the sharp pain of nails digging into her skin. Then he does something that catches her by surprise. In one fluent motion, he spins her and forces her into the driver's seat of the 4x4. The door's mechanism locks. Neos walks around the vehicle, unlocks the doors and slides into the passenger seat. He pulls out a knife from the glove compartment.

'Your phone.'

Reluctantly, she hands it to him, and he throws it into the glove compartment.

'Drive.'

'Where to?'

'Just drive the fucking truck, I'll tell you where to go. It's an automatic, so even you can drive it.'

Grace slides the gear handle into forward and they move off, slowly at first and then gain speed.

'That boyfriend, of yours, now he was a stubborn bastard. All I wanted was ten thousand euros, that's all. I could have asked for more, but I'm reasonable; unfortunately, he wasn't. You see, if I wanted to, I could have taken the girl, but it would have just got messy and complicated, so I took the money instead. It's what he owed me for stealing Natasha from me. You owe me too.'

Grace's hands grip the steering wheel. She glances at him. Her voice rises slightly. 'You killed him.'

'I apologise for that. It was not what I intended, but sometimes these things can get out of hand. As I said, he was a stubborn bastard. A shame, I know. Head out of the town.'

A shiver passes through her.

'Why didn't you go to the police?' He lights a cigarette. 'I knew you wouldn't, you see, you're just like me. Revenge is addictive. You and me, we're the same. We're addicts.'

'I'm nothing like you.'

'Shut the fuck up, you're what I say you are. And if I say you're a fucking whore, that's who'll you be.' He rubs the side of his head. 'You're giving me a headache. You'll only talk when I tell you to, alright?'

She stares at the road in front of her. She is shaking and scared, but with that fear comes a desperation and she doesn't care anymore.

Neos is looking out of the window. 'How is Natasha?'

'She's... better.'

He sighs. 'Good. I'm glad. After this, I might visit her. I've always wanted to go to your country and now I have a reason to... someone I can visit.' He turns to Grace and smiles. 'Take a left, just up here.'

They continue driving, through thickening countryside.

'What are you going to do with me?'

'You're talking again. Keep your mouth shut. You see, Grace, you stuck that pretty little nose of yours where it wasn't wanted. You took Natasha from me and for that, you owe me. From now on, you're mine. You're my brand-new Natasha. Just like she was my brand new, Drosoula.'

The name hits Grace like a wall. Neos is smirking. 'That's why things at the taverna got out of hand. I couldn't help myself. Temptations a bitch, but I like bitches, so I gave in to it.'

'Vasilis' wife left him for you?' Grace says incredulously.

'She loved me. Does that shock you?'

'What about the baby?'

'It was mine, not his. Stop here.' The earth and stone crunch under the tyres as the vehicle comes to a stop.

'You look unwell. Do you want some water?'

'Where are we?'

'Do you always answer a question with a question?'

'My God. What happened to the baby?'

'There was no baby. Not one that was born, anyway. It died inside her. We left the hospital without it. There was no funeral. No grave. Our life continued as before.'

'You mean she was brainwashed, or even still, terrified to leave. Even if she could, she couldn't, could she? She was just like Natasha. Imprisoned.'

Grace looks around her. They have stopped in a clearing. She can see an old stone farmhouse, the colour of its shutters, once blue, are fading with neglect.

'We'll be staying here for a few days. Even after all this time, all this waiting, I still don't know what to do with you. You see, Grace, I knew you'd come back. You loved Vasilis. I know what kind of person you are. I know what makes you who you are. I feel your pain, your sorrow, I can heal you. At first, I wanted to make you suffer, but over time and with your absence, I fell in love with you.' He reaches over and touches her face. Grace flinches. 'And given time, you will learn to love me.'

'What happened to Drosoula?' Grace's voice shakes.

'Grace, Grace. More questions. She doesn't matter. All that's important is right now, here... you and me. I care for you now.'

She feels like she has breathed all the air there is to breath. He still has the knife in his hand, but his grip around it has loosened.

The engine dies.

He has the key fob in his other hand.

In the time he has opened the door, slipped out, walked around the 4x4 and placed his hand on the handle of the door at Grace's side, her mind is set.

Her hand slightly wavers on the steering wheel.

She thinks of Vasilis.

There is remorse and everlasting regret.

She thinks of Pelagia.

Whose presence in her heart is everything.

As the door opens, she leaps from the seat. With the advantage of height and body weight, and with all the strength she can muster, Grace stamps on Neos's foot and her elbow breaks his nose. It is enough to give her the few seconds she needs. He stumbles backwards and falls onto his back, screaming in pain. She runs, as fast as she has ever done before. Neos is still on the ground, cursing her. He tries to stand, the pain seers through him, but he still manages to scuttle after her.

Branches tear at her face. Her lungs are bursting inside her. She slides down an embankment, crosses a stream, she slips, but gains her balance. She can hear Neos, but she is terrified to turn. Ahead, there is an olive grove. She can feel olives being squashed underfoot as she weaves a path through the grove. She leans her back against a trunk, catching her breath and listening. She can't hear him, worse still, she can't see him.

Around her, the air is still and quiet. All she can hear is her heavy breathing and a pulse in her ear. Then, from behind her, there is an audible crack.

The pain in her arm is excruciating, He's stabbed me. She can feel blood on her skin. He lurches towards her, grabbing her wrist. She pulls it away, but his grip is tight. He wrenches her wrist and she falls to her knees, the bone grazed by small stones, as she thuds to the ground. She is sure he will kill her now, but he is calm, in control, like he is enjoying the chase.

The solution to her predicament is right in front of her eyes and, when she realises it, there is no hesitation. She leans into his groin and bites hard, holding on to him and then tearing like a dog. His scream is high pitched, a

horrified shriek that pierces her ears. He releases her wrist.
He raises the knife and cuts the air towards her neck. Grace
rolls away from him and the blade sinks into Neos's thigh.
His eyes are wide with horror and disbelief and, by the time
he hits the hard earth hapless and confused, Grace is
already retracing her steps and scrambling back towards the
farmhouse and 4x4.

She leans against the bonnet, coughing and gasping. She
turns in the direction she came. He's not there. All she can
see are shrubs, and trees, and glowering clouds sliding
menacingly across the sky. She grabs the chrome handle.
'Please be open, please be open.' The heavy door moves
with her hand. She leans forward into the cab and reaching
into the glove compartment she retrieves her smartphone
with a relief that is so palpable her hands are trembling.
    She dials a number and lifts the smartphone to her ear.
'Police,' she says in a whispered cry as fragmented images
of Vasilis and drifting moments steal her mind.

The Present

Growing Together

There is a hushed surprise in Pelagia's voice as she holds
the piece of paper between her fingers and reads the words
her mother wrote. She looks up from the unfamiliar
handwriting and stares out, over the sea through tear-
stained eyes. A soft profuse breeze brushes her hair. She
holds it from getting into her face. The air is getting
warmer and the days are glowing in a different kind of light
now, with the promise of another summer ahead.

Grace wonders, briefly, as she stands beside the girl if
she has done the right thing. 'Do you want to go inside?'

'No. I like it here.'

As does Grace. It is here, amongst the shade of the
spreading vines overhead, that she often sat with Vasilis.
On one of these occasions, he told her of a letter that had
lain in a drawer for years. It was for Pelagia, written by her
mother, but only Vasilis' eyes had stared at the paper, the
words, the extravagant curve of certain letters, the ink...
until now.

'Your father wanted you to read it. When the time was
right. When you were ready. I hope I haven't let him
down?'

'You could never do that, Grace. Daddy loved you.'

'And I him.' She remembers the gentle touch of his
fingers. It was a pure sensation.

Pelagia nods and smiles. She holds Grace's hand.

Grace remembers the first time she saw Vasilis and,
looking back, she thinks even then, she loved him, if such a
thing is possible.

'Why did he have to die, Grace? Why is he not here,
with you and me? I don't understand. We could have been
a family together.'

Grace turns to face Pelagia. She squeezes her hand. 'You are my family now and I am yours.' Grace blinks the tears from her eyes.

The wind begins to pick up. Pelagia lifts her hand and releases the piece of paper into the air. It flutters and rises, unwieldy, like a dragonfly's fledgeling flight, heading out towards the sea.

The End

Get your FREE novella, Heartland, by Dougie McHale. Click on the link below

https://www.subscribepage.com/heartland

A note from the author

Thank you for taking the time to read The Flight of The Dragonfly. If you enjoyed it, please consider telling your friends or posting a short review. As an author, I love getting feedback from readers. Thank you for your kind consideration.

If you'd like to be first to know about any of my books, please visit me on my website and sign up for occasional updates about new releases and book promotions. I'd love to hear from you:

**Visit my website

http://www.dougiemchale.com

**Like me on Facebook

https://www.facebook.com/www.dougiemchale

**Follow me on Twitter

https://twitter.com/dougiemchale

The Girl In The Portrait

A novel by Dougie McHale

A story of the secrets we keep, and the power of forgiveness to heal even the most damaged souls.

London, 1905, The Quartet, a group of classical musicians are about to embark on a tour of Greece. When a celebrated artist paints The Quartet's portrait, no one foresees the drama that is to follow.

2016, in a small village on the coast of Fife, Mark tries to escape his past. When the woman he once loved, Abriana, unexpectedly contacts him, he accepts her offer to travel to Zakynthos and help her uncover the mystery of the heir to the portrait.

Abriana is a woman with a past she is determined to confront, at all costs. Forced to come to terms with the nature of love and betrayal, Mark discovers that the portrait's secret is about to play out its final episode.

**Buy From <u>Amazon UK</u> **Buy From <u>Amazon USA</u>

The Boy Who Hugs Trees

A novel by Dougie McHale

Everyone has secrets, but some can change your world forever.

Emily has a secret; 30 years ago, the choices she made changed her world forever. And now, it resonates in the present, threatening to reveal its truth.

When Georgia removes her son, Dylan, from a prominent Edinburgh school, she relocates to the family home on the Greek island of Corfu. The discovery of her late mother's diary immerses Georgia in her parent's troubled marriage, a story of love and tragedy.

Adam's life has become predictable, something is missing, and it has to change. When he answers an advert to home teach a boy with autism, he hopes his life will take on a new direction and meaning. But he hasn't bargained on falling in love.

Can Georgia and Adam continue to resist the profound attraction that draws them closer? Nothing will prepare Georgia for the diaries final revelation which will force her to question everything she knew about her mother and everything she knows about herself.

The Boy Who Hugs Trees is an intimate, compelling and intensely moving love story that unfolds and reveals the profound impact of impossible choices.

Buy From: Amazon UK * Amazon USA

The Homecoming

A novel by Dougie McHale

It only takes a second to change a life…

Louis Satriani, a successful architect, has a perfect life - or so he thinks, until he finds out his partner is having an affair. Distraught, he abandons his life and embarks on a journey that will take him through the landscapes of Greece and into a family's hidden past…

Maria Nasiakos, a young attractive tour guide, living on the Greek island of Zakynthos, feels that life is passing her by. When she meets Louis, a decision is made that will change both their lives forever…

Forced to confront past love and betrayal, Louis has to choose between his heart and head. As he unravels the truth about the extraordinary past of Maria's mother, can their love survive life changing events and the unfolding of a secret that can only be resolved by a homecoming?

Buy From: Amazon UK * Amazon USA

Acknowledgements

Heartfelt thanks to Sheona, my wife, for her continued support and constant encouragement. Thanks to Tracy Watson, Maggie Crawshaw and Lisa Richards who have been with me from nearly the beginning. As my advanced readers they have given me invaluable feedback on this novel. Finally, I am indebted to Katrina Johnston for her editorial skills, advice and time.

About the Author

In a past life, Dougie has been a dockyard worker, student, musician, and songwriter, playing in several bands, performing live and recording music. He has a degree in learning disability nursing and a post graduate diploma in autism. Dougie lives in Dunfermline, Fife, with his wife, daughter, son and golden retriever.

The Flight of The Dragonfly is his fourth novel, inspired by a love of all things Greek, her islands, people, landscapes, sea, light, and ambience all of which are important themes and symbols in his writing.

Printed in Great Britain
by Amazon